EV

SILVER LINING

BY

R.MUTHUKRISHNAN

WHAT IS POISON?

Anything beyond what we need is poison.

Every cloud has silver lining

It can be power, laziness, food, ego, ambition, vanity, fear, anger or whatever.

VOICE OF NORAH JONES

Voice of the Sunrise, singer of the dawn
On the horizon, of Those Sweet Words
In the Morning hours, a prelude of kindness
Creeping in an instance of moments and purpose
Every moment, every season, for every reason
the surface of song, Above Ground towards the sky
Forward your dreams, a walk with your Toes
Came a voice of the Blues, and Jazz so embracing
nward we sing together with The Handsome Band
member November, like the voice of Norah Jones
An amazing pianist and song writer
mble Me, yet you carry me hone for it's Not To Late
voice, harmony in blue, yet you Come Away With Me
the horizon we stay indoors, yet Don't Know Why
Name the voice that embraces the world
Embrace the Blues, the Jazz, the Folk of an angel
Singer you are, The Nearness of You we cherish
Don't know why?, but we know who you are
es, the voice of a Piano, echo of a guitar, the Norah J
Of Blues and Jazz-meant Dawn.

Dedicated to Norah Jones

ABOUT THE AUTHOR

Trichy Muthu Krishnan, a Bardolator, is a retired Professor whose native place is Tiruchirappalli and he started this professional career as a writer ever since his adulthood and has furthered his knowledge by writing plays for the College celebrations and then after his retirement from the service, delved into a full time writer of novels, especially Romantic suspense novels, based on human psychology, (Dr. William Stakel) and Shakespearean plays and sonnets. In all his novels, Shakespearean quotations are in spate significantly. His portrayal of characters in all his novels whether it is romantic or romantic suspense or Historical Romantic novels, are realistic and some real events are spun into a fixed form from his pragmatic life by which one can realize the reality of the situation in which the characters of the novels play their role accordingly.

About the book

R.Muthukrishnan

EVERY CLOUD HAS SILVER LINING

Every cloud has silver lining

By

R. Muthukrishnan

PUBLISHED BY
WRITAT PUBLICATION

310, PP TRADE CENTRE, NSP, PITAMPURA'NEW DELHI- 110034
WRITATLLC, A312, W. II Street,
#1880 CASPER, WY 92601
UNITED STATES OF AMERICA

PUBLISHED IN INDIA-2022
EVERY CLOUD HAS SILVER LINING
R.MUTHUKRISHNAN

ISBN............................
FIRST EDITION

ACKNOWLEGEMENT

Besides dedicating this novella, "EVERY CLOUD HAS SILVER LINING a Romantic

Suspense novella, to my grandsons, Chi. A. Pranav & Chi. A. Manvik and my granddaughters, "Sow. Tanushri &MahaLakshmi",

I would like to convey my deeper depth of thanks and gratitude to "Writat Publication", Its Editorial Committee and the "Support team "for encouraging me as well as the formation of this novella in its immaculate and impeccable form in printing and format.

RMK

PREFACE

EVERY CLOUD HAS A SILVER LINING" What does it mean?

It is usually possible for something good to come out of bad situation. A silver lining on a cloud is an ideation that the sun is behind it. The potential for something positive or beneficial to result from a negative situation. One can derive some benefit from every bad thing that transpires to one. An element of hope or a redeeming quality in an otherwise bad situation, as in "The rally had a disappointing turmoil but the silver lining was that those who came pledged a great deal of money.

8
Every cloud has silver lining

This metaphorical term is a shortening of" Every cloud has a silver lining." In turn derived from John Milton's"Comus"," A sable loud turns forth its silver lining on the night." There is always something hopeful about even the most difficult or unhappy situation. The worst situation has some element of hope or dome redeeming quality. John Milton appears to have been the originator of this metaphor as mentioned above. It was adopted by numerous later writers and so was already a cliché by the time it appeared in the popular magazines.

Joy and woe are woven fine,
A clothing for the soul divine;
Under every grief and pine
Runs a joy with silken twine.
It is right it should be so;
Man was made for joy and woe;
And when this we rightly know,
Thro' the world we safely go.

Who or what causes for joy and woe? Are we, or our circumstances, or both? It's easy for the philosophers to write or assert that one should be neutral to joy and woe. By dint of their ***megillah,*** one should be matured enough to apprehend the values of the aphorisms that have either been sermonised ***or*** read or outcome of their wisdom that have the power to realize the depth of these philosophies provided that he or she must be blessed by the Invisible. As the eminent William Shakespeare says that "The web of our life is of a mingled yarn, good and evil together "our life on this earth is the best experience earned to make

philosophy but very few act according to the philosophy.
"Look at the yonder field!
The farmer has tilled it and sown the seeds and watered it well. But this is not enough; He must fence it, lest the crop be destroyed by animals.
In the field of life, you sow the seed of 'karma', you water it with aspiration. But this is not enough, you must fence the field with satsang' (fellowship with god-men), else would your crop be destroyed by the animals of passion.
Well, can our passion be controlled by all by our reasoning power? There's always a qualm between passion and conscience but finally passion wins over the conscience.
Swami Vivekananda says in his discourse that "Money does not pay, nor name; fame does not pay nor bearing it. It's love that pays; it is character that cleats its ways through adamantine walls difficulties; the power of love is infinitely greater than the power of hated.
Love at first sight' (coupe de foudre) is always a matter of fascination which is usually the flaring up of infantile feeling-attitudes, the satisfaction of some infantile wish and the fascinated person falls suddenly in love with the fascinating objective, because the latter corresponds to the ideal. The flaring up of such a love with its enormous affect, at once conceals all critical faculties.
Man is a compound of manifold feelings that transform him in a particular manner in a given circumstance. Love, one of the manifold feelings is a strong feeling of caring about somebody and

being sexually attracted to them. It's a very general word and can be used in any context. It can sometimes refer to sex such as physical love or a sexual love but it is more often to do with feelings and the way these make one behave. Desire and Passion are stronger words and are much more to do with physical love and sex. Both desire and Passion can mean the feeling of wanting to have sex but only passion can refer to the act of having sex. But" Lust" is a very strong sexual desire, especially when Love is not involved. It's also related to attraction, a feeling of liking somebody especially in a sexual way so as to mean that sexual attraction is a large part of falling in love.
Kesavan, the protagonist of this novel, a romantic suspense novel, and his fellar, Jayasri, heroine, are not infatuated but attracted with each other in the beginning but Jayasri is found affected by Passion and Desire during tryst. After marriage, they are devoted to each other.
Lalitha is another character, clung to" Platonic Love, a supremely affectionate relationship between human beings,; here her relationship with her classmate, Jagan Moghan Reddy, in which coition is neither desired nor practised, a sheer homosexual relationship.
Another character is created as an example of "carnal Desire" in the name of Srinivasan, a widower but a perfect man without any bad habit but wants to use Lalitha as a caretaker of his lovely daughter.
I owe the debt of gratitude to the publisher of this Romantic suspense novel and submit this to my

readers as a Golden Necklace, studded with the Kohinoor Diamond of Kesavan and JAYASRI, carbuncle of Lalitha, Coral of Jagan Moghan Reddy, Emerald of Padmanaban, Lapis lazuli of Neelavathy, Pearl of Suganthi, Sapphire of Clairvoyant, Sardonyx of house owner and Topaz of his wife, to adorn the readers.

This novel is based on 'Human Psychology' and for the difficult terms, meaning is given within brackets for the sake of readers.

MUTHUKRISHNAN.
Published Author

CONTENTS

&&&&&&&&&&&&&&&&&&&&&&&&&&&
&&&&&&&&&&&&&&&&&&&&&&&&&

CHAPTER No: ONE:

LOVE LETTER (billet-doux)

It's Hemantha Rudhu. (Winter season)

THE hibernal breeze was levitating through the big town, Thirur, where the people were at the lap of Morpheus and the sun was hiding behind the horizon waiting for the dawn but was enjoying the pleasantness of the coolness of the hibernal breeze.

Except Agraharam, other areas of the town were immersed in silent atmosphere and the reason behind was the procession of devotees who were doing bajans during that early dawn and the hymns they were singing vocally with the devotional musical instrument namely,' harmonium' made

the people wake up who were still sleeping and among them was our heroine, Jayasri.
Yes, she's Jayasri, one of the charming girls, born in a family of toiles by the freakish destiny and her mother, Suganthi like her husband, Sankaraiyer was immersed in ***somnolence*** (deep sleep) like Oormila, wife of Lakshmana who accompanied with his brother, Lord Rama to the forest.(Please note down that Oormila didn't go to forest but her husband Lakshmana went to the forest with his elder brother, Rama)
The weather was foggy as it's on the pre-dawn that rendered the people cosiness to sleep deeply and our heroine, Jayasri was not exceptional to **somnolency** since she was a bit ***haggard*** (fatigue due to overwork) like her mother, Suganthi, a vicenarian as well as a housewife who was used to toil all day to earn a living by supplying idlies, a South Indian steamed cake of rice, usually served with onion broth, spongy idlies crispy dosa, crumpet varieties, aromatic vadai
and cookery opsonium(any food used as a relish such as chutney) freshly prepared coconut chutney and tomato chutney to many houses by which she earned sufficient income to make a living while her father, a middle aged man, was working as an accountant in an oil mill, far away from their hometown.
Her anxiety and concern over her daughter's marriage was growing as her daughter was growing to reach the ***nubile age.*** (Sexually mature; old enough for marriage.)

16

Every cloud has silver lining

The three souls had been living in that **minuscule** house (extremely small house) for twenty five years, a rented house with no facilities as the house rent was very low for their sake, Jayasri was working in a tutorial college as a part time tutor, teaching Mathematics to the dunces by which many times she felt it's better to tend the buffaloes than teaching them the rare art. With the income she earned, she was studying B.Sc. Maths under Correspondence course. She deposited a part of the amount to the Chit fund company without knowing that it was a fraud and cheating company. After collecting a huge amount the owner of the chit fund company, one day disappeared from the town*(absconded) and emplaned to a foreign country.

The shock she received was so heavy that she could not restore herself to the normal state for a long time. She attributed the incurring the heavy loss of hard earned money to the gods she relied on and inculpated the gods but not her capital foolishness in relying upon the incredulous chit fund company albeit her mother, a hard-headed woman advised her not to deposit the amount to the chit company but to the post office.

Nothing could be done against the cheat as the owner of the chit fund company was a political leader and no legal action could be taken against him. He settled his life with his wife and draughts safely in a foreign country with the money he swindled from the public especially from the poor. When she heard the bad tidings that the Chit Fund Company absconded with the money, hard earned

money of the people, Jayasri was in so despair that she was about to be fainted but what could she do when everything went against her like others?
Having seen her trauma, a tricenarian woman took pity on her and began to comfort her. She introduced herself as ‘Lalitha’ and spoke to her:” We’ve forgotten the home truth that **‘Covet all lose all’** and this harrowing incident teaches us a great lesson. I am also a depositor like you. What’s the use of crying over spilled milk? (To express regret about something that has already happened or cannot be changed). How much amount did you deposit?”
“Twenty thousand.” Her voice trailed away.
“Do you know how much money I lost? One lakh. I also felt a thunder struck my head on hearing this news. But what to do? What’s the use of lamenting for it washed away from our hands? On seeing you, it reminds me of my sister who is also like you. You’re a split image of my sister. Don’t worry. I will try my best to help you to compensate your loss. Before that, tell me what you are.”
Her soft words and benign tendency brought about Jayasri take a shine to Lalitha. She told her about her family and her biography.
“Oh, you are a Maths Graduate. Good. You’ve a bright future. The loss you incurred is going to be compensated within two months. I will arrange a Home-tuition’ for you. He is our neighbour having a son and a daughter. His son is studying Intermediate first year and his daughter is studying tenth standard. His daughter is somewhat better comparing to the son. But both are not good at

studies. Both are ineducable and hopelessly inept students. You can choose any time either in the morning or evening. Generally, morning hours won't suit to you as well to them. So evening hours will be suitable to you both. Here's my address. Take note of it and meet me today evening. I will introduce you to them. He is a business man and won't be at home for the most of the days but his wife is a kind and good lady. She is very anxious of the future of her children. They'll treat you well and pay the tuition fee regularly. They are ready to pay ten thousand per month. Do you agree?"

As the fruit slipped and fell into the milk Sharmila felt the delectation which was inexpressible as well as inexplicable too. From that moment onwards, she began to idolise Lalitha.

She readily agreed to her and received her residential address.

It's a blessing in disguise.

Jayasri told her parents about the accidental incidents, serendipity which conduced them to glee.

Jayasri realised the value as well as the truth of the discourse that His. Holiness, Sivasankara Baba discoursed that God is used to succour to His Devotees in the human form or any form. She believed that God succoured to her in the form of Lalitha and she thanked God.

On the same day evening, Jayasri went to the residence of Lalitha , matter of two kilometres away from her residence and at the sight of Jayasri, a beam of happiness spread over Lalitha 's face , held her hand lovingly and led her to the main hall.

Let's know the ***prosopography and Alembic*** **of Lalitha and Jayasri in the ensuing chapter.**

It's an individual bungalow with all facilities and comforts. Around the house on three sides of the compound wall, there were a number of tees and flower gardens and at the back of the house, there was a deep well from which the water for garden was used by pipe settings. There were two bed rooms and a kitchen and a dining hall and a main hall used as a reception hall.

Jayasri understood the status of her friend, Lalitha.

"Would you like to take any snacks now?" Lalitha asked Jayasri by sitting in front of her on the sofa.

"After fulfilling my work here…"

"Ok, let's go and meet the madam, now."

Lalitha took her to the next house where she had to tutor the dunce students.

The house lady was very generous and kind and provided them with hospitality.

Lalitha introduced the house lady to Jayasri and Jayasri greeted her.

In return the house lady greeted Jayasri and Lalitha and offered her a seat to be seated.

"She is Jayasri, my chum coming from Agraharam. She is a graduate in Mathematics and undertaking tuitions in that area. You have already told me that you have been searching for a good teacher to teach your children. She is the fittest person. I can give guarantee."

The house lady seemed to be pleased with her introduction. She asked Jayasri," Are you working anywhere?"

"At present I am undertaking tuition. I haven't tried for any job outside."

"What are your parents?"

Jayasri met the eyes of Lalitha who winked her eyes and spoke something through her eyes. Jayasri understood what she implied.

In a trice, Jayasri planned what should be replied to the lady's question.

"My father is working in TVS Company. My mother is a housewife. I am only the daughter to my parents."

"My son is Santhosh. He is always Santhosh except in studies. He has gone to play cricket. No problem that he has much interest in cricket but he doesn't have the same interest in his studies. His ambition is to become an Electrical Engineer but he has to work hard in that subject and very poor in Maths and English. That is his problem. My request is to make him fit for the entrance examination and fulfil his ambition. Next case is my daughter, Subha. She is very careless in all her works. She is blessed with deep sleep from the God as a boon. Even she doesn't know herself when she will sleep. She is a student tenth standard. Both are studying in the Central Government School, CBSE syllabus. But both don't show any interest in their studies. This is their problem in studies. So far, five tutors tried their level best to tutor these buffaloes but all tutors absconded without receiving their tuition fees. So, you are the sixth tutor. You try your best and do the needful efforts."

Jayasri and Lalitha tittered when the madam mentioned their children as 'buffaloes'

"Can you call your daughter to come here?" Jayasri wanted to see Subha.

"Have you ever heard anyone sleeping after taking bath? My daughter is the best example for exception. After school, she took bath and went to bed to sleep. Only God knows when she will wake up."

Now Jayasri sussed out why the Madam was ready to pay ten thousand rupees as tuition fees.

"Don't mistake me as I made fun of my wards calling them as buffaloes. Lakshmi is with us in this mansion but Sarasvati is not willing to remain with Lakshmi. What can I do?"

Jayasri assured her:" Don't worry, Madam. I have much experience in teaching the dunces. Day after tomorrow is an auspicious day and I start teaching them from six to eight in the evening. Once you handover the responsibility to me, hereafter you need not be anxious about your children in their studies.

Encouraged by her averment, Madam was very much pleased with Jayasri. So, she asked Jayasri whether she was in need of advance amount for which Jayasri replied humbly that she won't need the advance amount but it could be paid after a month.

On an auspicious day, Jayasri started tutoring or coaching the dunces and struggled with them. But the dunes struggled with her to learn Maths since they didn't know the fundamental knowledge. Now Jayasri understood rather realized pragmatically why the previous tuition masters absconded. She determined to continue teaching till she'd compensate the loss amount and in two months she received ten thousand rupees.

Lalitha suggested to continue tuition irrespective of the failure in inculcating in their minds fundamental knowledge in Maths.

Jayasri had been teaching, tutoring and coaching the dunces for six months but all her efforts were in vain. As a scrupulous girl she felt very sad but Lalitha directed her how to take the matter easily and emphasised that it's her duty to teach them sincerely but the result is to be left with the God.

SIX MONTHS PASSED.

One day "Rati" entered into her life and shot an arrow towards her.

(***Rati*** *(Sanskrit: रति, Rati) is the Hindu goddess of love, carnal desire, lust, passion and sexual pleasure. Usually described as the daughter of PrajapatiDaksha, Rati is the female counterpart, the chief consort and the assistant of Kama (Kamadeva), the god of love. A constant companion of Kama, she is often depicted with him in legend and temple sculpture. She also enjoys worship along with Kama. The Hindu scriptures stress Rati's beauty and sensuality. They depict her as a maiden who has the power to enchant the god of love. When the god Shiva burnt her husband to ashes, it was Rati, whose beseeching or penance, leads to the promise of Kama's resurrection. Often, this resurrection* *occurs when Kama is reborn as Pradyumna, the son of Krishna. Rati – under the name of* ***Mayavati*** *– plays a critical role in the upbringing of Pradyumna, who is separated from his parents at birth. She acts as his nanny, as well as his lover, and tells him the way to return to his parents by slaying the demon-king, who is destined to die at his hands. Later, Kama-Pradyumna accepts Rati-Mayavati as his wife.)*

A few seconds before her 'menarche', Pothos, god of sexual longing, yearning, and desire, glanced at her and made her ***fappable****.(Something that is sexually desirable, or deemed high enough quality that it can be used for masturbation purposes.)* while taking oil bath in the john. As she had obtained birds and bees at the age of ten, she was not affected by fear or shame but took it normal. The Nature made her to have acquaintance with the knowledge of "tickle the taco' during her solitary time. All her age mates with whom she befriended were the fetishist of iconolagnia (Iconolagnia = a paraphilia which consists in pursuing pleasure through pornography.) and se began to indulge in watching porno with them. Her mother was not aware of her secret watching as she was up to her brim as well welting in her domestic work.

Jayasri had a desire to get up early morning and paid a visit to the famous temple dedicated to Lord Krishna for **Hosanna** (prayer for blessing) where she happened to meet our hero, Kesavan who was also used to pay a visit to the temple, not for worshipping and praying.

To her surprise, our hero didn't turn to her or had a glance to her by which she was attracted to invite his attention towards her. But our hero who was affected by ***ennui*** (mental weariness from lack of occupation or interest) didn't respond to her amorous glances.

Suganthi got a suspicion on her for Jayasri made her wont to get up early morning, took bath in ice water and start walking to the nearby temple. "What's wrong with her for having abrupt devotion to Lord Krishna? Has Lord Krishna instructed her to come to the temple and worship Him daily? Any votive prayer? Being a slugabed, how she changed into a pious lady all of a sudden?"

When Jayasri was free, her mother asked her" Jayasri, I want to ask you one thing. Do you have any votive prayer to Lord Krishna?"

. Jayasri found out that suspicion had entered into her mother's mind. So she casually told her a lie," I want to be a dux in the university in Maths. The Final year examination falls on next Monday. So, I must ace the examination in distinction. That's why I am praying to Lord Krishna."

Suganthi tittered but she simulated as if she had believed her words.

As usual next day in the morning, Jayasri got up early, finished her ablution and walked down the street towards the temple dedicated to Lord Krishna with a resolution to express her love to him.

Lord Krishna was spectating at them from His **Adytum in the sanctum sanctorum.**

Every cloud has silver lining

As soon as Jayasri entered into the temple premises, her eyes were searching for Kesavan but he was late. Then after ten minutes, Kesavan in his dhoti and full sleeved shirt came to the temple where Jayasri was waiting for him. He didn't notice that a girl was watching him daily. He didn't know how long Jayasri had been longing for him.

Like our film world chooses Hindu temples for romantic scenes, Jayasri chose this temple for her amorous desires.

Yes, Jayasri was very much enamoured of him, his fair complexion and above all his unresponsiveness to her eager, amorous glance and lovely look. She didn't know how much he was vexed with his present life and he didn't know how far she was longing for him to propose him. The more he became unresponsive to her , the more she began to long for him and her love grew intense and she was expecting the moment to express her love to him for she had chosen the sentence," I cherish the day you walked into my life."

While Kesavan was circumambulating the internal sanctum, Jayasri followed him. Very few devotees were present at the temple and it was a right time for her to express her love or pop the question since there was none in the internal sanctum except them.

"Excuse me."

Her sweet voice made him turn towards her side. He was doubtful whether she called him or someone. So, he looked around him whether she

called someone else but when he found none, he confirmed that she called him. In a moment, he was *slack-jawed* and conveyed her same emotion through his look.
"Did you call me?" Kesavan's lips opened to utter such words while his eyes dilated by looking at her as her beauty tranced his heart. In a trice his mind captured her like a camera and her figure stamped firmly into his subconscious mind as an *engramma.* . "Oh! What a beautiful girl she is! "He exclaimed himself. Her face, stunning comely face, looked like a plenilune and like a cascade, her hair was on fleek, long and she coiffed her long ebony or sable curly hair. Her forehead was broad as if it were smoothed with sandal paste; a sandal paste stuck with vermilion at her glabella added to her pulchritude. Above all, her eyes, sable eyes like whirling wasps around the fragrant flowers, were a most alluring weapon to trance anyone's heart and drive them mad after her. Her eyes can display the"*Navarasas"* namely," Sringara (Love, Hasya (comic), Karuna (compassion) ,Raudra (anger), Veera (valour), bhayanaka (fear), Bhi Bhatsa) disgust, Adbutha (wonder), and finally Shanta (tranquillity).Kesavan felt that her eyes emitted amatory words at him. Her nose was sharp to imply that she was very strict and passionate in all matters. It seemed whether it was carved like the marble statue of Cleopatra or Helen. Her cheeks were of fair complexion with dimples on both sides by which it tempts anyone to osculate and basciate them. Her ears were like shell and were adorned with ear-studs. Her lips were pink to

seem as flake of orange fruit. She was ravishing in her *lehenga* and tight blouse so as to expose the contour of her *spathic and boobez. He found the excelity in her femininity.* In toto, she was a sylph. (*A sylph is a lovely, slim young woman or girl. You could describe a row of graceful ballerinas as sylphs. A sylph is always young, female, and slender, moving with an almost otherworldly lightness and grace. The original meaning of sylph was a mythical fairy-like creature, an air spirit that's mentioned by the poet Alexander Pope and appears in several Shakespeare plays as well. The 19th century French ballet "La Sylphide" is thought to have led to the use of sylph to describe slender girls, especially ballet dancers. Like 'toxophilite w*hen his *cupidinous* arrows of eyes were shot at her bust, the damsel felt as if his eyes pierced through her bust like a man cling to *Mazophilia, she felt horripilation* by which she could not reply to his question asked, 'Did you call me?"

As there was none in the surrounding place, he confirmed that it must be the sylph that she wanted to tell him something but when she saw her mettle, overwhelming mettle, he sussed out the reason and hence he reminded her of the question she posed to him. "Ms, is it you that you called me?"

On hearing his question, she controlled her emotions and nodded.

Next moment, he was shocked to see her further action.

Yes, the sylph slid her fingers insider her blouse and took out an office envelope, stretching out towards him, and said:" This is the envelope that fell from your book yesterday which you didn't notice. I tried to call you to remind you of this but you left the place quickly. "

With perplexed mind, Kesavan received the envelope from her and while receiving the envelope, his eyes found out her *fapworthy* fingers, which were nail polished. On seeing that envelope, he found out that it's not his envelope that he missed carelessly.

At that time, Jayasri smiled coyly and flexed her head by which Kesavan sussed out that it must be a *billet-doux*.

His doubt was not cleared off. "Is this *billet-doux* addressed to me or to someone so that I have to act as a messenger? Did she want me to use me as a messenger to give her lover in person? Is there anyone in the world to be enamoured of me? Is it essential for me to fall in love with any girl since I am jobless?"

Kesavan in his unusual tone asked her," Is it addressed to me?"

Jayasri was wreathed in smiles and nodded.

"What for?"

"You can understand after reading it." She darted amorous arrows at him

Kesavan was about to open the letter but Jayasri hurried to prevent him from opening the envelope and inhibited," Don't open it now. Leisurely open it and read it."

Kesavan understood what she meant and asked her," Your good name, please?"

She gesticulated to him that her name was in the letter. Then she began to circumambulate the inner sanctum while he stayed back.
Kesavan was burning with impatience to read the billet-doux; so, he walked swiftly towards Ibrahim Park where he could read the letter calmly.
There were some kids playing in the park and he found out a vacant seat nearby the tank and sat comfortably.
He opened the letter and began to read silently. It was written in English neatly calligraphically.

My dear Lover,

Trust this letter of mine finds you in the state of oblectation on reading this 'Love-Letter". I would like to introduce myself as Jayasri, born in a family of toilers and remain jobless for the past one year. Due to the poor economic status of my family, I couldn't pursue my studies in the college. I am only the daughter of my parents, my father being an accountant in an oil company at Gandhi Market, earns a meagre income and in order to make a living, my mother is supplying snack items to the needy. This is my family status.

I have been watching you in this temple daily .I don't know what makes me fall in love on you. Yes, I love you very much. You have tranced my heart. I tried my best to convey my love orally but some inhibition prevented me from doing so; so I am speaking my mind through this letter.

I am dotty about you,,,,,,,,

I don't find words to express my depth of love on you.

I will be arrided if you acknowledge my love. Moreover,
If you accept my love, I request you to have our tryst at the following address.
"MISS. D. LALITHA, 45, NORTH AGRAHARAM STREET, THILLAI NAGAR
Ms Lalitha is my chum, bread and cheese friend, and she gave me this idea to contact you by letter. I will be waiting for you today by ten. If you accept my love, please meet me there so that we can exchange our hearts and speak our minds.
If not ... No, I don't want to receiver negative reply from you. If you sweep aside my love or keeping silence to this letter, I have no other options except to commit suicide.
Your lover,
Jayasri

Kesavan read the letter many times and memorized every word in that letter.

(Continued)

CHAPTER No: TWO : UNEMPLOYMENT PROBLEM SOLVED

The fish knows not
The nature of the sea.
Knows not how wide,
How vast, indeed, is the sea.
Like unto the fish am I,
I know Thee not;
But I feel Thee,
I live in Thee,

And if, perchance,
I move out of Thee,
Sure, I die!

Like Gautama Buddha sitting under the Bodhi tree, Kesavan was sitting under the banyan tree and was reflecting on "Love Letter"

The birds were chirping and flying happily. "I would have taken the birth of a bird instead of human birth." He thought out of vexation as he thought whether it behooved him to reflect on that matter in the present position. Like a coin having both sides, he felt joy and grievance; Joy, to be enamoured by Jayasri and grievance, consent from parents in the amatory matters and his family status. He sighed and thought:" Every advantage has its own disadvantage. It's true in my life. When my mother comes to know my amatory matters what will she think of me? She suspects me since I am undertaking tuition to the girl-students and if she comes to know that I've fallen in love with Jayasri, it will corroborate her suspicion on me and ascertain that I am a useless fellow having no responsibility.

The Garden was yielding a serene atmosphere and was a vantage to him to meditate upon each and every word in Jayasri's billet-doux).

"What a pity! The girl who proposes is also same category. She is also pauper like me. So God has matched me with pauper family not at least middle class family. Albeit she was born in a pauper family, how beautiful she is! What a charming face! How ravishing she is in her simple dress, Flounce and shirt!

"I have been watching you in this temple daily .I don't know what makes me fall in love on you. Yes, I love you very much. You have tranced my heart. I tried my best to convey my love orally but some inhibition prevented me from doing so; so I am speaking my mind through this letter."-Ten years before, we, boys' used to stalk after the girls and were longing for them and slavered them but subversively modern trendy girls fall in love very easily upon the boys and chuckle the relationship as soon as their intention get fulfilled. There's an example in my life. My quondam lover, Vaishnavi popped the question and even after the popping cherry, she chucked my relationship for she got a *better Hand.*

Oh! What a ***beau siens*** these two have! How voluntarily she (Vaishnavi) dry humped on that fateful day!

Jayasri, in her letter, mentioned that I tranced her heart. Is it true? Am I so handsome and beautiful to trance her heart? It's Vaishnavi that she wheedled me by flattering me that I have ***beau corps***. Is it her carnal love that attracted her towards me? It's my pragmatic home truth that we should not rely upon the modern girls. Let me see when I become familiar with her. "

Next, she mentioned in her letter that," ***Ms Lalitha is my chum, bread and cheese friend, and she gave me this idea to contact you by letter. I will be waiting for you today by ten. If you accept my***

love, please meet me there so that we can exchange our hearts and speak our minds.
Who is Lalitha? Is she of the same type? Birds of the same feather flock together.Anyhow she mentioned the tryst and I am going to meet both by ten. How nicely she mentioned that we can exchange our hearts! On seeing the phrase,' exchange of hearts' it reminds me of the old lyric by anonymous

One-sided love broke the see-saw down
I got to get rough when I hit the ground
And you went your way and I went wild
And girl, you'd understand if your heart was mine
If we had an exchange of hearts
Then you'd know why I fell apart
You'd feel the pain when the mem'ries start
If we had an exchange of hearts
I'd never wished a lonely heart on you
It's not your fault, I chose to play the fool
One day may come when you'll be in my shoes
Then your heart will break and you'll feel just like I do
If we had an exchange of hearts
Then you'd know why I fell apart
You'd feel the pain when the mem'ries start
If we had an exchange of hearts
When time turns the tables and soon I'll be able
To find a new romance
And then you'll remember my love warm and tender
Too late for a second chance
If we had an exchange of hearts
Then you'd know why I fell apart

You'd feel the pain when the mem'ries start
If we had an exchange of hearts
"If you sweep aside my love or keeping silence to this letter,, I have no other options except to commit suicide." Does she stipulate me and force me to love her? I can't come to any conclusion unless I meet het at the place of tryst. "

Kesavan decided to meet Jayasri at the residence of Lalitha before ten. He returned home and drank a cup of flavour coffee, Kumbakonam Degree Coffee, ; then he performed 'Nithya Pooja' today special Pooja' and prayed earnestly.

By nine, he dressed up well and told his mother," I've some important work in the University. I may come late. Don't wait for me for taking lunch with me. Bye."

His mother was unaware of the fact that Kesavan was going to meet Jayasri at the residence of Lalitha in connection with meeting his new lover. Kesavan fibbed and started walking towards ThillaiNagar to meet Jayasri.

By ten he reached the North Agraharam by riding his father's bicycle and was searching for the door number. Soon he found out the house where a stout lady was waiting at the door sill for him. He guessed that the stout lady might be Lalitha, close friend of Jayasri.

When he stood before the closed gate, the stout lady nodded at him with an affable smile and was limping or hobbling down towards the gate to open it. Yes, she was a lame lady. Something must have crippled her leg for life.

Every cloud has silver lining

"Namaste, "Kesavan greeted her with an amiable smile. "Are you, Miss. Lalitha?"
She nodded and limping up to the main gate, she opened the gate wishing him," Namaste"
Lalitha, a crippled lady, a spinster was a *tricenarian* and it was revealed through her shrunken skin and sagged bosoms.
"My hearty welcome to you, please step in." She welcomed him.
Kesavan introduced himself and parked his bicycle by the side of the compound wall.
It was a medium sized house, an independent house, with all facilities and around the house were a number of plants and trees to give shadow and coolness during summer. There was a well at the back of the house and a small garden where different kinds of vegetables were grown. There were two bed rooms, one kitchen and main hall. In the main hall there hung a big photo of her mother adorned with a rose garland.. (Yes, her mother was no more)
Lalitha offered him a seat in the front hall and asked him what he wanted either coffee or tea. Kesavan offered a cup of coffee only and she went to the kitchen to prepare coffee. From the kitchen, she conveyed him that Jayasri rang up to her that she would be there before ten
"That's Indian Punctuality" Kesavan thought and smiled.
Kesavan was weary as he rode by bicycle and was sweating. So he wanted to refresh himself for which he asked Lalitha to show him the bathroom so as to fresh up.

Lalitha led him to the bathroom and opened the door.
Kesavan began to take bath and within ten minutes, came out freshly.
Lalitha helped him to prettify him by supplying him with necessary cosmetic things.
When he came out of the room, he looked like a young prince.
Lalitha was busy in preparing coffee while Kesavan was glancing over the newspaper.
Within ten minutes, Lalitha prepared a cup of coffee and brought it to the main hall in a tray. Kesavan took the coffee and sipped slowly.
By ten thirty, Jayasri came to her house and was surprised to see Kesavan waiting for her at Lalitha's residence.
Jayasri *dressed up* and *perked up* her outfit, *long skirt and shirt*, both matching colour, by which she was ravishing in her dress. At the sight of Kesavan who was waiting for her in the main hall, her visage disclosed riant feelings and wagged her right hand while her lips uttered, 'Hi" for which Kesavan reciprocated to her by wagging his right hand and said: "Hi"
Lalitha in her didactic tone admonished," You should not have come late to make him wait for you. He has been waiting for you for forty five minutes. "
"What to do, Lalitha? Did I come late intentionally? My mother wants me to help her in cooking as she is not feeling well. So, it's inevitable for me to help her in cooking and started from home by ten. Instead of waiting for the bus,

I feel it better to walk on foot. So it is late by thirty minutes." Then she turned to Kesavan and in an apologetic tone," Very sorry for making you wait for thirty minutes. When did you come here?"
"You mentioned in your letter the deadline by ten. So I came here by my bicycle at nine forty five. "Kesavan looked at his wrist watch
Lalitha fetched three plates of sandwich and kept it on the table and opened up the topic:" Let's discuss by taking sandwich." Then she cleared her throat and began to speak:" Mr. Kesavan, Jayasri is enamoured of you and *is dotty about you.*. We would like to know your idea in this amatory affair. What do you say, Kesavan? Would you like to accept her love?" She has been watching you for a month and fell in love with you. She is mad after you. She feels that she cannot live without you. Now the game is in your court."
Till Lalitha completed her sentiments on behalf of her crony, Jayasri was flexing he head and didn't look at Kesavan. But when Lalitha specified that,' *Now the game is in your court"* , she raised her head and met his eyes which conveyed him her love as well as aflutter disposition.
Lalitha and Jayasri were looking at him eagerly what he was going to tell them either positively or negatively.
"True to my heart what I would like to tell you is," Kesavan added:" she has already stolen my heart in the temple when she gave me her love letter. But I couldn't understand what has made her to be dotty to me. What is in me to be enamoured? I have never seen her before and I am a stranger to

her. I don't know anything about her or whereabouts. I don't know her residential address. "He paused and then glanced at her. Then, continued:" Before knowing my consent in this matter, I would like to reveal my family stratus. I don't hail from a rich family but from the same family what she mentioned in her letter. My father is a prohit and my mother is a housewife. We've our own house and by dint of rent and my father's meagre income, we are running a living. There is no other source of income. I am the pivot of their life. The only source of my income is Tuition only. Till I get government post, I have to undertake tuition which my mother opposes."

Lalitha smiled at Kesavan and asked him," Are you taking home tuition to girl students?"

Jayasri sussed out what Lalitha implied and so she also laughed at him.

Kesavan too laughed and said jokingly:" My mother drove the girls from my house when they came to see me in my house for showing the question paper."

It proves that your mother has foresight and a taciturn nature."

"It's true. I am only the pivot of her life."

"In this present situation, do you think your mother will go along with your decision and accept Jayasri as her daughter-in-law?

Kesavan gave his repartee:" Similarly, will her parents be ready to give their daughter in marriage to me who is fit for nothing and unemployed?"

His words touched their hearts.

"Never be despondent, Mr. Kesavan. **The darkest cloud has silver lining**. If your problem is unemployment, I can easily solve it. "

On hearing her words of assurance, both looked at her with wonder.

"If my unemployment problem gets solved everything will get solved. " Kesavan told her emphatically.

"If I get you a post in Chittoor in Andhra Pradesh, will you go and work there along with Jayasri? " Lalitha asked him.

"Are you fibbing?"

"No, I am not of that type. Seriously, I am telling you. Will you work in Chittoor if I get you a job there?"

"Certainly. No doubt."

"Promise?"

"By God's promise."

"Okay; you will get a job. Mr Jagan Moghan Reddy is my dearest friend. He is running an institution in Chittoor. He is in search of a dedicated teacher to take higher classes in his institution, "Maharishi Vidya Mandir". I think you are good at English. I will give you a letter of recommendation. You give him and join the duty. He will give you decent salary. My uncle is working as a supervisor in Government in Vellore. I will give his residential address. He will give you accommodation. From Vellore you can travel by train daily. Moreover, Jayasri is also good at English and Maths. She will also be appointed in that institution. Both can work together. If you earn his goodwill, then he will take you as the partner of the institution. Your financial problem will be over. What do you say now?"

On hearing her words, Kesavan was overwhelmed very much and with bleary eyes, he joined his two hands towards Lalitha and saluted her. "I will be grateful to you for the succour you do in my life. I don't know how I am going to repay the debt of gratitude."

"If it is true, then, you marry my soul, Jayasri and treat her well. Be careful not even a drop of tear should be dropped from her eyes. Promise now in my presence at my Pooja room."

Lalitha was gratified when she saw Jayasri's face bloomed like a fresh flower. She asked her friend," Jayasri, what do you want to say?"

Jayasri replied humbly: "What's there to say? I get serendipity to win my love. I don't find words to express my gratitude. What else can I say?"

Lalitha spoke to them: "In this world it is common for all lovers to be enamoured of each other for some other reasons. But how far they are successful in their life by marrying their lovers is very rare and meagre. I met failure in amatory affairs and was cheated by ungrateful fellow. God only knows how much I suffered. I pray God that no one should be afflicted like me. Love Failure is worse than perditions. So, I made up my mind to help the lovers, known lovers, to make them success in their life and get them married. I used to feel happy in their happiness. My soul, Jayasri, conveyed me that she has been enamoured of you and sought my help. So I made her write to you billet-doux and made you come here to speak your

minds. Now the problem is solved. What I expect from you is: 'Take a service in your life to unite the lovers and make their life successful by your possible help. "
.Both promised to do according to her will.
Gratified with them, Lalitha asked them," If you wish to discuss or exchange your ideas, you can go there and open up your views overtly. After discussion, come here if any is left unsolved. Now you both go to that room and discuss there.."
Then she asked Jayasri to come with her and led him to her private room. Then in a whispering voice, Lalitha asked Jayasri," During sweet-nothings, don't lose your self-control. Be careful! Never allow him to reach the culmination point."
Jayasri with her erubescent face and coy smile, nodded and went to the room as directed by Lalitha. In a few seconds, Kesavan paced towards the room where Jayasri was waiting for him.

(Continued)

CHAPTER No: THREE
(KESAVAN'S ROMANCE)

There's none in the city who didn't know Ramamurthy Sastrigal, famous for potency which he proved by having four daughters and four sons. The house in which they were living was neither a hut nor a cottage. It's very difficult to identify which's kitchen and which one, bed room or reception hall. He was a rival to Kesavan's father who was also a prohit.
One day, he paid a visit to Kesavan's residence.

Every cloud has silver lining

Neelavathy, mother of Kesavan, was surprised to see him there and she sussed out that he was expecting something from them. But she nodded and offered him a seat to sit in front of her.
He was always used to beat about the bush.
"Where's Anna? (It means, father of Kesavan) Last week, I saw you taking medical treatments from Dr. Dharmarajan. How do you feel now? Where is your son, Kesavan? He is known to the whole city for his excellent teaching in English Grammar. My second daughter, Vaishnavi, has been weeping bitterly for a long time for she is not able to understand what the lecturer teach in English. She is Tamil medium background. But she is a final year student in Maths. I think she is B.Sc. Maths Third year student. She is very good at Mathematics but subversively poor in English. She has been pestering me with her requests to contact your son, Kesavan for teaching her English but I am very busy and so far I haven't remembered her insistence. Today morning, she reminded me to contact your son and arrange for tuition in English. One month enough. My daughter is very shrewd and learns very quickly. It's left to his convenience either he can teach at my house or here in your house. Kesavan decides the time and I will send her at that time. Please help my daughter and it is in your hands, sister."
Neelavathy thought of herself: "Oh, that's the reason you've come here! Without expecting advantage from one, you won't step into one's house." Then she gave her repartee to Sastrigal:"

It pleases me to hear that your daughter, Vaishnavi is very shrewd in Mathematics. Generally Tamil medium students find it difficult in Colleges in their further studies because they have to study through English. My son is a dux in the University and a gold medallist. (Really, Kesavan was not a dux and not a gold medallist) As you said, his fame as the best tutor in teaching English has spread far and wide. He wants to work not in Government colleges or schools because, all are Tamil medium only. He has forgotten speaking Tamil but English. He has applied to St. Joseph's College and is expecting appointment Order. Till it comes, he doesn't want to waste his time. That's why he is undertaking tuition, home tuition. Even God knows not when he comes and when he goes out. He is up to the brim. At present, he is not at home. (But Kesavan was in his room studying an English novel and was eves dropping) As soon as he returns home, I will ask him the possibility whether he can take tuition or not. Give me your contact number and I will send the message."
Ramamurthy couldn't talk more than this and finally he requested her to show consideration.
Next day in the morning, to her shock, Vaishnavi appeared at the door sill of Kesavan's residence. Her presence baited Neelavathy and concealing her hatred, she told her politely:" Very happy to know that you are very much interested to learn English from my son but unfortunately, he is not feeling well. So, after he gets cured, I will send the message. Yesterday your dad came here and I replied what is to be done next. But he misheard

what I said and now he sent you here.. No problem. He is still sleeping, lazy fellow. Would you like to take coffee?"
Vaishnavi was not as stupid as Neelavathy expected. She understood what Neelavathy implied. "Sorry, aunty. " She didn't speak afterwards and went berserk.
Neelavathy reported to Kesavan:" Have you seen how she came here with skimpy dress:" Has she come to learn or for any other intention? It's better to give up taking tuition to girl students. I gave her a perfect answer. One word is enough to the wise. "
In the evening, Kesavan received a message from Vaishnavi by dint of his cell phone which mentioned:" I regret to inform that I was ill treated by your mother for no reason. Is it wrong to learn from you? My poverty has made your mother behave rashly and mercilessly. Had I been rich, I would have been treated well. But I am born in a poor family. If you think I am not guilty, please teach me Grammar at my home or anywhere but if you think I am wrong, do as you like. It's left at your discretion."
He replied immediately; "In the present situation, it is not advisable or I to take tuition at your residence and you are not in a position to come to my house. So, I will recommend you to Krishnan to whose children I am taking tuition. He is a genuinely a gentle man. He will oblige to my request. Being you are a girl, there won't be any problem to him because, I am taking tuition to his

daughter. If it's a boy, he may hesitate to accept my request. So, I will message to you before six. " Kesavan made a request to Mr. Krishnan to permit Vaishnavi to learn along with his daughter and he accepted his request without hesitation. But the next day, he received a repot rom Mrs. Krishnan that it would be better not to allow Vaishnavi to their house as she's a chatter-box and was afraid of whether Vaishnavi would spoil her children character wise. So, Mrs. Krishnan regretted to inform that she sternly condemned Vaishnavi not to step into her house hereafter.

Vaishnavi rang up to Kesavan and vented her anger on Krishnan family. "Is it my fault to be born in the poorest family? Is it wrong to have thirsty to learn from the gent like you? Had I been rich, the fat lady would have welcomed me by circumambulating the camphor plate in front of me. Because of my poverty only, the fat lady neglected me and humiliated me. What wrong thing did I do at Krishnan's house? I learnt a good lesson from the society. Unless one is rich, he or she is trampled down in this evil society. ***A cat may look at a king* =யானைக்கு ஒரு காலம் வந்தால் பூனைக்கு ஒரு காலம் வரும்.** I will teach them a lesson one day or other. Is Latha more beautiful than I am? I understand that you are undertaking tuition because Latha has enchanted and tranced your heart. Is she better than me in all aspects? What's lacking in me comparing with her? Don't I have charm? Don't I have attractive organs? I

hate you, I hate the world, I hate the entire society….."She was bitterly crying.
Kesavan tried to placate her anger. "Vaishnavi, cool yourself. I was reported that you were chit-chatting with Latha. You may not know that Latha is an innocent girl though physically matured. She is seventeen but doesn't know the world around her. In short, I can say that she is a frog in the well. I wonder how you dragged the matter of sex irrelevantly. Who under-rated you or your charm? Do you think I've no other work other than comparing the sexual organs of girls with others? I am a Guru to them. I don't have such kind of base feelings in my mind and heart. If I am not wrong, I am sure that you are affected with inferiority complexity. ***Can a leopard change its spot?*** Jenma புத்தி செருப்பால் அடித்தாலும் போகாது. Realize the words what I said." He rang off his cell phone.
As usual, Kesavan started for taking tuition at about five thirty in the evening with necessary books and walked down the road towards Thenar via,. Raja Theatre. To his surprise, at the corner of the road, Vaishnavi was waiting for him and at the sight of Kesavan, she came near him and said:' Hi!" and said in her unusual tone:" Extremely sorry for I have spoken stupidly. Nowadays, I am aware that I am insensible. But I don't know how to avoid. Can you spend a few minutes for my sake? I would like to open up my mind with you. Shall we go to Marakadai Park?"
Vaishnavi was in her college Uniform dress, weekly twice, Monday and Friday, maroon colour

tops and white bottoms. Gently she was carrying some books to mean that she's a college student. Kesavan could not meet her esurient eyes of an avid curiosity when she made a request for tryst. He'd to take tuition to Jayasri, a tenth standard student, English medium, at six in the evening and then by seven to nine to Latha and her younger brother, Savannan , eighth standard student, (CBSE syllabus.)

"I have to take tuition at six." Kesavan said Kesavan hesitantly.

"Where?"

"Tennur."

"At what time?"

"At six."

Then?

………

"After six, Latha tuition, am I right?"

Kesavan nodded.

Today, declare Holiday to them. You are going to be with me till eight. I have a lot of matter to discuss with you, Kesavan."

"Please, Vaishnavi…."

"No more request, Kesavan. Take your phone and inform them in my presence."

Please, Vaishnavi."

"Please, Kesavan for my sake. Today only." She fondled.

Like Sage Viswamithra, he broke his grit of mind. Vaishnavi, like the celestial angel, Menaka, made him accept her stipulation and inevitably, he rang up to Jayasri and Krishnan to inform that due to inevitable work at home, he could not take tuition.

"Now only, you're my Kesavan. Please come with me." Vaishnavi walked him to the big park.
Marakadai Park is also known as 'Lovers' Park' and one could see lovers here and there sitting in different poses in the park.
After he sat on the grassy floor, Vaishnavi sat very close to him and opened the conversation.
Now, Kesavan could not consider Vaishnavi as his student and he won't be Guru. He is also a man of flesh and blood. So he succumbed to the temptation and behaved like a doll in her hands.
Vaishnavi fondled his hand and uttered words passionately:" "If I am not mistaken, why won't we be the true lovers?"
As soon as she held his hand, dextral hand and kept it in her sinistral hand, Kesavan didn't oppose. He stammered:" What… you mean… we… lovers…?
Have I uttered any vulgar or obscene word to discommode you, Kesavan?" Saying, Vaishnavi kept his dextral hand at the protruding part of her tops very gently which he didn't expect to happen. His palm perceived her bandeau she was wearing inside her tops.
Then appressing his palm to the protruding part of her tops, she asked him," I haven't received response to my question.. Why?"
"I don't remember anything now. I don't know what baffles me." Kesavan was overwhelmed and could not respond to her question.
"Shall I remind you of my question?" Vaishnavi caressed and slid his arm inside her tops.

It was the maiden experience to both of them. Vaishnavi and Kesavan watched a number of love scenes, read smut stories and watched a number of porno films by which they had acquired theoretical knowledge. Now they acquire pragmatic knowledge in that 'Lovers' Park.

No sooner did her hand slid his arm inside her tops, than Kesavan felt a sense of inexplicable pleasure pierced through the vessels of blood and felt the edge of her cleavage. His palm was hot.

Similarly, as soon as his fingers perceived the edge of her cleavage where the cup of her bandeau welcomed his fingers, she felt pleasantness and her face turned into rubicund.

"Is it interesting, Kesavan?" The dialogues what he had to ask her, she was asking him.

Kesavan felt his eyes burning and blabbered:" I am very much excited by this maiden experience, Vaishnavi."

"I've seen you a number of times crossing the Vinayaga temple and know that your father is also prohit like my father. But my father is the rival of your father and there is no cordial relationship between our families. I have a school mate namely Jayasri. She is also studying Mathematics but under correspondence course. We, both are ***Philomath.*** She has also been watching you when you were going to the temple daily. She used to enquire you for the details but I didn't respond to her. I know she is infatuated with you like me."

Kesavan had never expected that he was going to meet Jayasri and acknowledge her love. When she mentioned about her co-mate, Kesavan was not interested to know much about Jayasri because he was not in a mood to know about her as his rapt attention was towards her boobs. "What a happenstance to feel the boobs of a girl that too, who voluntarily picked my arm and slid inside her tops! Suddenly, he remembered the oracle of His. Holiness, Sivasankara Baba who said: "Our relationships on this earth are not new but continuity from our previous births. Your mother in the present birth may be some kind of relationship with you in your previous birth. And this relationship may vary in succeeding births. So, my relationship with this girl may be due to some kind of relationship during my previous birth. "He thought himself

When Vaishnavi asked for his abrupt silence, he mentioned the oracle of his Guru. Vaishnavi nodded and said:" Yes, it is logically accepted because we don't know each other but something attracted me towards you and I voluntarily brought you here for playing foreplay. I believe that our relationship has continued from our previous birth."

Kesavan pulled her tops to some extent to peep through her tops inside where his arm was resting as a haven. But, Vaishnavi resisted and said sternly:" There's a time to see whatever you like to see but this is not the time to see what you like to see."

Kesavan tried to take away his arm from inside her tops but at once, Vaishnavi seized his arm and said laughingly: "No need to take away your arm from there."

"What sin have my eyes committed for being interdicted like the apple that Eve was crazy to pluck the forbidden apple?" Kesavan asked her.
Vaishnavi didn't know who Adam or Eve was and she didn't know anything about John Milton's Paradise Lost and paradise Regained. So she asked Kesavan about them but Kesavan told her. "There's a time to say something but this is not the time to say what you wish to know." He gave her repartee.
"Oh, tit for tat?" Vaishnavi sighed and after a pause, continued:" That's why I want to learn the classic Literature in English. Can you teach me the English classical literature?"
Albeit she used the terms wrongly, he didn't point out them. He tittered and said convincingly:" I will tell you classical novels written by classical English writers. "
"If it is so, when are you going to take tuition to me?"
"Do you want me to come to your house and take tuition?"
"Do you want me to come to your house for taking tuition? Vaishnavi replied in the same way.
"It's impossible to take tuition in my house for my mother will knock me out. But will your mother allow me to take tuition when she came to know that my mother is against taking tuition to you? Won't she suspect me?"
"If you're ready for taking tuition in my house, I'll do the needful steps. Are you ready? When are you going to take tuition to me?" Vaishnavi fondled

tightly so that he could not take it away from her cleavage.
"From tomorrow?" Kesavan extended the space of his fingers which had been resting at her cleavage Vaishnavi felt his palm cupped her dextral boob profoundly. She looked at him lusciously.
Kesavan whispered:" Is it interesting now?"
Vaishnavi nodded with lascivious smile adorning her rubicund face.
He exclaimed: What an orbicular shape is yours!. What a lubricious mound! Albeit it's in a dense form, it never sags. What complexion, what shape your areola and tit…I can't see visually whereas my fingers got a luck to feel it."
Vaishnavi laughed and replied:" Tomorrow."
"At your house?" Kesavan asked eagerly.
Vaishnavi shook her head and said calmly: If my mother identifies us, she 'll besom me strongly."
"Then, where?"
"Valli Malai." She said calmly and looked at his face eagerly what he was going to say.
"What! Valli Malai! It's nearly ten kilometres from here. "
"Let it be even hundred kilometres. Can't we go? It's the safest place for us." She paused. It's due to his squeezing her boob.
Kesavan apologised and said:" How long are my fingers kept idle? They're always active."
Vaishnavi laughed and wielded her ribald:" Let your active fingers prove their agility tomorrow."
Kesavan pecked at her cheek pronto in the wink of the moment and asked Vaishnavi," How do you know all about these things?"

My friends mentioned it that it is a place for orgy and promiscuous bath play can be done by skin-dipping. Don't ask me for more details. Even if I know, I won't let you hereafter. Let's be ready to catch the train by nine at the Fort station. We've to alight at the third railway station, walk five hundred metres across the groove and reach the valley. During weekend holidays, one can see crowd of lovers camping there. So, Valli Malai is our tryst tomorrow. I'll be waiting at the Fort station for you. If you fail to come using some lame excuse, I can't excuse you. Keep in mind." Vaishnavi spoke didactically.

Now Vaishnavi is his teacher and he is her student. All turned subversively in a moment.

Kesavan nodded silently.

"Any problem?"

He shook his head and then he asked her hesitatingly," If I am not mistaken, shall I ask you a peculiar question to get the true answer?

Vaishnavi was so quick to understand what his question was going to be entered. She smiled at him and asked him, "Any personal question?"

Kesavan nodded.

Vaishnavi guessed rightly. She laughed and said calmly: "Okay, ask question to get the true answer."

Kesavan posed the question. "When do you start masturbation?"

Vaishnavi laughed shyly and then recounted her experience:" Well, I had my first orgasm when I was 10 years old. It was totally unintentional and not knowing what it is orgasm. I was sitting in the bathroom and I took the water pipe just casually and put my finger on the vent from which water comes out half and the water was coming as stroke and suddenly it got on my clit and I felt A FEELING which I didn't know what it was and I put the pressure of water on my clit again for few mins and then I orgasmed and I didn't knew at that point that I had AN ORGASM because I was a kid. After that I kept doing this whenever I used to take a long shower because it gave me pleasure and reduced my stress. I felt good. When I was 16 years old, I once started to rub my clit with my fingers in circular motion and I orgasmed. I discovered a new way at that point to give me pleasure without water. I first watched porn when I was 15 years old during my exams to release stress. At that point I used to feel wetness in my underwear but I didn't knew why it was happening. But whatever it was I was feeling good. When I was 17 years old I used to masturbate quite often after I discovered that circular motion rubbing my clit thing. I used to watch porn videos and read erotic novel to masturbate.

Now when I'm proper adult, I masturbate daily 2 - 3 times. I can't go without it. It reduces my stress level and helps to go to sleep peacefully. That water pressure thing I still do whenever I take long shower. I watch porn videos a lot. But I doesn't let this habit of mine interfere with my daily life.

I'm still a VIRGIN though.

have the opportunity - is go online and watch some hard-core porn. Then I masturbate just with my fingers, sticking my middle finger deep into my pussy. Stereotypical masturbating, I guess. : P takes me a while to come... probably because I'm enjoying it so much! I only do this every month or so.

Hope I helped you out.

Kesavan nodded and then asked her next question:" Have you ever heard or have been told their experience? For which Vaishnavi started recounting:" I don't want to mention the name of the girl. But she recounted to me her experience in this field.

I remember her first time having an orgasm very vividly, she was 12 and had won a kindle at school, so she was getting all the free books she could, and reading them at night, she started reading some erotic novels and in one she was reading about a girl fantasizing about a man while fingering herself and she wandered what she was rubbing that felt so good, so she reached her hand down and she was soaking wet and she touched her clit right away and a shudder went through her body so she rubbed it a few more times and had a very intense orgasm. After that she'd read an erotic novel every night and masturbate, after each orgasm she'd wait 30 seconds before rubbing again. When she got a phone she discovered incognito and watched porn. She started a game with herself to see how many orgasms she could have in one night before it was too sensitive to touch. The summer she was 15 she'd spend hours just having multiple orgasms, she guessed she was addicted, it felt so good. Now she didn't need porn or anything to have an orgasm, she is 19, and she does it at least 3 times a night to relieve stress and help her sleep. Not as much as when she was a young teen but plenty often."

Then, Kesavan and Vaishnavi engaged themselves in sweet nothings till the gardener drove the lovers out of the park as it was the time for closing the park.

Before parting, Vaishnavi osculated him and reminded him of the tryst the nest day morning.

Kesavan nodded and asked her," When shall I get the fortune of having 'Holy Dharshan" of seeing you completely?"

Vaishnavi laughed and replied:" I never expected that you will acknowledge my love albeit you're a tutor. I am a lucky girl to have you as my tutor." She wheedled. Then she flexed her head and with wreathed in lovely smiles as he overtly asked her," ***When shall I get the fortune of having 'Holy Dharshan" of seeing you completely?"***, Vaishnavi understood the pun he played and smiled at him:" If you're very particular in worshipping the Holy Dharshan", it can be done as you like but it is not a suitable place to fulfil your desire. Had it been the solitary place, I would have shown you the Holy Dharshan. Anyhow, you are going to see me completely tomorrow at Valli Malai, isn't it?"

Her lustful implication tempted him and he said in a passionate tone:" How interesting it was, you know when my palm cupped your mounds!"

"Vaishnavi sighed and replied lustfully:" It's very interesting to you but I could not endure the pleasantness caused by your manipulation and my veins were burning with desire. I don't know how I am going to sleep tonight. Because your manipulation stamped as an engramma and it can't be erasable from my mind till my death."
Kesavan replied:" I am also a human being made of flesh and blood. Is there anyone in the world who can conquer his feelings of lust in the modern world? Our love affair is not platonic love but infatuation. But because of this, we are not losers and we are not going to change our ways. As I said before, our relationship continues from our previous birth. It is the master plan of God. "
Vaishnavi could not understand what he said but simulated as if she had understood what he said and replied:" As per your wish, you can have the "Holy Dharshan" tomorrow morning. Is it okay?"
Kesavan nodded and wagged his hands at the time of parting from her.
Kesavan returned home and his mother, Neelavathy was surprised to see him come early and so she asked him:" Didn't you take tuition?"
"Now I am affected by 'Migraine". Please give me a cup of hot coffee. I want to take rest." He fibbed and resorted to his reading room.
In five minutes, Neelavathy gave him a tumble of hot coffee and then asked him," Is there any problem?"
Kesavan nodded..
"What's the problem?"

"I have written the Railway Service commission and the officer concerned for appointment is expecting bribery. If dad uses his influence and approach the CCS, without bribery, I will get the post. But dad has not aptitude to influence the officer. I don't know how to make him understand my position."
Neelavathy comforted:" What to do? Had he the aptitude to influence the offices, you would have got the best positon in Government service. I will try my best to make him take steps in your case. Don't worry."
Kesavan tittered. Till late night he couldn't sleep.
(Continued)

CHAPTER NO: FOUR
(BATHING SPORT)

Kesavan, as an insomnia patient couldn't sleep that night. His mind was haunting around her, her lovely looks, rubicund face, and spathic boob's perception and her sweet-nothings-all made him sleepless. Albeit his eyes didn't catch sight of her cleavage or the boob his hands cupped, his thoughts sweetened his memories and the time he spent with her in the Lover's Park. He was unaware that his mind was filled with lust but not with love. After he ***wanked*** only, his stress got relieved and had a sleep.
Next day in the morning, he woke up with the thought of Vaishnavi. After ablution, he said to his mother:" Maa, I've to go to the University Library for reference. So I will be a little bit late for lunch."

What did Neelavathy know about their amatory affairs? So, she believed in his words. As usual, his father got up early in the morning and went away for performing 'House warming ceremony' as it's an auspicious day.

He walked down the street and crossed the Raja theatre and walked fast towards Fort station where Vaishnavi was waiting for him. Yes, she came there a little bit earlier.

Vaishnavi was ravishing in her ghagra dress with transparent Lehenga choli, gifted by a rich person on the eve of Navaratri Festival while Kesavan was in black pants and blue sleeved shirt.

"Did your mother say anything?" Vaishnavi asked eagerly.

Kesavan told her how he fibbed to his mother in order to make her believe in his words. Then he asked her," How did you manage in your house?"

Vaishnavi showed her books and said" Special Class at eight. So, they won't suspect me."

"What's our plan today?"

"In ten minutes, the Passenger train is going to come and I am going to travel in the lady's compartment. You travel by the next compartment. At the third station, we have to alight and walk down the road across the rails. In thirty minutes, we can reach the valley through the little forest. "

Kesavan nodded and then asked her," After reaching the valley, what is our plan?" His naughty wink and words pleased Vaishnavi who smiled charmingly and gave her repartee:" As soon as we go there, you will learn there."

Every cloud has silver lining

"Las night I had no sleep," reported Kesavan to Vaishnavi and added," I spent the night by thinking about you only."

Vaishnavi smiled and said:" Last night, I tossed and turned on my bed for a long time till it beam wet. Today morning, I washed well "

"I wanked secretly indulging in shacking with you."

"But you haven't seen it till now. But how did you shack with me?"

'My eyes are made of x ray eyes."

"Let me prove what I am wearing inside."

"No bandeau and no thong or briefs, am I right?"

Oh, God! How do you come to know?"

"That's why I told you that I have x ray eyes."

Similarly both indulged in ribaldry till the passenger train arrived on the second platform.

There was heavy crowd and all compartments were full of heads and no place to stand. Both managed to entrain the compartment, in the same compartment on footboard inevitably.

At the third station like many youngsters, Kesavan and Vaishnavi detrained from the compartment and walked across the rails along with other youngsters who were also going to the Valli Malai.

Nearly one hundred youngsters, both boys and girls, all lovers, were travelling by the passenger train. Some lovers walked in the trodden path while some entered into the groove and made a way through the rugged path. Some prefer to walk through the safety path.

Every cloud has silver lining

Kesavan and Vaishnavi were treading on the rugged and thorny bushes by encircling their waists each other. Lust and lubricity were burning glowingly in their minds. Both were aware that ten set of lovers were following them.

The climate was gorgeous and the lovers enjoyed the day.

Till they reached the foothill they engaged themselves in ribaldry. On the way to the foothill of Valli Malai, Kesavan and Vaishnavi saw one or two denarian and vicenarian lovers lying on lap of the lover in their skimpy dress and were loving to distraction. While Kesavan and Vaishnavi were crossing them, the *inamorata* (a person's female lover) was stripping down her petticoat by herself and after seeing them, she turned to opposite direction. Vaishnavi smiled at Kesavan amorously and asked him to carry her to the foot hill as she liked to be carried by him. Then Kesavan was carrying Vaishnavi in his arms and was walking down the trodden path while Vaishnavi was encircling her flowery hands around his neck to poise herself.

While carrying her, Vaishnavi asked him whether she was too weighty to be carried for which Kesavan replied:" Yes, it's due to the pair of mounds and callipygous nates."

Hearing his lewd and ribald comments, she bopped on his head kittenishly and commented that he was a maven in persiflage.

In the meanwhile another pair of lovers who saw Kesavan carrying Vaishnavi in his arms, the inamorata asked her lover to carry her in his arms.

Kesavan pecked upon the protruding parts of her tight bosom and perceived them and found out that there was no bandeau inside and the contour of her boobs and erect thelium was exposed through her bosom.

It tingled Vaishnavi and it showed through her countenance.

There was curved path and a small brook was found where there were a number of lovers bathing, skin-dipping. Kesavan forded and dropped her in the stream. Then Kesavan also immersed himself up to his neck in the stream. Along with other comrades, Vaishnavi and Kesavan were dabbling in the brook.

Their dresses were wet. Both stripped down their dresses and slightly washed in the running water, rinsed them and hung them on the branches of the trees to dry them.

Now Kesavan got a chance to see Vaishnavi in her stark naked position and Vaishnavi, vice versa,

Both were stark naked and Vaishnavi saw him ogling at her. She asked shyly:" Why are you looking at them so keenly? Your looks are like arrows darting at my body and they pierce through my body."

'What a charming boobs you have!" he exclaimed and was ogling at them.

Vaishnavi was very proud of her dense boobs she'd and she liked Kesavan ogling at him and lauding them as the bathykolpian beau siens. Her face turned to rubicund when his eyes were swarming around her beau corps. She involuntarily constricted her thighs tightly and hid

the sign V formed at her interfemoral region, thus leaving behind the protrusion of her Coleus Feminus exposed to his eyes that bobbed up him.
Kesavan thought whether Vaishnavi was a celestial angel, Urvashi, standing in puris naturalisbus and thus enslaver his mind. Her physical structure was so captivating that he was sure to go mad after her. From her neck to her ankle, the sun's rays couldn't perceive by which it remained untanned and protected her fair complexion. Her entire body was soppy as if the flower had been recently watered to fresh up it. Her orbicular boobs were heaving rhythmically in accordance with her inhaling and exhaling and it seemed to Kesavan that they welcomed him to enjoy them. Albeit they're fleshy mounds, they never sagged unlike other girls who were skinny-dipping in that brook. Like a buxom, she had a curvaceous body structure that tempted him to perceive her naked body.
He imprinted an enduring kiss on her erect boobs and his hands hid the shape like the black clouds clouding the sun and the moon. Her boobs had lost freedom once again as his palms imprisoned them but rendered her boobgasm due to his manipulation at her erect boobs by which Vaishnavi closed her eyes passionately and involuntarily. Lapping her naked boobs like a cat, one of his hands descended towards her navel and perceived the stubble grown around her pubic region.
Vaishnavi jerked a little when his middle finger ran over the curved path of her constricted Labia,

perceiving the lubricated region and was searching for the possibility to enter into the Gates of Heaven.

Having known his intention, Vaishnavi was so generous to open the Gates of Heaven for him to see and enjoy. So, she dilated her thighs a little so as to allow his middle finger only, admission a single point only, and his middle finger, craving for entering into the Heaven, was penetrating into her lubricious path smoothly.

Next moment, Vaishnavi flinched back as the middle finger impaled and popped the cherry pronto in the wink of the moment, thus deflowered her virgin very easily thus causing the hymenal haemorrhage.

Unlike other girls, she did not weep bitterly but endured the piercing pain patiently and when he asked with much concern whether she was hurt very much and felt uneasy, she shook her head and allowed him to do as he liked.

He lifted her naked body and carried her to the edge of the brook, placed her on the edge and washed her pudendum well while some of the lovers were spectating at them. While he was laving her pudendum the hymeneal haemorrhage mingled with the stream of water and the sanguine blood was carried along with the course of the running water.

While the skin-dippers were spectating at them, Kesavan flexed his head towards her chest and whispered something for which Vaishnavi nodded, tacit consent, and Kesavan, feeling gratification, penetrated his erect Phallus into her

distended pudendum, as the Gates of Heaven was distended giving access to enter into the Heaven.
Vaishnavi asked him," Shall we do it in the water?"
Kesavan nodded and took her to the shallow place of the brook and pursued the Dramatic Play and she enjoyed.
It was the first experience to them to realize what Heaven is. What Orgasm is! Kesavan and Vaishnavi realized pragmatically why even the celestial deities incarnate to enjoy the pleasures of orgasm. Though its duration and orgasm is mortal it is immortal.
Then they began skin-dipping in the brook.
It's a pleasant experience for them to play bath-sporting in the brook and moreover, it's a maiden experience to skin-dip overtly in the midst of other lovers who were also skin-dipping.
Vaishnavi caught the sight of a pair of lovers who were effing in the water and she turned to the side of Kesavan whether he was drooling over them. As expected, Kesavan was eyeing up the lovers, effing lovers, in the water and both forgot their surroundings.
The skin-dippers were splashing water and were yelling happily and joyfully, laughing boisterously.. Vaishnavi immersed her body, ***au naturel***, in the water up to her neck which looked like a lotus floating in the river.
When others start leaving from the brook to catch the Down Train, Vaishnavi and Kesavan had to start from there inevitably. By the time, they were about to leave, their dresses were dry and they

dressed themselves and got ready to start from the brook.
"Do you feel pain even now?"
Vaishnavi nodded but did not speak verbally.
"Extremely sorry, Vaishnavi,""
'Without breaking the coconut, you cannot get its kernel."
"You're always practical."
"My period starts from tomorrow. So there should be the gap of at least a week for our next meeting." Vaishnavi said with a sigh.
"I see."
"If I go in this manner, my mother will find out the secret. So I must get the help of any girl here to comb my hair and plait properly and dab cosmetic or talcum powder on my face so as to look fresh."
Vaishnavi got the help from one of the girls who was also nakedly walking along with her lover and she helped her in combing her hair and plaited. Moreover, she gave them plantain fruits and biscuits for which they conveyed her thanks and got familiar with them.
They caught the train and returned home by two in the afternoon.
&&&&&&&&&&&&&&&&&&&&&&&&&
&&&&&&&&&&&&&&&&&&&&&&&&&
&&&&&&&&&&&

CHAPTER No: FIVE
ENTRY OF NEW RELATIONSHIP

A swelling with a disposition of qualm brought about Kesavan a battle field between lust and love. He pondered over whether he was right in his action in view of amatory affairs with Vaishnavi who enslaved him by her lust and tempted him to manipulate her boob in the park, Lovers Park. Further, ***she trysted*** Valli Malai, a haven and a heavenly place for the lovers the next day morning to accomplish her lubricity for which she darted the arrows of lust at Kesavan by which he agreed to her proposal. But being scrupulous, his conscience seared him and could not sleep for a long time. At last he decided to meditate upon Sivasankara Baba, a celebrated and holiest Clairvoyant and siddha who succoured to him many times.

It was very simple practice; by lying on the bed, he began to chant the mantras, 'Sankaram Sivasankaram and eventually, Baba appeared in his mental screen and replied thus:" discontentment is her soul in many births in many forms and it follows in the present birth to seek contentment. ***Unfit as your spouse as she over indulged in lubricity abnormally (nymphomania) fittest person was born to bring mascot and light your life glowingly.***

"What kind of relationship with her? Kesavan asked the Siddha.

"As tigress, hen, cobra and concubine and finally lover in your previous births and in the present birth, the soul wanted to fulfill the latent desire through you. "Was the telepathized message.

What! I was born as a tiger, cock, kept her as a concubine and finally as my lover?"

"Seven birth relationship."

Remaining two births?

"Incestuous relationship."
"Thanks, Baba."
Kesavan opened his eyes. Now he bent on what should be done next. He blocked her calls Vaishnavi was flabbergasted for he blocked her calls. She suspected that it must be the graceful work of Neelavathy as she would have smelt the rat. She tried to contact him by different numbers but all those numbers were blocked, and attended by Neelavathy, mother of Kesavan.
The following day in the evening, she sent her sister, Geeta to see whether he was in his house or not and if he could be seen, she would communicate to him to meet her in the college. But his mother was waiting to receive Geeta as her guest. As soon as her sister, Geeta entered into the entrance gate, Neelavathy welcomed her gracefully, very kindly and affectionately and spoke very kind words:" If I see you or your sister another time entering my doorsill, I will not hesitate to besom you both. "
After this incident, many unwanted things happened and the enmity between two families grew more to the worst.
In the meanwhile , Kesavan had to go to Mysore to appear for the M.A. English final year examination and Krishnan helped him financially for the travel and Kesavan left for Mysore, But unfortunately, he flunked World Literature paper for he didn't prepare well. In other papers he scored just pass marks but declared fail. Since he knew the result, he didn't bother about his failure

but strove hard to engross his attention towards that paper. Yes, he had a flair of perseverance. In winter, Kesavan had an amatory experience by meeting Jayasri at the temple.

&&&&&&&&&&&&&&&&&&&&&&&&&
&&&&&&&&&&&&&&&&&&&&&&&&

Jayasri unlike a rustic lass, appeared to be an urban sylph and was a slim and tall Vicenarian, had a raving beauty and was a ravishing sight in her ghagra dress. Her ruddy complexion, her lovely eyes, and her sharp nose like that of Shakespearean's Cleopatra, pink lips like those of her vertical labia but her labial mouth was in horizontal position. Which looked like that orange flake, might have tranced their hearts. No wonder that her rubicund face would enslave the opposite sex.

Jayasri coiffed her hair for the party; her cascade of ebony hair without plaiting them but left spreading out as a modern trend. Her temple was broad which reminds us an axiom that those whose temples are broad are of highest intellectual persons and it is true in the case of Jayasri in whose broad temple, her fringe hid the half of the area of her temple. A glittering Tilak adorned at her glabella. Next, many poets metaphorised the arched eyebrows as a rainbow but her pair of eyebrows were of the size of her pair of breasts, semi-circular size with black hair as if they,,' re the stubble of her pubes when they were left devoid of depilation or epilation.

Above all her eyes were lovely, through which she could express what she thought in her mind and at the same time, had the power to enslave the opposite sex. Like Shankar, she is bisexual and her lovely look was enough to make others dotty about her. Next, her nose was sharp similar to William Shakespearean Cleopatra whose nose was sharp like that of bronze Idol of Goddess Durga. Below her nose was a pair of orange flaked lips corresponding to the vertical structure of her pudenda Labia, their dimension and softness and when she opens her mouth, her lips get dilated similar to the dilation of her Labium Majora when thighs are spread wide or got to dilated. Moreover, her nose tip looked like the protrusion of her Coles Feminus, the most sensitive organ of a female.

Her dental structure was of uniform type and were of milk white adding to her pulchritude when they were exposed while speaking. Her pink tongue similar to the smoothest organ of her vaginal walls, used to swish stylishly when she was talking. Her chin was strong and was apt to her oval size of her bright face. Her ear ornaments were made of gold covering, pea cock design were dangling from her ear rings and her ears ornaments used to wiggle like those of her voluptuous boobs wiggling while walking or galloping or moving. Like her eyes having sharpness, her ears had also sharp aural power.

Next, her neck was as butyraceous smooth as that of the foramen of her Crotch while sopping the profound area during cunnilinction.

A few centimetres downwards from her neck was a fascinating region where all look at to see the dimension of the pair of mounds formed in her chest. They are called as pleasure pillows in the slang term and her boobs were of orbicular in shape, having ruddy complexion. In her early years, she had heard from her friends circle that by massaging the boobs, their size would be augmented and she wished to have optimum size breasts for which she developed the habit of massaging her boobs with oil buy she hadn't known the fact that genes and hormones determine breast growth and they can keep growing and changing into her late teens.

Generally her caste ofi girls have naturally well-developed breasts due to genes and their hormonal secretions are also responsible for their well-developed breasts growth.

Jayasri habituated to wank during bathing and felt immense pleasure known as **boobgasm** while squishing her rotund breasts and then clit- flicked to obtain orgasm.

Initially she had developed an inhibition **to beat the beaver** but after reading an article on ‘masturbation” she got clarified and eradicated that qualm.

Apparently, Jayasri kvelled to have the eminent breasts and it reached its zenith when, during her school life, her class mates started ogling at her mounds.

Next was her midriff region having the same ruddy complexion and was even till her navel, a long slope like a valley from the pair of hillocks.

And her navel was deep to feast with those who are obsessed by **Alvinophilia,** a nice pit stop between her breasts and genitals where one can circle the area with light touch, dabbing, and lapping and during foreplay, a middle finger can be penetrated into her vagina and stimulate her G. spot using a "Come hither" motion. While the other finger can be used to rub her abdomen and appress to her navel by thumb. Moreover, when her navel would be rubbed around like massaging her pubic region, one can witness that her abdomen gets lightly stimulated following contraction of abdominal muscles which are connected to the vagina and these contractions make her feel aroused- even orgasm.
Next region is a region of fascination for all the boys. Like a whirlpool, a concavity in the surface of her midriff produced a depression in her navel and there was a declivity towards her vestibule, Mons Veneris, which was niftily depilated or epilated to expose its original ruddy complexion to beautify the eyes of its spectators. Serving as procreative organs, this strange organ is used for manifold purposes such as the source of orgasm, centre of coital plays foreplays, and an ejector of unwanted things in the body. When her thighs are constricted it forms the shape of V" between her groins and serves as a gate to Heaven. Like a Gate Keeper, her Coleus Feminus was guarding and peeping out of the Vulva remaining at the edge of the curved cleft. Generally the skin on female's intimate areas is darker than the rest of their skin and it is normal because of the melanin to cause

variations , epilation and exposure to sun But Jayasri used ***Toskani Radiance Intimate Cream*** to counteract the flaccidity and pigmentary changes helping the skin recover the natural tone and appearance.

Next, her pair of thighs were like the colour of the flake of jackfruit and as smooth as butter and **glabrate** to allure the opposite sex. Moreover the biceps of her thighs were enticing and were so smooth that it facilitated to lap them cozily. Further her knee- cap parts were not dark like other gents but fresh having the same colour of her thighs. Her ankles were glabrous as they were niftily epilated periodically.

It's a pleasant experience to her fella to **goose** het callipygous nates and were strong as her thighs. If she would perform Anasyrmos one can see the muscular hills a pair of hills having the glen. Like her hips, her muscular hills of nates wiggle while walking or striding. Usually Jayasri won't be without enduing with her briefs or thongs by which the contour of camel toe can be seen through the crotch.

Like all girls Jayasri was not exceptional to wank or **beat the beaver** especially during bed time and mostly she used to indulge in **breassturbation,** *The act of a girl or woman sexually stimulating herself by **fondling**, rubbing, licking, and sucking her own breasts and/or nipples as well as using a dildo or **vibrator** to simulate **tit fucking**.*

In a nutshell, this bangable blonde was over sensitive and emotional and a passionate girl.

Every cloud has silver lining

KESAVAN ENTERED THE BED room where Jayasri was waiting for him by sitting on the bed. At the sight of Kesavan, Jayasri stood up on the floor and flexed her head. Her face was rubicund. When Kesavan came near her, he called her lovingly, 'Jayasri'; that word sweetened her ears and she raised her head to look at him. "Come here; let's speak our minds."

Jayasri batted her eyelids and eyed up him. Then she rested comfortably in the bed by sitting near him after which he encircled her waist and drew her near him.

"Aren't you astonished by the *enigmatic happenstance*?"

To his reply, Jayasri leant over his shoulder cozily and opened the '*sweet- nothings*" with him. """Yes, many unexpected things happened. I've one doubt but I'm afraid whether you will mistake me." She inhibited.

Kesavan smeared her back and said calmly:" I know what you are going to ask me. You're doubtful whether I like you very much or not. Don't you think it is a silly and trivial question to make you fuss over it?"

Jayasri chuckled and said:" I have been watching you crossing me but you never turned to my side, I mean at least a glance. Why?"

Kesavan laughed heartily and said:" If I tell you the real reason, you will laugh at me. Do you know the mason, Arumugam, son of Natesa Maestri?"

"Yes, I know his father and his son also. Why do you relate it with this?"

"Do you know Arumugam is *nouveau—riche?"*

Jayasri shook her head to mean that she didn't know.
"The sins he committed has an impact through his son namely, Jambu to whom I am the tuition master. He is as asinine as Karunanidhi. All efforts were made to din in his clay brain but all are in vain. So I used to be in an upset mettle. That's why I missed to see you.".
"But I thought that you're arrogant and haughty. I thought that you simulate and intentionally avoided seeing me. "She chuckled.
Kesavan, caressing her shoulder, asked another question:" What makes you to be enamoured of me as I am not as pretty as you expect?"
When his hand caressed her strong shoulder, she was erotized and yearned for his osculation. After that, she felt his fingers flitted through her neck and drew it to French kiss her.
"Who said you're not pretty? You are the most handsome boy to my eyes. "Saying, she basciated on his cheek.
"Which place do you want me to osculate?" His hands descended from her neck.
Jayasri whispered softly:" Yes, that's the place."
"Where is it?"
"It's the place where your fingers descended."
"But like dark clouds hiding the sun, your *tops* are hiding it."
"The Sun can be exposed when the dark clouds get dispersed, isn't it?"
Okay, dear; Let the sun be exposed by dispersing the black clouds." His hands cupped

her *babylons* along with the tight shirt she was wearing.
Jayasri guessed that he might be a Mazophiliac. So she asked him in a whispering tone," Are you *fetishist for* babylons?"
Kesavan replied by fondling the protruding parts of her tight shirt: "Yes, because they're *bootylicious,* "and he found out that her face became erubescent since his foreplay stirred her latent feelings.
Then she didn't continue her *sweet-nothings* because Kesavan buried his face into her upper part of the tight shirt which was protruding out. His lips felt she was wearing brassiere.
As soon as his mouth appressed to her *babylons*, Jayasri, for a fraction of minute, closed her eyes and then was looking at the walls of the room vaguely. It could be possible for him to unbutton her shirt and expose her brassiere but he, without unbuttoning her tight shirt, his mouth clipped the mass of her protruding part of her shirt which concealed her spathic boobs. Then, he made her lie in a supine position on the bed. As Jayasri was lying supinely the contour of her *babylons* was explicitly visible to his eyes to stir his imagination.
"Are they towers? Or they twin hillocks? Are they really big or because of wearing brassiere, do they appear big in size? How *bootylicious* they are! How true that having bathykolpian add pulchritude to the woman folk! I must enjoy with her boobs and render her *boobgasm ...* "
As she expected, he laid his body on her to form missionary position so that he could play with her

hidden boobs. He moved his body through her smooth body and French kissed her which she reciprocated. She rained kisses on his face till he descended his mouth below her neck.

Kesavan asked in a whispering tone," May I see your boobs?"

Jayasri, smiling at him, unbuttoned the first button of her tight shirt so that he could see her spathic cleavage.

Kesavan could see the edge of her *archetypal breast* and a part of her green colour brassiere. He joined her two hands with his hands and buried his face into the verge of her boobs. When Jayasri inhaled, her bosom heaved and ebbed when exhaled. Her hot breath corroborated for the intensity of her salaciousness. Then Kesavan buried his face into the middle of her bosom and nibbled the verge of her breast which she felt musky. Then he released her hands and unbuttoned her two buttons out of five in her shirt. Now he could see the profound view of her brassiere that covered her chubby breasts like white frosts concealed the steep hills. At the sight of her brassiere he could see the bulging of her *bathykolpian* babylons, he had a doubt whether they were real in size or false due to the cups of her brassiere she was wearing to protect her breasts from sagging.

It's an enigmatic experience to him how she read his mind when she asked him," Do you have still doubt in it?"

Kesavan simply smiled without answering to her question.

Next moment, she unbuttoned her shirt and without stripping her shirt, she parted her shirt to expose her brassiere that was used to conceal her boobs from seeing but the contour of her boobs was visible explicitly to his eyes which he saw avidly the parts of her brassiere she was wearing such as: *front strap; apex; cups; under band; channel and underwire; wings; sliders; neckline; hook& eye closure; centre front gore; adjustable back strap; sliders; rings.*

Jayasri slid her hands back and unhooked her 'Hooks and eye closure' and stripped her front straps of fixed to her shoulders by which she bared her breasts now. *Once her brassiere got freedom from her boobs, now they looked like fresh a twin bloomed flowers.*

No male can be free from the sense of Mazophilia as the centre of attraction or psychologically termed as a paraphilia.

Kesavan cannot be exceptional to be a *majophiliac*, and ergo, he *deported like a voyeur* who wallows *at* the sight of bare breasts. His voyeurism arrided Jayasri and she was proud of her spathic and perkiest boobs.

At the sight of her amazing • astonishing • awesome • staggering • breathtaking • miraculous • stunning • sensational twin boobs, he was stirred to *cop aphelia* and in the next moment, he grabbed her twin boobs lustfully and *nuzzled* against her neck and rained kisses. Then he asked in a whispering tone," How do you want me to handle your boobs?"

Jayasri smiled at him and replied: "*Mild stroking and gentle squeezing followed by osculation. Onanism in the case of... ..... Below my navel.*

"Are you penchant for 'cunnilingus'? Kesavan winked at her with a sexy smile on his face and fondled her tits.

"No girl in the world abhors cunnilingus since it stimulates much and conduces to the apex of orgasm. So, when Kesavan mentioned the word,'*cunnilingus*', Jayasri readily *concurred* in his view and his desire, lascivious desire. For the past one month, from the day she met Kesavan, she had been *maritating (Latin word: to manipulate one's vulva by hand)* and in her mental screen, there filmed the paraphilia of Kesavan who performed coition with her and consummated her. Kesavan started *lambereing* her erect thelium till Jayasri heaved her waist from her bed to certain height and Kesavan sussed out how the intensity of lasciviousness brought about such kind of movement. Unlike others, he didn't ask her whether she was gratified with his mores of foreplay as it's obvious from her sibilating and wriggling like a worm on the bed while he was lapping her thelium, sensitive part of her boobs.

Her *wagging and twitching* augmented his *lascivious desire.* He saw her fair complexion colour of her skin like that of the flake of jackfruit, changed into sanguine colour and especially her face that added to her pulchritude. Prior to his lapping her boobs, they were *flabby* (soft and fat) but gradually it became stiffened due to gorging of blood vessels and stimulated nerves. Kesavan thought whether they're apple fruits, a pair of apple fruits since they turned into sanguine colour also like her face. Similarly, her thelia or papilla became erect to be *thelerithism (erection of nipple)* . As he was lapping her sinistral papilla, thelium, which looked like a cat licking or lapping a cup of milk, Jayasri sibilated now and then wagging her face and waist above the surface of the bed. Sometimes she rose from the bed to form a sitting position and pressed his face against her bosom whispering in a soft tone," It's really interesting, Kesavan."

Her *encomium (formal expression of praise)* as a maven in the realm of 'sexual foreplay' gratified Kesavan. Like air horn *twinged* (press tightly between fingers), Kesavan fondled her *dextral dense* boob (right side boob) while lapping other boob, *sinistral boob*,(left side boob) for some time. Soon Kesavan was tired of mono foreplay but wanted to switch over to another kind for which he should strip her dress completely. So he asked her whether she could pose *in puris naturalisbus*

With a wreathed smile adorning her face, Jayasri got up from her supine position on the bed and stood on it. Then she unhooked her petticoat and stripped it down which fell down through her bare thighs. Now she was in her single dress, *Thong, (A thong is an undergarment which has more cloth on it and it used as an underwear as well as swimsuit. In the shape, the thong resembles a bikini bottom but there is very less cloth at the back making the hips almost visible. It is only worn by women who use it as a garment which is able to protect all the body parts which are considered sensitive. They some in a variety of shape and sizes and are one of the most worn among women.)*

When Jayasri was standing on the bed in her 'Thong' dress, the only dress on her golden body, she appeared to be the sexiest figure to trance the hearts of youngsters to ogle at her and drool over her sexual organs.

Jayasri was standing semi nakedly and *overtly* in her skimpiest dress to be a *cynosure* (*person who is the centre of attraction or admiration*) in front of Kesavan who was stunned to see her pose and lost his sense and *gaped (look with amazement)* at each and every part of her body. He was astonished to know that she neither felt coyness or shame to pose semi nakedly in his presence. Though it's a few hours of familiarity with him, yet she deported as if she was his wife and swept aside her inhibition to remain *au natural*, which he considered it *copacetic (fine, completely satisfactory)* to render him *oblectation* (*a pleasant state of feeling very satisfied and happy)* and stir his latent feelings emotionally and her body structure was *bootylicious, voluptuous, curvaceous,* and *bangable (sexually attractive).* Like an ordinary layman, his eyes struck to her 'thong' by which one could see the '*Camel-toe'* (*slang the visual effect created when a woman's trousers cling too tightly to the crotch, emphasizing the shape of the pudenda)* which he hadn't seen so far.

Her semi naked pose reminded him of the ''Angel' Menaka, who enticed the sage Viswamithra by her willowy charm and grace and semi naked, exposing her graceful breasts, bare breasts. Similarly, she looked like an *Aphrodite (What other female deity as Aphrodite to not only illustrates her power in the mythological world of Greek religion through her nudity, but also to explicate Aphrodite as more than just a beautiful goddess. Aphrodite in all was more than just the goddess of love and beauty)*

"Is she the celestial angel, Menaka, or Urvashi, or Rambha, or Tilottama or Ghritachi who are the most famous for beauty? It's true that beauty depends upon the view of onlooker, but is she beautiful or sexy or over sexed, or steamy or coquettish or prurient? She is stunningly beautiful in this semi-naked pose. How will she be in stark naked pose? There is difference between the Sun and the Moon but both are of rotund like her breasts. How small are her thelia comparing to the big size of her breasts! It's the right growth of her breasts in accordance with her age. It can easily sussed out how intensity of her lasciviousness and prurient desire she must have to pose semi nakedly in my presence! Now I behold at her 'Thong' which exposes the contour of her vulva which is called 'camel-toe'. What a sex appeal in her skimpiest dress! ......

The more Kesavan brooded over this matter, the more she became impatient and finally asked him in her mother tongue,"? (Is it enough to see or continued to be seen?"

Kesavan smiled and replied:" I am not cloyed with ogling at your semi naked pose Jayasri."
"How long will you be ogling at it?"
"As long as I am satisfied with *your sexy appeal* since it provides me with an epulation."
"If you take longer time to ogle at it, then, when can you see other item?"
Her last words, *"If you take longer time to ogle at it, then, when can you see other item?"* made him know what she implied.
"It's you that must inaugurate." Jayasri expressed her mind without looking at him but flexed her head smiling.
Kesavan chuckled and inaugurated what she expected him to do.
Both Kesavan and Jayasri neglected to see the 'Thong' as an unfaithful human being as it had protected her sexual organ, *cunt.*
Engrossed in her '*Mons Veneris"*, an area of flesh covering a woman's pelvic bones above her sex organs and then, "Mons *Pubis "the rounded eminence, made by fatty tissue beneath the skin, lying in front of the pubic symphysis. A few fine hairs may be present in childhood; later, at puberty, they become coarser and more numerous.* Kesavan *perved* (*looked at with amorous intentions*) that her Mons Pubis and Mons Veneris are *glabrous (hairless)* otherwise called as '*hardwood floors' (shaved genitalia)*
While Jayasri was in the *stance*, *(standing position*) Kesavan was sitting on the bed comfortably and ogling at her pudendum which was *gamboge (lemon yellow colour)* unlike the

Indian ladies whose pudenda are of sable colour which Kesavan disliked. Like the lips of her mouth-size, her *Nymphae (Labia Minora)* were of vertical shaped lips, having a little curve with projection of *Coleus Feminus (clitoris)*, one of the most sensitive parts of her sexual organs and the profound area was not visible because her thighs were constricted but exposed the projection of her Clitoris

Next moment, her anticipated moment knocked at the door. Yes,

Kesavan genuflected before her and imprinted his kiss upon her *escutcheon* region.

Jayasri closed her eyes as she knew what he was going to do next.

Jayasri felt his fingers cupping her escutcheon region and his palm appressing her labia pudenda. Afterwards there was no *sweet -nothings.*

His dextral palm appressed at the curve of her pudendum and smeared for a few minutes till she began to sigh and moan. He felt his palm wet because her *Skene's glands, also known as the lesser vestibular glands, Para ureteral glands or homologous female prostrate , these glands are located on the anterior wall of the vagina , around the lower end of the urethra . They secrete a fluid that lubricates the ureteral opening and are surrounded with tissue that swells with blood during sexual arousal.*

His hand palm rubbed her Coleus Feminus for some minutes by which her entire body became erubescent and she moaned ecstatically.

Kesavan was an *"Acomoclitic" (a fetish for hairless genitalia) and he was aflame (very excited)like Jayasri whose cheeks were aflame with coy as* Kesavan whispered softly into her ears:" Could you lie down on the floor so that I can look at your vagina and its inner parts?"

Jayasri nodded even though she knew it's his freakish desire to leer at her vagina and its inner parts. Next moment, she lay down on the bed stretching out her legs straight.

Kesavan knelt before her and dilated her thighs profoundly so that he could see her *vagina* vividly.MajoraLabia, LabiaManora, the vaginal opening a*nd Bartholin's and Skene's vestibular glands.* Th e urinary meatus is also included as it opens into the vulval vestibule. Other features of the vulva include the pudendal cleft, sebaceous glands, the urogenital triangle (anterior part of the perineum), and pubic hair. The vulva includes the entrance to the vagina, which leads to the uterus, and provides a double layer of protection for this by the folds of the outer and inner labia. Pelvic floor muscles support the structures of the vulva. Other muscles of the urogenital triangle also give support.

As there was no sufficient light, he used his cell torch to examine her vaginal organ like a Gynaecologist. His eyes sighted at her hypo gastric tract, a starting point of erogenous zone and slid his eye below her navel where her Vulva could be seen that contained Mons Pubis, LabiaMajora and Labia Minora, Coleus Feminus,

Vaginal Vestibule, vaginal orifice, bulb of the vestibule, greater and lesser vestibular glands.
Kesavan knew that the Mons Veneris, the name given to the bulging portion caused by the pads of fat above and on the other sides of and surrounding the Labia Majora that was glabrous and it acts as a cushion during coition and prevents causing bruises caused by the impact between the pubic bones
It's the wont of Jayasri to epilate her pubic hair periodically by dint of' Electro Epilator' presented by her chum, Lalitha. During the process, "Electrode" is placed through a special needle and is attached to the hair follicle. After epilation, she used unguent to heal irritation creams that consists of derivatives from papaya, pineapple, walnut, horsetail and soybeans which have influence that delay for the growth of hair. These components are also included in the ingredients of epilators. Their action can be aggressive since they are capable of affecting the bulb of the hair.
Kesavan, after dilating her thighs, perceived her Labia Majora which he felt soft, fatty skin covered tissue that encloses and protects the rest of the Vulva, swell and gorged during sexual intercourse.
Jayasri, by dilating her thighs and exposing her pudendum, was watching him how he was examining her genitals. She derived pleasure while he was leering at her inner parts of her Vagina.
Kesavan was focusing his cell phone torch towards her dilated vulva and exclaimed:" How

beautiful it is! I'm really lucky to see your genitals, Jayasri. I must thank God and you too."

"Thanks to me?" Jayasri wondered and added," Really, I must thank you for I have never obtained such kind of orgasm in my life.

"The eye- minded scene was haunting my mind from the moment I saw your pudendum and I never dreamt that I will see your naked body in this pose in this eventful day. It's an engramma in my mind, Jayasri. I love you so much." Kesavan was overwhelmed and kissed on her patulous vulva.

Jayasri acknowledged his osculation and requested him to keep his mouth at the vestibule of her vulva. "Could you cunnilingue my organ?" Kesavan understood that Jayasri was penchant for cunnilingus. So he was ready to cunnilingue her vulva. "Are you penchant for *cunnilingus*?" Kesavan asked her with a smile.

"Having seen the pornographic film where two students engaged themselves to cunnilingue her in a wood, I have been penchant for it." Jayasri replied cravingly.

In the next moment, Jayasri saw him dilating her thighs still further and kept his face on her escutcheon region so that his mouth touched her patulous vulva.

Her escutcheon region was of rose complexion and was smooth as it was well shaved, which is called as "*Hardwood floors" (shaved genitalia)* and he smeared it with his hand to find its smoothness. He said:" Your pubic region is as

fair complexion as that of your boobs. Both regions are sexually attractive, I like it, Jayasri."
Jayasri blushed and smiled but didn't say anything; she acted as a silent spectator.
Kesavan began to *lambere* her groins first. Then her thighs. Without lapping her vulva, he was *lambering (licking)* from her crotch to knee joint. She came to know that he purposely lambering from her groins to knee joint without cunnilinguing her vulva so to make her crave for it. Jayasri could not control her feelings for which she murmured: Let your tongue play with my pussy." She made an appeal overwhelmingly.
Jayasri was as crazier as Kesavan in cunnilingus and when she expressed her wish for cunnilingus, Kesavan readied himself for the foreplay. As a first step, he smeared the profound area of her pudendum and while his fingers came into contact with her Coleus Feminus, she jiggled that had an impact upon her erect boobs.
Jayasri who was in ***puris Naturalisbus*** saw Kesavan ***leering at the structure of her Vulva*** *(*The **vulva** (plural vulvas or vulvae; derived from Latin for wrapper or covering) consists of the external female sex organs. The vulva includes the Mons Pubis (or Mons Veneris), ***Labia Majora, Labia Minora, the*** *vaginal opening,* ***and*** *Bartholin's* ***and*** *Skene's* ***vestibular*** *glands.* The urinary meatus is also included as it opens into the vulval vestibule. Other features of the vulva include the pudendal cleft, sebaceous glands, the urogenital triangle (anterior part of the perineum), and pubic hair. The vulva includes the entrance to

the vagina, which leads to the uterus, and provides a double layer of protection for this by the folds of the outer and inner labia. Pelvic floor muscles support the structures of the vulva. Other muscles of the urogenital triangle also give support.
Then Kesavan ***began to flick the beans*** (*to masturbate by stimulating the clitoris)* and while he was flicking her clit, she jiggled and moaned by tossing her head on the pillow and sometimes, jiggled her hip and chest to convey him the intensity of her ***clitorism.*** While Jayasri was ***beating the beaver*** (*female masturbation*) while taking bath in her bathroom, she felt ***clitorism*** but the intensity of the orgasm felt by her was lesser than the present manipulated by Kesavan.
After a few minutes, she felt his fingers dilating her ***Labium Minora*** and one of his fingers was prodding into the foramen, probably his middle finger. Kesavan beheld at her vulva which was small in size though it must be big in size in according with her age. While his middle finger was prodding into her vaginal passage, his fingers glided through her vaginal area as it was moistened by the secretion of glandular secretion. Kesavan assumed that her hymen would be ruptured as his finger but her vaginal passage allowed his fingers to glide freely and smoothly so as to touch her ***G.Spot*** so as to stir the "***Haptephilia"*** *(sexual arousal when touched presumably in erogenous zones.)*
No sooner did his finger touch her G.Spot, than her clunis ***jounced*** *(moved up and down) since the* ***Nymphet*** *(a young girl who is sexually precocious*

and desirable) ***was*** *burning with* **tumescence** (orgasm) and she began to stroke her breasts and sometimes ***twinged and tweaked*** *(pressed tightly between fingers and squeezed*) her babylons and looking at the celling vaguely she moaned and sighed.

After seeing her reactions to his foreplay, Kesavan penetrated his index finger along with middle finger into her smooth and glassy vaginal passage and it allowed his two fingers; then he penetrated his ring finger also along with his middle finger and index finger together into her vagina which glided through her vaginal passage and touched her G.Spot by which Jayasri ***enjoyed*** and tossed her body on the bed moaning and sighing. Eventually he performed 'Fingering and Fisting" *(Fingering is one when one or several fingers are placed inside vagina while Fisting is the one when the whole hand is inserted into the vagina to give pleasure)*

Kesavan expected that his fingers would rupture her hymen and hymenal blood would be oozed through her vagina and stuck to his fingers but quite contrarily, no haemorrhage ***transpired*** (*happened)* He didn't' ask her for the reason for the loss of her hymen but he guessed it must have been ruptured when she ***flicked the beans.*** She had already ***popped the cherry*** (*lose one's virginity as hymen gets ruptured)* by herself as she was accustomed to ***flick the beans.***

You're killing me bit by bit, Kesavan." Mumbling, Jayasri was raking her fingers through his hair and fondling him.

Arrided by her emotional words, Kesavan engrossed his in his foreplay. He splayed her thighs still further very well that cannot be extended any more. If he would dilate her thighs still further, he's afraid that her cunt would be split into two . Since Kesavan dilated her thighs very well he'd a vantage point to place his tongue over her erect clitoris and inserted his three fingers only into her vagina. Now, he began to lap her ***coleus Feminus*** like a vat lapping a cup of milk. His tongue was very active in lapping her sensitive organ and he lapped it horizontally and vertically while his fingers, three fingers were jigging inside her vaginal passage. Whenever, his fingers grazed her G.Spot, Jayasri ***jounced (moved up and down repeatedly*** her entire body emitting her moaning and sigh.. Kesavan understood that it was her ecstatic moans.

The more and more Kesavan played with her Coleus Feminus and G.Spot, the more was her orgasm and ecstasy. When she felt that it was impossible to endure the pain or pleasure, she whispered softly to have vaginal intercourse by which Kesavan readied himself to penetrate his Phallus into her patulous vulva.

Next moment, Jayasri felt that his phallus was ready to dart at her patulous vulva as it was grazing her Clitoris, his glans was grazing her ***clitoral hood*** and like a plane taxying down the run way before "Take-off", and his boner was penetrating into her patulous vaginal passage slowly and gradually. Then it increased its speed.

Every cloud has silver lining

Both Kesavan and Jayasri were ***levitating*** *(float in the air)* in the Paradise of Lust.
How long they were levitating in the Paradise it's not known but both felt that were in Euphoria for many yugas. In the meanwhile, she requested him for her chance to remain in the ***"Cowgirl pose".*** For which, Kesavan remained in the supine position on the bed while she began to ride on him till she squirted.
NOW THE PLAY IS OVER

It was mid-day
Jayasri was in her cowgirl position lying on his bare body while her sinistral breast was adpressing to his mouth.
Kesavan heaved a sigh and eyed up at his wife, Jayasri which asked her, "Are you consummated now?"
By his look, Jayasri read his mind and answered through her eye contact: "I am very much satisfied with your sexual mores, darling."
"Is my part in the play satisfactory?"
"Immensely satisfied, darling."
"Which one do you like very much in mine?"
"Everything in you was very fine in its excellence."
"Specifically which one do you like very much?"
""Clitoris."
"I thought you would prefer my boobs to my clitoris."
"I came to know that cunnilingus rendered you more *orgasmic pleasure* than boobgasm, am I right?"

Jayasri nodded with a timid smile and asked him," How did you find it out?"
"During *venereal* play, you evinced much response when I was *clit flicking*. But there was less response when I was fondling with your Babylon."
Jayasri chuckled and said: "Yes, it's true; while you were cunnilinguing my clitoris, I forgot the entire world and felt as if I was levitating in the air. I have never in my life felt such kind of orgasm as that of todays. Oh! What an orgasmic pleasure. "After a pause, she added," But now, I feel '*Lumbago*' (pain the lower region at the back)
"It's my maiden experience, Jayasri. When I eyed up your stark naked pose, it has been an engramma, darling. Still it dwells in my sub-conscious mind,"
"I felt a *tad-bit* (a little bit) shy when I was semi-naked but I inhibited when I was to be in stark naked position when you were ogling at my cunt. After my menarche, even my mother hasn't seen my sexual organs but you're only the person to whom I exposed my secret."
"I'd never seen in my life such scene. So I was very much tempted and I was not aware of my environment and didn't know what I was doing."
"Your final play was superb which I can't forget in my life, darling. I feel hereafter I can't be without you, Kesavan. Every day I want it to be done. I have become sex crazy….."
"I too feel so but can we do it tomorrow also?"

"I don't think so it's possible because she has to go to college. For our sake, she applied leave. Let's have our tryst form our tomorrow meeting."
"Where?"
"At the foot of the Hill."
"At what time, Jayasri?"
"""The same time."
"Okay, it's done."
By the end of their conversation, Kesavan's mother rang up to him.
Kesavan attended the call. "A sweet tidings to you, mummy; I am going to get a job in Chittoor and in connection with this, I am discussing with that person. The entire details cannot be conveyed through phone. Within an hour I will start. I will let you know the entire details in person. Bye, mummy." After this, Kesavan asked Jayasri," Jayasri, are you sure that your chum can get us post in Chittoor? "
"There's no doubt in it, Kesavan. She is not a cheat."
"I don't know anything about her and the life she leads. Can you tell me about her?"
"Please wait until I wear this dress." Jayasri rose from his body to wear her 'skirt 'which was slung to the corner of the room but Kesavan prevented her from wearing her dress by pulling her hand and detain her saying, "Please do remain without dress till you finish her biography about Lalitha.
"What's the relevance to telling her biography and wearing dress? You deport like Karunanidhi. He used to *blather (idle or foolish and irrelevant talk)* for publicity. …" She made fun of him.

Comparing him with the *smatchet (a contemptible and unmannerly person), a rantipolea (wild reckless quarrelsome person), flumadiddle (foolish and worthless) and asinine* Karunanidhi, Kesavan did not like it and his countenance expressed his dissatisfaction.

Jayasri noted his *peeved expression* (got annoyed and resembled in one's facial expression) and rued for the comparison she made with Karunanidhi. Next moment, she apologized for her slip of tongue and said:" Extremely sorry, Kesavan. I don't know that he is your *betenoire (person or things that one abhors.* Hereafter, I won't make comparison with him. "

"Okay; that's all light; now tell me about her biography."

CHAPTER No: SIX

PROSOPOGRAPHY AND ALEMBIC OF LALITHA

Sometimes people area beautiful not in looks
Not in what they say
Just in what they are.

Lalitha was not aware of the fact that her *fella (male lover)* was a *snake in her bosom (meet with ingratitude or receive evil for good) and a spive boy (man skilled in dishonest ways) and there's no sherift* (paava mannippu) for he *spoofed her* (*sth intended to deceive; deliberate trickery intended to gain advantage)* to *wreak Thamatos (cause to happen as a consequence an unconscious urge to die,)* when she *popped him the question (asked him to marry) as he belittled her.*

Every cloud has silver lining

Lalitha was born in a rich family having four sisters namely Malathi, Banu, Swetha and Gowri who settled their life in foreign country. Malathi settled her life in Texas by marrying her husband, a software Engineer, Banu married a doctor, love marriage settled in Australia, Swetha fell in love with Electrical Engineer and settled her life in Dubai while the last daughter, Gowri married a Christian doctor and settled in London.

Her father *was a prickmedianty (an affectionately nice person, fop)* but till her *menarche (onset of first menses)* she had been a *matrophilic (has more affection or love for the mother than the father)* *Lalitha, when she was five years, was affected by viral fever followed by polio attack by which she became lame. Her father, an Executive Engineer, spent a lot of money for her but doctors declared that God only could cure her lameness.*

Her father gave her the best form of education in reputed institution and she *boned up (*to *learn as much as she can do for a special reason*) and was good at studies. But she was teased by her colleagues in schools and colleges *for her physical handicap by which she was tormented mentally than physically.*

Weal and woe *(prosperity and adversity*) in one's life is common and after the period of adversity, followed the life of prosperity as she completed her Ph.D. successfully and B.Ed. also.to get the post as a teacher in a Government school where she found it's a *haven of sinecure and she* saw the Headmaster in his seat on the date of joining duty but afterwards she didn't see him. When she asked one of the teachers, he hesitated at first and then he disclosed the secret.

It's an urban school and the atmosphere was favourable to the teachers who wanted to spend time joyfully.

There was no teacher to take English subject and the teachers who know teaching English didn't take class but instead, a brilliant student was selected to handle the class. That brilliant student was none but our heroine, Jayasri who had earlier studied in Kamakoti Vidyalaya English medium. But she couldn't continue her studies there because her parents could pay the school fees and so she had to join the Government school, one English medium group was running but only three students only joined.

Lalitha observed her teaching by hiding behind the class. She could handle the class effectively though she committed mistakes here and there. A good impression was formed on her. She collected information about Jayasri.

The Government teachers assembled in the Staff room said:" Jayasri is only the dux in this school and it is her ill fate that she discontinued her studies in the illustrious institution, Kamakoti Vidyalaya for her parents were so poor that they could not pay the school fees. So, Jayasri was sent out of the school and there was none in that school to take pity on her and help her studies. "

Lalitha bent on to help her studies and asked her whether she liked to continue her studies in Kamakoti Vidyalaya and her reply shocked s well *slack jawed* (very surprised) Lalitha

"Sorry for refusing your help, Madam. There was none in that old school to take pity on me and help me. So I am not ready to continue my studies in that school. I am satisfied with this school and I am going to prove myself as the best student in this school.. Thank you, madam."

Her reply astonished Lalitha and other teachers. Soon she was in her good books. She took special interest in her and began to tutor her daily during her spare time.

In every man there has foible and forte and Lalitha is not exceptional. Her foible was *Cellcoholic (addict to cell phone; Nomo phobia* (*cell phone addiction)* and she was unaware that this would be the *peripeteia (sudden and unexpected change of fortune or reverse of circumstances) in her life.*

Through 'Face Book', she got a friend to whom she disclosed her contact number. That Face Book friend introduced himself as Mathematics teacher working in Government school and wanted to meet her for which she agreed.

Initially, Jayasri was used as a messenger between them to convey the love message.

A tryst was made for meeting. During the meeting, he wheedled her and gained an advantage over her. Gradually he expressed his love telling her emotionally that he won't live without her. She believed him without knowing that he's a *sandbagger (One who deceives you about his true nature or intent in order to take advantage of you.)* Love burgeoned between them.

From that moment onwards, Lalitha became *ebullient (overflowing with enthusiasm)* and as a stupid damsel, she wanted to court him. By the time her face Book friend *conciliated* from her (*gained good will from her)*

Gradually Lalitha attended the school two days per week and her liberal absence to the school did not affect her work.

Their *amorant* life (romantic) was very smooth and continued for one year and her face book friend didn't touch her. This freakish quality attracted her soon she began to yearn for his touch. She had been *petting the poodle (female masturbation)* since her fourteenth year and it got intensified when she transpired to watch pornography films.

As he maintained distance from her, she began to yearn for her and she regularly petted the poodle during bed time. During the process, the *Eros* (sexual desire) augmented to *Aphrodisia* (*violent sexual desire*) and squirt after the tumescence reached

Next day, Jayasri *intented o*n herself to pop the question to her fella at the time of the tryst. So, on the fateful day, she *groomed* herself (*cared for her external appearance) to resemble as a bonny lass (beautiful and healthy lass* and looked at the mirror to confirm whether she had *togged up (dressed in her best)*

Lalitha wanted Jayasri as her companion to that place where he was to wait for her arrival. As anticipated, her fella was waiting for her but he never expected that Jayasri would accompany her. Then he realized that with the help of Jayasri she could walk and she was used as an *adjuvant.* (Helper) to her as she was lame in her dextral leg. Afterwards, Jayasri left the place and walked towards a hillock and sat and waited till her return. Even after an hour, Lalitha didn't return. So struck by anxiety, Jayasri scurried to the spot where she saw Lalitha *in pubis naturalisbus eagle spreading* on the ground (*spread both hands and legs) and he formed a missionary position like her.*

Jayasri hid herself behind a tree and as a *voyeur and a peeper* she was spectating their *humping.*

Every day their humping occurred witnessed by Jayasri till one month.

After a month, Lalitha raised the issue for marrying her as a *suitress*

Now the time ripened to reveal that her fella was a *cupboard lover* (*one who insincerely professes love for the sake of gain*).

From that day onwards, her fella shunned away meeting her by which Lalitha consternated and became despondent.

Her father came to know about her affairs and the reason for her despondency. Her mother felt very much and left her to assist her second daughter who was pregnant. Yes, she went to Texas, Los Angeles, in USA.

Her failure in love spread to her sisters and they began to mock at her. After six months, her mother's dead body retuned to India.

Her sisters attributed Lalitha to their mother's death.

Her fella's last words were ringing in her ears: "*I cannot marry you legally but can keep you as my concubine if you agree with me but if not, I can't help.*

JAYASRI RECOUNTED TO KESAVAN WHAT SHE WITNESSED

The door of the Thalamus opened and Jayasri stepped out of the room.

Lalitha who gazed at her with mischievous smile on her face held her hand and walked towards the kitchen room and asked her, "Tell me completely what all occurred in the bed chamber. It seems that he squeezed you."

Jayasri recounted all in details in a whispering tone.

Lalitha hugged her and said:" I think Kesavan won't jilt you like the *Perfidy* fellow (treacherous). I have contacted Mr. Jagan Moghan Reddy, Chittoor. He wants to see you both tomorrow. So, you both should be ready to start to Chittoor tomorrow morning. There will be no problem in getting post there. My best wishes to you, Jayasri. "

After thirty minutes, Kesavan came out of the room.

Lalitha made fun of him and then she conveyed the good tidings what she told Jayasri.

Kesavan was overwhelmed and held her hands affectionately and shed tears happily.

After lunch, both left the place with tears.

LET'S WAG OUR HANDS TO LALITHA WHO WAS WAGGING HER HAND TO THE COUPLES.

CHAPTER No: SEVEN
A NEW LEASE OF LIFE

Every cloud has silver lining

As soon as Kesavan reached home, he informed the good tidings to his mother that he would be appointed as a Teacher in a school in Chitoor. As he contacted the Chairman of 'Maharishi Vidhya Mandir ', the person concerned was pleased with the details he told him and asked him to appear for an interview the next day. So he would be ready to start for the journey to Chittoor next day by train. His mother was immensely happy to know that her son would be appointed as a teacher in a school and she conveyed the same news to his father when he returned home in the evening His father, being a prohit, wanted to enjoy the retired life with his son and when he came to know that he was going to be appointed as a teacher in Chittoor, he released a sigh of relief.

Similarly, Jayasri informed her mother about her appointment in Chittoor as a teacher for which her mother was very much pleased. When she told that after joining duty, she would take her parents to Vellore after shifting family. Her father was very happy to learn that his daughter was going to get a job in Chittoor and the family would be shifted to Vellore.

Next day morning, Jayasri and Kesavan met in the Junction and caught the train to Chittoor. Their parents also came there to send off them but they didn't know each other. Jayasri's father and Kesavan's father requested the TTR for reservation and the kind TTR, sanctioned them the reserved seats in reserved Compartment. So the journey was quiet comfortable.

Every cloud has silver lining

During train travel, Kesavan and Jayasri planned about their future life. They exchanged their views about the matter concerned with their marriage with the consent of their parents.

They reached Chittoor station by four in the evening and they freshened up in the station and came out of the station.

Maharshi Vidhya Mandir was in the Industrial colony and when they reached there by share-auto, it was five.

They met Jagan Moghan Reddy who was ravishing in his white jippa dress welcomed them and offered them snacks and tea.

Maharshi Vidhya Mandir was a very big institution having the strength of more than a thousand students and there was a hostel attached in the school. Some teachers from various States, stayed in the hostel and each teacher was assigned the duty of hostel students for their studies and the teachers were responsible for their upbringing.

It was a two acres area and the main building was used for the Administration and the adjacent buildings were used for classes.

By six in the evening, a 'Demonstration Class' was arranged with hostel students.

Kesavan was the first to demonstrate in presence of teachers and Principal.

He took class excellently; particularly English Grammar and the students were satisfied with his teaching. Then he asked the students to ask him doubts in the Grammar lesson. . One girl student, namely Padma Priya, tenth standard, asked

Kesavan:" What's the meaning of the word, "invisible'?
Kesavan explained the synonyms of the word by writing on the blackboard.

Invisible ***adj.***

Invisible • out of sight • inconspicuous • imperceptible

These words all describe sb/sth that cannot be seen.

PATTERNS AND COLLOCATIONS

Invisible / that cannot be seen

The tanks were camouflaged so that they were invisible from the air. ◇ *There are countless stars that are* ***invisible to the naked eye*** *.*

He was a wizard who could make himself invisible. ◇ *She felt invisible in the crowd.*

OPP visible ⇨ visible

▶ **invisibly** ***adv.:*** *He moved away invisibly into the background.*

out of sight ***phrase***

in a place where you/it cannot be seen

If you leave the camera in the car, put it out of sight under the seat. ◇ ***Keep out of sight*** (= Stay where you cannot be seen) . ◇ *She never* ***lets*** *her daughter* ***out of her sight*** (= always keeps her where she can see her) . ◇ ***Get out of my sight*** *!* (= Go away!)

OPP in view ⇨ visible

inconspicuous not attracting attention; not easy to notice

She tried to look as inconspicuous as possible.

These small birds have a dull brown coat which makes them inconspicuous.

OPP conspicuous ⇨ marked

imperceptible (rather formal)

that cannot be felt, seen or noticed because it is very slight

There are imperceptible changes in temperature occurring all the time. ◇ *The differences were imperceptible to all but the most trained eye.*

There was an almost imperceptible pause as she gathered her breath to speak.

▶ Imperceptibly ***adv.*** : *The daylight faded almost imperceptibly into night.*

Then Kesavan explained: If capital Letter is used it means the Almighty and if small letter is used then it is used as an adjective to mean that something cannot be seen.

Mr. Jagan Moghan Reddy was immensely satisfied with the performance of Kesavan and asked him to wait in the office room.

Then it's the turn for Jayasri.

Jayasri taught the fundamentals of 'Trigonometry' in a very simple manner.

All the students were not only satisfied with her teaching method but also spoke to Jagan Moghan Reddy to select her as their Mathematics teacher for they liked her teaching method.

Their salary was fixed.

Their salary was three lakh per annum and every four months one lakh rupees would be paid. during working days, lunch is free and they 're entitled to take only one day leave per month and if they take more than one day, it is subject to 'Loss of Pay" Within three days, they have to join duty.

Kesavan and Jayasri never expected such a *lucrative* salary for which they felt themselves levitating in the heaven for they thought that their life style would be comfortable without pecuniary problems.

In a trance, they imagined the life of Heaven with the power of money. Yes, they began to build a castle in the air. They bought a big house in the centre of the city, demolished it and reconstructed a palatial building and multi storied building and rented for commercial business men to yield high profit rent and deposited in the banks to buy some other flats. They bought three cars, one for Kesavan, another for Jayasri and another for their children. Daily, they used to go to Chittoor by their car……..Their imagination attained the apex of the ambition.

When Jagan Moghan Reddy asked them," Are you satisfied with this salary?" their imaginary world came to an end and realized that they are on the earth.

"Thank you so much, sir." Both, at a time, conveyed their gratitude to him.

Jagan Moghan Reddy continued:" You will be given free meals in the afternoon. Every day snacks and tea will be provided to all the teachers at three in the afternoon. Moreover, according to your efficiency, your salary will be increased every year. What I expect from you is the sincere and dedicated service to this institution. What else do you expect from me?"

"Sir one request," Kesavan opened the topic and added," We don't know Telugu and request not to compel us to learn Telugu and teach the students through Telugu if they don't understand the meaning in English. "

On hearing his words, Jagan Moghan Reddy was immensely *kvelled (felt happy and proud)* with his reasonable question and said very happily:" Very good. I need such candidates only. We compel each and every teacher to speak English only and train our students speak in English. Every Saturday we don't have classes, instead, debate, training the students to speak in English and extracurricular activities,. Etc., are conducted. Hope you enjoy teaching and atmosphere here very soon."

Kesavan and Jayasri felt that it was a suitable place for showing their efficiency.

Both promised to join the duty after three days and left the place with composure.

Then they planned to meet the uncle of Lalitha in Vellore for rented house and then return immediately to their native place,

Kesavan informed the entire details to his parents and Lalitha and specifically thanked to Lalitha for the succour she did.

His parents were in glee when they heard the stroke of luck cast to him and he further mentioned that he would contact the man the Chairman mentioned for the rented house. On any account, he didn't reveal that due to succour of Lalitha only, he got the job and high salary. So he fibbed that the chairman recommended him to his friend in Vellore city for the rented house.

When they reached Vellore, it was eight at night.

Vellore, it is famous for its extreme climate, during summer, the temperature is very high and on the contrary during winter, it is extremely cool. Vellore Fort, the temple situated inside the fort and police Training cater and the garden in front of the fort…. are very beautiful for tourist attraction.

The house Lalitha mentioned was far away from the bus station for which they hired an auto and reached the place.

The paternal uncle of Lalitha was a middle aged man living with his wife in a big house and his sons settled their life in USA and he was leading a life unhappily with his wife as he could not live with his sons and grandsons. The reason is obvious.

There was no mutual understanding between his wife and daughters- in law for which his sons didn't care him and his wife like their wives.

Lalitha had already contacted him and informed the entire details about Kesavan and Jayasri and requested him to help them and he promised to do his best. So when Kesavan and Jayasri got down from the auto, he recognized them and welcomed them with his wife.

His wife was very kind and the best in hospitality; they showered hospitality on Kesavan and Jayasri by giving them dinner and then they showed the portion in his house for rent. It's an old house but spacious building and ventilation facilities. The walls of the house were not whitewashed and they're shade. The kitchen room was big enough to cook comfortably and even they could dine in the kitchen room and there was a mini 'Puja" room adjacent to the kitchen room. There was a big hall and in the centre there swung a swing attached with iron chain. There was a number of old furniture occupying the entire space. However, they didn't have any other option except to accept it inevitably. Bath room was common and at the back of the hose was a deep well full of water and they had to use for washing and drinking.

"Are you satisfied?" When the house owner asked Kesavan and Jayasri, they nodded simply and then he continued," Regarding the house rent and advance amount, Lalitha undertook the responsibility she has already sent the entire amount in my account through online. So as you said, after three days, I mean on Thursday, you occupy the house and in the meanwhile, I will make this house spic and span and whitewash the walls. Don't travel by night. Stay here and take rest in our room tonight. Tomorrow morning by eight, you catch the express train to Tiruchy. Before four in the evening, you can reach home. Wash your face and make refresh yourselves Get ready to dine with us for dinner. "

Actually they had no plan to stay there in the night but continue their travel to their native place. Since the house owner and his wife offered them the hospitality lovingly and affectionately to stay in their house to spend the night, they could not reject their words but agree with them.

During supper, the house owner told them his family story and his achievements and failures. Then after words he began to tell them the features of Vellore city.

CHAPTER No: EIGHT
VELLORE CITY

Vellore, the Head- Quarters of Late North Arcot District and Current Vellore district situated in 12′ 35′ N and 79′ 9′ E, has a very interesting History of its own. A strategically located City, it is well connected by Rail and bus routes to major towns of the neighbouring states like A.P. Karnataka and Kerala. The History of the city assumes a great significance and relevance, as we unfold the glorious past. It was under the sway of various dynasties and rulers, the prominent among them being the Pallavas, Cholas, and Rashtrakuta dynasty of Malkhed, Sambuvarayar, and the rulers of Vijayanagara, Nabobs of the Carnatic and the British. The Monuments found in the district give a vivid picture of the City through the ages. In the 18 th Century Velloqqwas the scene of some of the decisive battles fought in Ambur (Tirupattur district) (1749) A.D Arcot (Ranipet District) (1751) A.D and Vandivasi (Tiruvannamalai district) (1760A.D) as a result of the long -drawn struggle between the English and the French for SuLalithacy. One of the monuments of Vellore is the fort and its exact date of construction could not be established, in the absence of proper records. A very close examination of the stone inscriptions suggests that the fort in all probability might have been built during the rule of Chinna Bommi Nayak (1526 to 1595A.D). The fort is one of the most perfect specimens of Military architecture in

S.India. The Jalakandeswarar Temple inside the fort is very fine example of Vijayanagar architecture. The Kalyanamantap, on the left of the entrance, with intricate caring and delicacy of exaction, bears testimony to the engineering marble and advanced state of sculpture of the times. Another land mark that has put Vellore on the centre stage of Medical world is the Christian Medical College Hospital. Dr. IDA Scudder, the American lady, with a missionary zeal, started her Medical work in 1900 A.D. by setting up a very small Hospital, which in the last hundred years has grown into a premier Medical Institution of international repute. The central prison in Vellore, set up in 1830 A.D. is another historically important land mark as some eminent personalities and Freedom Fighters like Thiru. Rajaji, R. Venkataraman had served their prison terms here. The other noteworthy monuments are the Mausoleums located in Aruganthampoodi area on the Vellore – Arcot road, where the family members of Tippu Sultan were buried and the Muthu mandapam on the banks of river of palar, a memorial raised by the Tamil Nadu Government to honour Vikarama Raja Singha , the last Tamil King who ruled Kandy (Srilanka) from 1798 to 1815 A.D. He was imprisoned in Vellore fort for 17 years.

Vellore Fort

The Vellore fort even withstood Hyder Ali's siege for two years from 1780-82 CE

The fort of Vellore was built around 1566 CE by the chieftains of Sadashiv Raya of the

Vijayanagara Empire. In the mid-17th century the fort passed through many hands. First the Aravidus, the last dynasty that ruled Vijayanagara lost Vellore to the Bijapur Sultan then in 1676 CE, it was captured by the Marathas after a siege that lasted four and a half months. Eventually the fort came under the charge of Dost Ali, the Nawab of Carnatic, before passing on to the British in 1760 CE. From this time, the fort would be linked with the fate of Tipu Sultan's family. Vellore fort withstood Hyder Ali's siege for two years from 1780-82 CE, and would later become the base for Lord Cornwallis' march on Bangalore to defeat Tipu Sultan.

When Tipu Sultan was killed at Sringapatam during the Fourth Anglo-Mysore War (1798-79 CE) and his kingdom handed back to the Hindu Wodeyar kings of Mysore, the British exiled Tipu's surviving 13 sons, several daughters, their respective families and their entire entourage to the Vellore fort. They stayed in the palaces in Vellore fort and so played an important role in the Mutiny of 1806.

The Day of the Mutiny

Indian Sepoys used Tipu's daughter's wedding as an excuse to enter the fort

On 9th July 1806 CE, one of the daughters' of Tipu Sultan was getting married. The sepoys used this as an excuse to enter the fort. As a sign of the revolt, they pulled down the British flag and hoisted the Royal Tiger Flag of Tipu. They also announced Tipu's son Fateh Hyder as the new ruler. In the early hours of July 10, the Indian sepoys attacked the European barracks within the fort, and by late morning they had killed over 100 British soldiers and ransacked their houses. On receiving the news, the British commander, Colonel Robert Rollo Gillespie rushed with the Madras Cavalry, based 20 kms away in Arcot, and charged through the gates attacking the Indian sepoys. The revolt was suppressed by noon resulting in the execution and court-martial of most of the mutineers.

Attack of the Mutineers on the Redan Battery at Lucknow, 1857

Tipu's family would be moved away and objectionable dress codes retracted.

As a result of the uprising, a court of inquiry was setup by the British, who decided to shift Tipu Sultan's family to Calcutta, in isolation, so that they could be as far away from Vellore as possible. Meanwhile the objectionable orders related to the dress code, that triggered the mutiny were also retracted. The news of the uprising shook up England so much that the then governor, William Bentick, and the Commander - in - chief of the Madras army, John Cradock, were both dismissed from their positions. Sadly however the British didn't quite learn from the Vellore mutiny about the need to be sensitive to Indian ways. Decades later, reports that the British were lining cartridges of the newly introduced rifles in animal fat would send soldiers across Meerut, Lucknow and the North up in arms!

Both were hearing his words very interestingly. Afterwards, the house owner's wife made arrangements to provide them with a separate room for them to sleep.

It was a spacious bed room having an old model cot and the couples had to sleep on the old bed without pillows. There was an old 'Crompton Company fan' hanging in the centre of the central beam of the bed room. He switched on the fan and it started rotating at a normal speed.

Kesavan was not accustomed to sleep without pillows and when he found out that there was no pillow available for the old bed, he was discommoded and did not feel ***gemutlich****(comfortable and pleasant)* for which he asked her how he could sleep without pillows.

"You see, this is not a lodge to get all kinds of facilities. We are at the mercy of the house owner and are provided at least with these facilities. We've to be contented with what we get." Jayasri advised him.

Kesavan gave her repartee by smiling at her:" Yes, what you said is true. We must be contented with what we get. When you are here, then why should I worry about pillows?"

Her eyes asked him, "What do you mean?"

His eyes glued at her pyjamas where it clung damply to her body clearly revealing her callipygous curves and the entire shapely length of her legs. She understood pronto that he meant her callipygous structure.

With the expression of quasi anger on her charming face, she uttered lovingly," you, knave. How dare you mention it?"

"I said what is real." Kesavan replied by encircling her waist and drew her near.
"What is real?" Jayasri asked him eyeing up his eyes lovingly.
"You're a sylph. It is real." Kesavan lifted her and carried her in his arms and laid abed.
"Sylph"!
"Yes; 'sylph' means a slender graceful young woman." Kesavan defined it.
"Woman or girl?"
Girl is often used to refer to a young woman in informal or friendly contexts. However, some young women find it offensive and lacking in respect when somebody refers to them as a girl in a more formal or professional context.
"Not both but an Angel." Kesavan eulogized her and French kissed her after switched off the light. Now dark swayed the room and they could not see with each other.
Acknowledging his 'French kiss' she smiled and remarked, 'It's so dark that I cannot see your face."
"Why worry when darkness is our companion?" Kesavan touched her navel.
"Do you like pitch darkness?" Jayasri asked him French kissing him and allowing him to strip her tops.
"Darkness is comfortable for this matter." Kesavan stripped her brassiere.
Jayasri then stripped her bottoms along with her thong and lay bare on the bed.

Next moment, she felt him ***nuzzling*** *(rub or push against gently with nose and mouth)* against her pair of boots.
At this, Jayasri, in return, held his hand and placed against her pubic region.
Like a snail, his hand crept through her velvety pubic region and descended towards the Mons Veneris.
There was no pillow talk between them.
In the pitch black room none could see what was going on there but could hear her moaning out of orgasmic ecstasy.
Next day morning some rays of the sun pierced through the gap of the tiles in the ceiling to disclose their position.
Both were in ***naturalisbus; Jayasri was in the prone position while Kesavan was sleeping by using her clunis as pillow.***
By six, Kesavan was awoken by the noise made in the street by hawkers. He opened his eyes wide and understood his position. Then he remembered the timing of the train they had to catch. He got up from her bare body and shook her to wake her up. Jayasri attired her old dress neatly and got ready to open the door.
The house owner's wife welcomed them and directed them to the bath room for ablution.
After ablution, both got ready for break fasting with the house owner.
After breakfast, they took leave of them and reached the Vellore cantonment Railway Station.

The Express train was not as crowded as they expected. They had comfortable seats and made a comfortable travel up to their destination.

No sooner did Kesavan step into his door sill of his house, than his mother and then his father hurried to welcome him and hugged him lovingly by shedding happy tears.

"Is it true that your salary is four lakhs per annum?" His mother could not believe her ears and his father replied to his wife," Kesavan won't tell lies. It's true. God won't upset us. Vellore is a very nice city and I am going to continue my profession there."

Kesavan impressed his father by his kind words:" There's no need for you to work hereafter. Here I am going to support our family and you, as the head of the family guide me how to lead the life there, I will follow your footsteps. First of all, I am very hungry. I wish to eat lunch food. Please serve the dishes first." Saying, he went to the bathroom and took bath in five minutes.

During eating the dishes with main food, he began to narrate how he got the chance to meet Jagan Moghan Reddy and get the post as a teacher in Maharishi Vidyalaya. When he mentioned about Lalitha, his mother asked him how he came to know about her for which Kesavan had to mention about his amatory affairs with Jayasri and after revealing the entire matter, he asked his parents whether it's wrong to fall in love with Jayasri who helped in getting him a fine opportunity. Finally he appealed to his parents," Dad, mummy, it's true that I have fallen in love with her. But if you don't like her to accept her as your daughter-in-law, then I will not meet her any more. I won't join the duty and I will try somewhere to get the post. Now the decision is in your hands,"

His parents brooded over this amatory affair of Kesavan and discussed with each other. Next day morning, his mother replied positively:" If Jayasri wears the ornament of chastity and treat us as her parents and obey the elders, we have no objection. Can you give us the guarantee?

Kesavan replied:" It's better for you to decide this question by yourself. If you feel that she deserves to be your daughter-in-law, then we'll proceed further but if you feel that she doesn't deserve for the position as your daughter- in-law, then I will chuck the relationship with her. If you say positively, I will join the duty day after tomorrow otherwise, I will resign the post and seek the job somewhere because she is going to continue her service there in Chittoor. After chucking the relationship, I can't continue my service in Chittoor along with her." Kesavan asserted.

"Did you promise her to marry her?" His mother asked him.

Kesavan cleverly replied to this question: "I told her that marriages are made in heaven. If my parents and your parents agree with each other and understand mutually to decide the matter positively, then let the marriage be conducted. Like me, she would have told the matter to her parents. There's nothing in my hands but in the hands of you.. Above all, it is in the hands of God to decide. "

His mother believed in ***'Cleromancy" which*** is a form of sortition, casting of lots, in which an outcome is determined by means that normally would be considered random, such as the rolling of dice, but are sometimes believed to reveal the will of God, or other supernatural entities. But Kesavan had no belief in this trivial matter as he considered it as a superstitious belief. So he told his mother when she applied '***Cleromancy***" in the puja room "Mummy, I challenge that you will get different kinds of result when you apply it. See what I say. Miraculously, when his mother kept two small bits of paper written as 'yes' in one paper and 'No' in another paper and kept at the feet of the God's image and she earnestly prayed, she asked her husband to take one after praying earnestly.

His father took one paper from the feet of the God's image and when it was opened, the verdict was "Yes."

Dissatisfied with the verdict of God, another time, it was cast and this time, his mother closed her eyes piously and uttered some mantras and took one paper from the God's image and this time, the God's verdict was ' No"

Kesavan laughed and said: See, the God has been confused by your question. If you apply another time, then it will be 'Yes' See what will happen."

His mother again tried. To her perplexity, the verdict was "Yes.

Kesavan then clarified his mother's perplexity. "I tried a galore of times the same kind of ***Cleromancy*** but every time, I got different answers and nothing happened really. So, I lost confidence in this way of knowing the verdict of God. It is unshakeable faith in axiom that' Marriages are made in Heaven. If Jayasri is to be my partner in my life, none can prevent it ; similarly, if she is not to be my wife, then whatever we try, she won't be my wife. It's true."

His father was in favour of him and conceded to give him in marriage to Jayasri but his mother was little bit hesitant.

In that evening an unexpected event took place.

Yes, Jayasri's parents arrived at the door sill of Kesavan with a plate containing plantain fruits, betel leaves with betel nuts, some jasmine garland, turmeric powder and vermilion powder and coconut.

"May we come in? "Both, at a time, asked permission to enter into the house.

Kesavan's parents didn't expect their arrival even though they were not familiarized with them. Similarly, Jayasri's parents were not familiar with Kesavan's parents.

Kesavan's parents guessed that they must be Jayasri's parents. Inevitably they welcomed them by hiding their real feelings.

They were offered seats to be seated in the main hall for discussion.

Kesavan's mother asked Jayasri's mother what the matter was.

Jayasri's mother introduced herself and began to tell them her biography and her husband's biography. Then she began to impress them by ***prevailing upon*** his parents *(to persuade one to do* *something that they don't want to do)* by dint of her humble approach.

"Either knowingly or unknowingly both of them fell in love with each other. I think it is not a crime that they did. What I feel is that it is galore times better to have amorous affairs with our caste people instead of other castes to encounter many problems. Both of them got job in Chittoor with high salary and they can live happily with us. I mean, we all can live together happily. There is nobody to help us in our old age except my daughter and if you consider this case sympathetically, there is a way for happy life for all of us. I have brought up my daughter properly and on any account she won't ***pit*** (oppose) to your advice and prove to be a faithful daughter. I can give guarantee for my daughter. I have told you all necessary things and expect your answer, favourable answer."

Kesavan's parents were very much impressed by her way of approach. Kesavan's mother knew very well about her son who is in deep love with Jayasri though he simulated to be indifferent in this matter.

If you feel that she deserves to be your daughter-in-law, then we'll proceed further but if you feel that she doesn't deserve for the position as your daughter- in-law, then I will chuck the relationship with her. If you say positively, I will join the duty day after tomorrow otherwise, I will resign the post and seek the job somewhere because she is going to continue her service there in Chittoor. After chucking the relationship, I

can't continue my service in Chittoor along with her." His words were ringing in her ears.
She chuckled when she reminisced that her son followed the same steps that she followed during her teen age. Yes, her mother fell in love with his father and against the wish of her parents, she married him. She remembered how her mother ***anathematized*** her (*cursed her)* She knew very well that neither she nor her husband can do anything if Kesavan would elope with her. If it would happen, then their life would be more miserable than ever. So she began to speak very carefully to Jayasri's parents.
"I really appreciate the sense of your words. I was under the impression that he must settle his life permanently either in the government jobs or Banks. But when I come to know that it is not possible for the Brahmins to get Government posts as well in Banks, the present post is many times better than those jobs. He told me that like your daughter, his salary is four lakhs per annum. So totally they can get eight lakh. Per month they get sixty six thousand rupees approximately. After one year, their salary will be increased to five lakhs that is ten lakhs per annum. So, he is going to settle his life in Vellore. Next step is marriage. He has chosen his life partner in advance. There is nothing wrong. Like you brought up your daughter, I too brought up my son properly. I can give guarantee that on any account, he won't jilt your daughter. Further, as you said, let's live together with our children happily in Vellore. Let's conduct their marriage on an auspicious day

in a very simple manner. I have no relatives but friends only. Let's conduct the marriage on any temple, old temple either here or in Vellore. Let's decide afterwards. First of all, let them join duty and get the advance amount from the institution. I came to know that Mr Jagan Moghan Reddy is a good person. I think they have selected a very good place. The entire credit goes to Lalitha madam. I want to convey my thanks to her for she played as an adjuvant to our children. Without her succour, our children can't get the post as well as the rented house in Vellore. So the affair occurred happily .Tell me if there is anything you want to say."

The parents of Jayasri were very much arrided with the words and behaviour of Kesavan's parents who ***lionized*** them. They told her:" "Today you please come to my house and speak with my daughter. Then you will understand the truth of my words."

His mother chipped in and said:" ***We are sure to come to your house not to test your daughter but to know the selection of my son.*** Moreover, they have to start tomorrow night train to Chittoor, I feel either of us accompany them to make arrangements for their food and guidance. At present, I can't move anywhere. So, it'll be better if you accompany them to Chittoor and make necessary arrangements. By Sunday morning, we would like to come over there and stay for two or three days and return immediately. I would like to rent this house to a suitable person. Till then, I can't move anywhere. After settling here, we would like to come there with our luggage. What do you say?"

"Okay; it's left to your will and pleasure. Now we'd like to take leave of you. We are waiting for your arrival to my home very eagerly."

Jayasri's parents got up from their seats and were about to leave.

Kesavan's parents exchanged a plate containing with coconut, betel leaves with betel nuts and some flowers. They took leave of the house happily.

Kesavan, who was eaves ***dropping*** *(listening secretly to the private conversation of others)* the conversation held between the two families felt the sense of Euphoria and levitating in the sky with his fella. 'Am I relieved from the grip of seven and half Saturn? Do the impediments towards my progress get vanished? How does my obstinate mother change immediately? What a foolish plan I made if my mother disowns to my reasonable request! God has saved me from swerving from the path of Adharma. How foolishly I planned to elope with Jayasri if my parents disagree with my request! It's incredible that my mother concurred with the parents of Jayasri. God is great. So far I've been under the illusion that the God also is bound by the imposing of perditions by Saturn but now I realize He can change my ***kismet*** *(fate)* through Jayasri and Lalitha. I am indebted to Lalitha and in return I should do such a great succour which she never forgets me. What should I do and how should I help her so as to keep it memorable throughout her life?"

CHAPTER NO: NINE
PLEASANT LIFE

All that was harsh and dissonant in his life melted into one sweet harmony

While Kesavan was swimming in the ocean of ***oblectation*** *(a pleasant state of feeling very satisfied and happy)*, Jayasri was dabbling in the ***ford*** of dream land, ruminating the raunchy scenes in which she played a pivot role with Kesavan who popped her cherry previous day. She brooded how she was yearning for Kesavan for three months and how she attained the fruition of her longing in a day and how she made a pleasant journey with her fiancé .She realized that hadn't Lalitha aided as an adjuvant, she wouldn't have accomplished her avid desire. She brought forth the scene in which her parents played an important role when she ***wore her heart on her sleeves (divulged** her amorous affairs with Kesavan*) and informed her parents politely that she bent on to marrying Kesavan who also trothed to her with the aid of Lalitha.

Her mother, Suganthi couldn't believe her ears but confirmed it by asking her whether she heard was true or fib. At first she stewed as every mother feels, smote her hands upon her forehead and ***wreaked to be groggy.*** She posed a question to her mother whether loving is a curse to the humanity and persuaded that she didn't ***goof*** *(commit a faux pas or a fault or make a serious mistake)* but what every girl normally feels and falls in love. With the intention of lessening her burden in the family and keeping them in a pleasant atmosphere by marrying Kesavan and earning huge income so as to lead the life pleasantly. She disclosed the entire details how Lalitha helped her in this amative play. Jayasri wheedled Suganthi how she faced perditions in bringing up her in the life and she determined to do away with her strain and burden so as to smoothen the life.

Eventually Suganthi had to nod and then she informed her husband to come home as she had an important affair to deal with him. Her husband applied leave and hurried home. It's very easy for Jayasri to persuade her father and made him concur to her opinion. He realized that in the stream of pressure in his job, he had no time to think about the future of his daughter and the duty ahead of him. When he came to know about the economic status of Kesavan, he concurred with her and made arrangements to meet Kesavan's parents.

Jayasri had unshakable faith in Kesavan as he was a Brahmin, and was waiting ***atiptoe** (eagerly expectant as anticipating a desire event or arrival)* for the good tidings from her parents. When her parents arrived, she found out the trace of happiness on their lit face and her mother hugged her saying," You're really lucky to marry him. Our economic status coincides with his. There won't be any problem in your marriage. Today evening, Kesavan's mother is coming to our home to see you and discuss with you. Try to earn the good name from her and be ***in her good books.***

Jayasri and Kesavan attended the interview on Monday, stayed in Vellore that night and started from there (Vellore) on Tuesday and reached Tiruchy on Tuesday evening. Next day, Wednesday, morning Jayasri's parents confirmed their daughter's marriage with Kesavan on Wednesday. Two days glided quickly and on Friday morning, they had to join the duty in Chitoor.

Kesavan's mother came to Jayasri's house on Wednesday evening by four.

When she entered by four in the evening, Jayasri's parents gave her a warm welcome and offered her a seat in the main hall. At the sight of the hall, she understood their poverty stricken position. ,

Jayasri emerged from inside the room with a plate containing some snacks and a tumbler of coffee. She greeted her with an affable smile and stretched out towards Kesavan's mother who acknowledged her greetings with a smile on her face. Her simple dress impressed her and asked Jayasri to take her seat on the chair but Jayasri, curtseyed at her feet to seek her blessings by which she was very much impressed.

"May I know about you?" The interview started.

"Of course, Aunty," came her reply pronto and added, "I think you know very well that I am only the daughter to my parents and studied up to Intermediate in the Government school. I have been in the good books of my teacher namely, Madam, Lalitha by whom I got an opportunity to get a job in Chittoor. Jayasri replied ***laconically*** *(effectively cut short)*

"Good. When are you going to join the duty?"
"On Friday."
"Where are you going to stay, I mean in Chittoor or Vellore?"
"In Vellore with you and my parents together." Jayasri smiled and answered prudently.by mentioning the word," ***In Vellore with you"***
His mother, ***Neelavathy***, arrided by her encomium and prudent answer, said:"It's not possible at present for me to come to Vellore because my house is to be rented to a good person. Till then I am very busy.'"
"..............................."
His mother continued her interview questions: "When did you start your amative affair with Kesavan?" Neelavathy overtly asked he toughest question.
Jayasri was little bit shocked since she didn't expect such kind of question so soon. She controlled her emotions and replied calmly:" Three months before, I fell in love with your son as I was very much impressed."
"What did you find in him to get impressed?" Though she posed a foolish question, yet, she had to answer. So she answered correctly: "He won't stalk after the girls and never talk unnecessarily with anyone. These qualities impressed me, Aunty."
"Do you have staunch faith in my son?" Capital foolish question was asked to Jayasri.
"Yes."
"How?"

"Because he is your son." She gave the apt answer.
His mother was very much impressed by this reply and nodded smilingly. "We are about to reach the stage of senility and can't adapt ourselves to the new circumstances. Sometimes, we may be irritated and dart arrows of resentment at you. Can you bear it?"
"If my mother scolds me, can I show my anger to my mother? Like this, when you are equal to my mother, how can I resist you, aunty? We need your guidance for the smooth living and execute your orders immediately. Till you handover me the responsibility, I will never meddle with your acts. This is my promise."
Though Neelavathy knew very well that it's flattery, yet, she acknowledged it to be true and asked her, "Do you have any question to ask me?"
"Yes, aunty."
Her sharp reply made her stare at Jayasri and asked her," Yes, ask me what you want to ask me./"
"Do you like me?" Jayasri asked her mother-in-law which she never expected.
She could not answer immediately for she was stunned. Then she laughed. "I came here not to conduct an interview but to know your opinions and see how you are. I confirm that you are the suitable girl to my son. He has many peculiar qualities. He can't endure hunger, He won't like hot in the food items but very much fond of eating sweets. Therefore he is nicknamed as 'Sweet boy' "She laughed and then added "Kesavan told me about Lalitha. I want to meet her and pay my

gratitude for the immense help she did to my son in getting job, that too with high salary…..Could you accompany us to her residence?"

"Certainly,"

"We are indebted to her for the succour she did to our family. So I want to help her in such a way that our help should be higher than her help. It must be a turning point in her life. What is your idea, Jayasri?"

"Really Great Idea, Aunty. It doesn't strike my mind." Jayasri bopped her own head.

My husband, being a prohit (prognosticator), is well acquainted with many people in this city. At Thennur, there resides a middle aged man namely, Srinivasan, a lawyer whose wife expired ten years ago leaving her female child in the hands of her husband. He is not only a millionaire but also a perfect man. He has no bad habits. He is a widower. At present, his daughter is being looked after by his sister. But he is not satisfied with the upbringing of his sister so he is in need of a widow or any lady to take care of him and his daughter. If God is willing, we can unite these two in marriage. Lalitha had already reached menopause and there is no chance to give birth to a child and no support after the death of her father. So, if both are willing to marry each other, let us conduct their marriage along with your marriage. What do you say?"

"Splendid idea." Cried Jayasri in glee. She added," I can persuade Lalitha to marry the man you mentioned.

"The purpose of my visit here is fulfilled well. Let's all go together to her residence tomorrow morning and try our level best. I am now taking leave of you." Neelavathy took leave of them and walked down the street.

Waiting **a tiptoe** for the arrival of Neelavathy, Kesavan was pacing up and down the hall and at the sight of his mother, he simulated as if he were not interested in knowing the verdict of his mother. But her husband asked Neelavathy what the matter was.

Neelavathy cleared her throat and nodded. Then she said:" Jayasri is of curse a plaint personality and suitable to our family. Some one of us, being elders, should accompany them to Vellore. Sugandh's husband, working in an oil mill company, can't quit the job because he has not received his salary. Moreover, they don't have money to send his daughter to Chittoor. Moreover, we, to, are in the same boat. So we can't accompany with them now. Let Kesavan explain the position to the Principal and draw some advance amount to spend the remaining days in Vellore. By next month only, it is possible. So, our programme to Vellore is cancelled. " she said sadly.

Kesavan was not sure whether Jagan Moghan Reddy would consider their case sympathetically and give money as an advance amount. So, they had to depend upon Lalitha to borrow some amount as a loan.

In the evening, both families went to the residence of Lalitha by walk.

Excited Lalitha welcomed them and pointed the seats to be seated. Her father luckily was in the house and it was a good opportunity to open the topic.

Her father, Mr. Padmanaban, a ***septuagenarian*** *(age between seventy and seventy nine)* was a tall, lean man, a retired employee from the State Government service, with his usual ***Duchene smile,*** but an ***ECCEDETESIAST*** (one who fakes a smile or hides a pain behind a smile) for her daughter, eldest daughter, had been left to be a ***spinster*** who spent an arid life as her youth was over-ripened with the passage of time by which she was to lead a despondent life.

Neelavathy conveyed something to Jayasri by dint of her eyes by which Jayasri nodded and walked Lalitha inside the room.

Kesavan's father introduced himself and then the remaining *officers* introduced themselves to Padmanaban and after introduction was over, he opened the topic:' Sir, in view of the marriage alliance for your daughter, we have come here to discuss with you and we would like to know whether you have made any arrangement in this connection and if you haven't made or all efforts have been in vain by extraneous reasons, we've a good and apt alliance for your daughter. Now we expect from you a favourable answer."

On hearing the words, his face changed from vapid smile into gentle smile and said:" ***Woe is me***. (***Showed he felt distress or misery, often used humorously)*** She had already missed the train. Her mind is filled with an abandoned hope in life.

Your message looks like a ***guerdon*** **.**If it get accomplished, I am the first man to dabble in the ocean of Euphoria. "

In the meanwhile, the *lady officers* were persuading Lalitha inside the room while Kesavan's father and Jayasri's father were narrating him about Srinivasan, a lawyer by profession.

"Something is better than nothing." Her father said:" I have no objection in this matter and if she concurs with your arrangement and lead the happiest life, I will be much thankful to you.

After thirty minutes, the army led Lalitha to the hall to convey her ***volition (***willingness) She, at first adamantly shook her head with a view of ***Nolition (unwillingness)*** to their proposal**.**

Except Jayasri, Kesavan and Lalitha, other officers marched towards the residence of Srinivasan to discuss with him in view of marriage alliance with Lalitha.

Till their return, Kesavan, Jayasri and Lalitha were discussing about the further steps to be followed in Vellore.

By nine, the army returned to the native place with a smile of victory adorning on their faces like the army returned from the battle field after victory attained.

Suganthi conveyed the good tidings that Srinivasan gave his heartfelt consent to take Lalitha as his life partner provided that a mutual understanding prevails. The date of Betrothal also was fixed the next day.

THE WILTED FLOWER WON'T BLOOM AGAIN BUT IN THE CASE OF LALITHA, IT BEGAN TO BLOOM.

Padmanaban ***blissed out*** *(to cause to become or feel great joy or happiness) since* this marriage would light the glee for eve in his daughter's life. He ordered supper online for all of them that night. When they had their supper, it was eleven.

Before they're going to leave, Lalitha requested their parents to allow Kesavan and Jayasri with her since she had to talk much about the job.

Lalitha asked them," Could you do me a favour?"

"Favour! Don't use that term but tell us what we are to do and we are at your service." Jayasri's parents and Kesavan's parents were so emotional that they need no demand servile obedience from Lalitha but they were overwhelmed

"Please don't be melted with emotion and impulse. I have a lot of instructions to give Kesavan and Jayasri how to behave with Jagan Moghan Reddy in Chittoor. They have to catch train at two in the afternoon and by the time they reach Vellore, it will be ten. They have to take rest at night in my uncle's house. Next day morning they have to join duty." She paused and then she turned towards her father's side and nodded with a smile.

Next minute, Padmanaban went inside his room and returned with a cover and gave it to Neelavathy saying," Take this amount with you as a loan amount. Whenever possible, return this amount to me. This is not a free amount but borrowed amount which can be paid at your

earliest convenience." He gave the amount to Neelavathy.
In the beginning he mentioned," **Whenever possible, return this amount to me. But at the end he mentioned," This is not a free amount but borrowed amount which can be paid at your earliest convenience."**
Kesavan and Jayasri family learnt a new lesson from Padmanaban.
"***Money makes many things. Neither be a borrower nor a lender,***
You've to pledge your prestige to your lender. The holy passion of friendship is of so sweet and steady and loyal and enduring a nature that it will last through a whole lifetime, if not asked to lend money.
On hearing his words, that were like a stung with the lack of ***urbanity***, and made them realize the ***home truth,*** Suganthi and Neelavathy exchanged ***dekko*** (*a quick look)* with each other and then spoke to Padmanaban:" We are already indebted to your daughter and we don't know how to repay our little gush of gratitude. But we tried to compensate it by making this alliance to your daughter. They say it is unique and the apex of virtue to unite the couples or lovers by marriage. We'll be blissed if Lalitha marries him and lead a happy life with him. How we can't forget the succour she did, similarly you also can't forget the succour we have done. So we are immensely satisfied with this alliance and we will help in all possible ways. "

This crisis bewildered everyone including Lalitha who had never expected that her father deported in a silly manner and a ***faux pas.*** She realized that her father, being a State Government employee, had already been poisoned by corruption and bribery due to the heist Karunanidhi that spoiled the entire world. She couldn't help but controlled her resentment. She felt that her father behaved like a man who fed a sparrow with a lot of food and then finally wrenched its head to kill it.

Suganthi ***spurned*** the offer which Padmanaban did as succour to them.

There are still a galore of ***Padbhanabans*** in this State who are ingrained in the ditch of corruptions and bribery.

Readers, please note, Padmanaban is not portrayed here as an Antagonist where in each novel, there exist villains to test the valour of hero. Padmanaban is an example how a man with money hoarded usually behaves towards the needy.

When Lalitha recounted everything about Jayasri and Kesavan and how she succoured to them by recommending to Jagan Moghan Reddy, Padmanaban simulated to sympathize them but swollen with pride and haughty . And when Lalitha had requested him to help them with finance, he looked down upon them as they are dependents. Lalitha rued for the behaviour of her father and thought that she became wise after the event.

When Suganthi spurned the amount he offered, Padmanaban received it with a smile on his face that resembled his cunningness and said calmly:" Don't feel I have hurt you. Money estranges even the best friends. That's why I spoke like that." He thought that his logic was perfect.

Neelavathy gave her repartee:" **There's nothing wrong in your chop logic**. Will anyone succour one for the job besides financial help? Is it right to expect both from the helper? Actually when Jayasri mentioned your family position, I bent on to help your daughter by making a suitable alliance with the recommendation of my husband. Lawyer Srinivasan gave his consent to marry Lalitha after discussing with her. If this marriage takes place, we will be very happy. "

Her words," **There's nothing wrong in your chop logic' baited** Padbhanabhan but observing the situation conducing to debate which might turn at any time into thoughtless tiff, she put an end to the argument.

"Daddy, it is the time for you to go to bed and take rest. I will deal with this matter. Don't worry. Good Night." She coerced her father to leave the place and take rest in his bed room.

Inevitably, Padmanaban returned to his bed room. After he disappeared from the spot, Lalitha said:" This is the attitude which every Government employee possesses. All due to the ***betenoire*** Karunanidhi. Does money ***compensate*** for the succour? *(do or give something to somebody in return)* I think it can't. Further, though Jayasri is my student yet we don't habit like teacher and student but chums. A truest friend can be identified during distress only. I wish to be true to my friend and it is also possible for me to help financially. Wait here till I return." She went inside and returned with a cover containing twenty five thousand rupees. Then she stretched out the cover to Suganthi and said:" This is my hard earned money but not corrupted money. His money is corrupted and bribed amount. Keep this amount with you, "saying, she turned towards Jayasri and instructed: "On any account, never keep the entire amount inside the travel bag but in your pant pocket. Tomorrow, you have train at eight and reach Villupuram by ten thirty. From Villupuram, you have direct bus to Vellore via,. Thiru Annamalai. Before five you will reach Vellore. Take snacks at Vellore famous hotel, Ananda Bhavan. Take complete rest in your rented house and convey my enquiries to my uncle and aunt. He will tell you the complete details when you reach Vellore. You need not stay now with me since the situation is not favourable to all of us. At first, I had an idea to detain you here to have a hearty talk but……" She did not complete her talk but stopped without completion.

Jayasri and Lalitha cuddled with bleary eyes.

Then they parted. Lalitha wagged her hands when they took leave of her.

Both families walked towards their houses. On the way they were planning what to do next in Vellore.

Neelavathy asked Suganthi," Can you accompany them tomorrow with necessary things?"

Suganthi sarcastically replied:" Mami, necessary things! What I have cannot be taken with me because all are worn out and very old. What I wish to do is, pack all the things and therow it into the Cauvery River. Not even a single thing is useful for the new family. We have to buy A to Z for the new family. "

Her sarcastic remarks made them to convulsive laughter.

Neelavathy gave her repartee:" Tell me when you are going to sling them into the Cauvery River so that I can also sling all the domestic things into the river. Not even a single thing is useful to anybody. The darkest cloud has silver lining. Now through our children, the darkest cloud will be cleared."

Suganthi said:" Do you have any idea how to conduct their marriage?"

"Very simplest way. Let's all start to Vellore day after tomorrow night by train and reach Vellore on Sunday morning. Gold chain is very costly. So, let's buy 'covering chain as "Thaali' After ablution, let's all go to 'Jalagandeswarar temple, at the Vellore Fort. .Buy two garlands. Let the couples garland each other and tie the covering chain in front of ***the sanctum sanctorum*** of Agilandeswari temple. Afterwards, let's go to a good hotel and have our feast. Marriage is over. On Sunday night, let's all travel by train from Vellore to Tiruchy. As soon as they receive salary, let's all say good bye to Tiruchy and settle our life in Vellore. "said Neelavathy.

"You must be an Economic Professor in your previous birth. Well planned. "Suganthi praised her.

They were planning how to lead a comfortable and economic life in Vellore.
They shared the amount twenty five thousand into two so that each got twelve thousand five hundred rupees.
Both families had a comfortable sleep and peaceful sleep that night.

CHAPTER No: TEN
CLAIRVOYANT

*Born in a family of toilers, Jayasri, a sylph, by human nature of her age, was tempted **"Avoir le coup de foudre"** (to fall in love with at first sight) with our **Adonis,** Kesavan, a Post graduate student in English Literature, Delhi University by Correspondence course, **reciprocated***
her love when she ***devised*** (*to invent sth new or a new way of doing something)* to convey her love to him by dint ***of billet doux*** by which he was enamoured with her. Both never expected that Lalitha would be their mascot or '***un coup de chance*** (*a stroke of luck)* in uniting them in marriage and lit their life with a decent job so as to make them earn a decent income for a smooth living in Vellore and shatter the kismet that afflicted them due to the rubs and worries of life and teach them a lesson to lead the life of ***condignity*** **(status obtained through honest work)*

Every cloud has silver lining

When Jayasri appeared in her blue churidar at the Railway junction, she was ravishing in that dress and above all Kesavan never missed to note the ***hickey*** (a temporary red mark on her cheek resulting from kissing or sucking by him) and when Suganthi asked her about the mark on her cheek, Jayasri fibbed that it was due to some insect bite.

Like a bloomed and fragrant flower, Jayasri was as fresh as a rose soaked with a mantle of dews. Her mother, Suganthi, and Kesavana's mother Neelavathy came to the railway junction to give them a good send -off.

Kesavan gave them an effusive welcome by dint of gesture and countenance. Jayasri shook his hand enthusiastically though Suganthi was embarrassed by her act.

Madurai-Tirupathi Superfast Express train arrived on the platform No: one at eight.

They found out that nearly ten passengers alighted at the station and they were sure of reservation allotment if they approach the TTR. Kesavan approached the TTR and requested to provide them with two seats in the reservation compartment. The TTR looked at Jayasri up and down and then said:" Go and occupy the seats No: 30 and 31."

Kesavan and Jayasri released a sigh of relief and entrained the reserved compartment and kept the luggage in the allotted seats. Then they got down to talk with their mothers.

Kesavan stooped and touched the feet of his mother, Neelavathy and then Suganthi's feet.

Then he spoke his mind to Suganthi:" I will protect Jayasri as my eyes. Don't worry about her. Anyhow, we are all going to live together in Vellore. It's temporary parting. "

His words comforted her soul. Then he spoke to his mother:" When I was unemployed, I hate Tiruchy and was anxious when to abandon the place but now I feel so much why I should leave my native place, leaving you all as an orphan. . However, it comforts my mind that we are all going to live together in one place. "

Jayasri ***bosomed*** Suganthi (hug tightly with pressure with arms usually with fondness.), blubbing with bleary eyes:" Mummy, This is my maiden experience in my life to be away from you as I am going to part with you now till we are united together .I am not able to ***endure the heaven of hell.*** I will be expecting your arrival with dad on Sunday morning."

By this time, the guard whistled and wagged the green flag and the announcement for departure of the train was made..

After the announcement, the train began to move slowly from the platform. Jayasri, was wagging her hands and ***blubbing*** (*shed tears*) as she was going to leave her native place. Kesavan wagged his hands to them with bleary eyes as he tried to control his grief. Like the ***ephemeral*** (*transitory) jo*ys of childhood, their joy and pleasure lasted for a short period.

Those who are ***penchant for*** their native place can understand the ***disgruntled*** mettle of our hero and heroine as they were going to leave their native place.

Kesavan and Jayasri were peeping out of the window, wagging their hands towards their parents till they ***evanesced*** *(fade gradually from one's sight)* from their sight and they saw Suganthi and Neelavathy shedding tears by wagging their hands.

The superfast train was carrying the passengers of different tempered persons; some are happy while others are unhappy but the train as a stoic man was carrying them towards their destination.

Jayasri felt pragmatically how parting brings about grief.

Jayasri couldn't control her tears and she buried her face into his neck and sobbed. Kesavan tried to console her as he was aware of other six passengers gazing at them.

Kesavan felt someone was staring at him and his eagle eyes ***went out to have a gander*** to that side. (Directing the eyes towards somebody or something and perceiving it visually,) The man who was in 'Jippa' was smiling at them seraphically. It seemed that he had known what made her ***dysthymia*** *(the tendency to be very sad)* and he cleared his throat before speaking at them:" If I am not wrong, your name is Kesavan and her name is Jayasri. Am I right?"

That man was a **CYNOSURE** (person who is the centre of admiration) to all eyes. Kesavan and Jayasri felt that his eyes ***glued*** on them.(be fixed as if by glue) "Who is he ? He is a strange man to them but how can he know their names? They have never seen him in their life. With perplexed mind, they looked at him and asked," we haven't seen you already. Can you tell me who you are and how do you know our names?"

"It's true that you don't know about me. None knows in this compartment about me. It's needless affair now. Could you tell me that you are Kesavan and she is Jayasri? Am I right or wrong?"

"None knows in this compartment about me"- His words invited the attention of other passengers and all looked at him admiringly.

The strange man darted his look towards the passenger who occupied the set number, 34. "I think your name is Santhanam, C.A. and your purpose of your journey is to see your daughter in Salem who has given birth to a male child. Am I right?"

The passenger by name, Santhanam was ***flabbergasted*** **by** his words. He nodded at him admiringly.

Then he turned towards our hero and said:" ***The happiness and unhappiness of men depend as much on their turn of mind as on fortune. The mind is its own place, and in itself can make a heaven of hell a hell of heaven. It's the same mind that once abhorred your native place and it is the same mind that is longing for it when you are leaving your native place towards northwest to join the duty with your newly married wife, Jayasri. With the help of your chum, you got a job in a school run by a gentle man. You both felt***

indebted to your bosom friend for whom you chose a lawyer as her life partner, isn't it?"
Hearing his vatic pronouncement, Kesavan and Jayasri were struck in wonder and were gaping at him. Both unconsciously nodded at him.
The strange man continued:" The lawyer you chose is not a suitable match to your bosom friend who is physically handicapped. God has chosen another man for her life who is residing at the place you are going to work under him. Moreover, the rented house you selected is not a suitable place but a jinx. You will get a decent house in New Colony, Vellore. You try and you get it. Good luck is going to knock at your door. Yes, by this marriage, you are going to be the partners of that institution." He paused.
At this time, the TTR with his documents arrived at the spot for collecting passengers fare from Kesavan and Jayasri. At the sight of the clairvoyant, strange man, he didn't hesitate to stoop his body and touched the feet of the clairvoyant saying, "*Swamiji, Here's my obeisance to you. Bless me, my Lord.*"
The clairvoyant blessed him and asked him," Has your son joined the Medical College?"
"Yes, my Lord. It's a miracle that he has got the Medical seat without bribery. It's my virtue that I did in my previous birth to have the Dharshan of His Holiness. I never expected that I will have the dharshan of the Holiness in this compartment…."
The Clairvoyant smiled and said in a mild tone," I am ordained to help you and your family. Your daughter is going to marry very soon. She has

fallen in love with a boy who doesn't deserve to marry her. I will change her fate and mind. Your daughter's marriage will happen as per your will only. There is no doubt in it. Are you now satisfied?"

The TTR shed tears of joy and joined his two hands together to worship him and he was overwhelmed.

The Clairvoyant blessed him and took out the travelling ticket from his pocket with money and gave it to the TTR saying," Take the fare amount and give me the receipt."

"Please allow me to pay the fare amount, Your Holiness."

The Clairvoyant shook his head and patted his back saying," No, it is not correct. Receive the amount and give me the receipt. Moreover, don't forget my words:" The more you help the deserved, the more you will get blessings from the God and your life will be prosperous. " The TTR nodded and touched the feet of the Clairvoyant and gave him the receipt for the fare amount. "When can I have dharshan again?"

At any time at any day as per His will." He pointed his index finger towards the sky.

The train slowed down and halted at a small station for want of signal.

Some of the passengers got down from the compartments to see what hell made the train stop at a small station.

The Clairvoyant was little bit irritated and said in a serious tone:" Your Department has to face the music as the undeserved people are employed under the Reservation policy. It's incorrigible." He got down from the compartment as other passengers did like hum.

There was a long road by the side of the rail track. The Clairvoyant crossed the railway track and mounted up the road and then disappeared.

The TTR, while collecting the fare from Kesavan he asked the TTR who the stranger was.

The TTR replied:" He is a great Theurgist. Some years before, I happened to meet Him in the same train and he uttered vatically what the problem I faced. Then he predicted that my son would get Medical seat. Without bribery, it is not possible to get the Medical seat. But miraculously, my son got the medial seat without any bribery. He solved all my problems. But I don't know who he is and what made him predict and why he is doing. But he is a clairvoyant and mascot."

After the TTR left the place, Kesavan and Jayasri brought back the vatic words ***foredoomed*** by the Clairvoyant:" ***The lawyer you chose is not a suitable match to your bosom friend who is physically handicapped. God has chosen another man for her life who is residing at the place you are going to work under him. Moreover, the rented house you selected is not a suitable place but a jinx. You will get a decent house in New Colony, Vellore. You try and you get it. Good luck is going to knock at your door. Yes, by this marriage, you are going to be the partners of that institution."***

The sorrow melted into bliss. Kesavan exclaimed:" Good Grief! (Used to express surprise) How incredible it is! Can anyone believe if we narrate what has been transpired today in this compartment? Lord Sri Ranganatha has guided us though this theurgist. Are we born under the Lucky Star! Is it credible to believe that we are going to be the partners of the institution? If we say to anyone, we will be admitted into the mental hospital. …"

Jayasri chipped in:" Incredible it is! He predicts that Jagan Moghan Reddy is going to marry Lalitha. How can it be possible? "

Kesavan replied:" Why can't it be possible? In the life of TTR, what he predicted happened perfectly. Haven't we witnessed it?"

"Till it happens what he predicted, nothing can be ascertained."

"Why do we incline to negative attitude?"

"Okay. All is well that ends well."

The remaining passengers also partook of this discussion.

The train arrived at Erode Junction at 11-00 A.M. By the time, Kesavan and Jayasri took a ***siesta.*** Jayasri was napping on the lap of Kesavan ***cozily***. *(Comfortably)*

Till they reached Katpadi Junction, they didn't take any meals but biscuits, tea only.

There were four busses waiting to load the passengers into the bus and along with the load of passengers, Kesavan and Jayasri joined them and reached the Vellore bus station comfortably.

When enquired a stranger, he suggested that Adyar Ananda Bhavan hotel is the best hotel in the city and they believed in his words and travelled by walking to the hotel.

It's fortunate for them to have ***ambrosial*** food items at Anandha Bhavan hotel.

Kesavan ***smacked*** the items of tiffin verities *(press the lips together and open them nosily as in eating)* especially tasting savoury condiment items. Tasting them, he asked Jayasri," Can you prepare such kind of savoury items Do you know how to prepare?"

Jayasri laughed and said:" I have forgotten to tell you a truth. I don't know cooking. Please excuse me for hiding this truth. "

Kesavan said convincingly:" No problem. Till your mother returns, let's take meals or savory items in this hotel. Bye the by, learn cooking from your mother."

"Thank God, I was afraid whether you will ***reproach*** me *(to feel guilty about sth that you think you should have done differently)* for I don't know anything about culinary things." Jayasri sighed.

At this, Kesavan eyed up and exclaimed:" What! Reproaching you! What hell you're talking! Do you think I ***am a nine days' wonder? (****Be a cause of great excitement or interest for a short time but then quickly forgotten)* I will never in my life ***objurgate*** (chide) you on any account for you are an apple of my eyes. This is my promise." Kesavan impulsively promised.

Chide and reproach: both are different terms of usage. Chide is used to tell somebody gently that you disapprove of something that they have done while reproach is used to tell somebody that you

blame them or are disappointed in them because you think they have done something wrong or to feel guilty about something that you think you should have done differently.

Arrided by his promise made impulsively, Jayasri expresser her glee through her visage and in a caressing tone asked him," As soon as my mother comes, I will ask her to prepare different kinds of sweet items for you as you are penchant for eating sweets."

"Did my mother tell you this?"

Jayasri nodded with a smile on her rosy lips and eyed up at him.

"Shall we buy some sweet items so that we can take them before retiring to bed?" Jayasri asked Kesavan casually.

"Okay; you choose as per your wish."

"Which kinds of sweet item do you like most?'

"All items from sugar to jaggery." (Jaggery is a sweet item an unrefined brown sugar made from palm sap)

"Specifically?"

"Wheat Halwa."

Okay; let me order for '***wheat halwa and Gulab jamun"***

'Why do you choose two items?"

"For some purpose." Jayasri flexed her head coyly by which her face became rubicund and erubescent

Kesavan sussed out pronto but simulated as if he were ignorant of her ambiguous terms.

"You're very poor in this matter." Jayasri played ribaldry. Her face was ***fapworthy*** to look at.

(Attractive). She blamed him as a ***sex-manqué.****(one who has tried to do a particular activity but is not successful)*
Kesavan ***bonked*** on her head with his fingers. *(to hit somebody playfully not hard)* and said:" I am a ***lion*** in this matter. *(One who shows strength and courage)*
"It's very easy to say anything but is difficult to prove in action, isn't it?" Jayasri spoke in '***double entendre'*** which refers to a double meaning usually shocking or risqué in its sexual suggestiveness.
"To night I will prove in action." Defied Kesavan playfully.
"Let me see." She challenged.
When the waiter asked them what they needed more, Jayasri ordered for 'Wheat Halwa' and 'Gulab Jamun' for 'parcel'
The waiter directed them to choose the particular item of sweets displayed in the show case. To their amazement, they saw different colours and different shapes of sweet items displayed in the show case.
Finally, Jayasri chose quarter kilo 'wheat Halwa' and quarter kilo 'cylindrical shaped Gulab Jamun. When she selected the 'cylindrical shaped Gulab Jamun' Kesavan smiled mischievously.
They reached their house by share auto.
The house owner asked them the first question:" Don't your parents accompany you?"
Jayasri replied calmly:" On Saturday morning, they're coming."

"Well. Did you take supper or shall I provide you now?"
"Thank you uncle, just we have had our supper on the way home in the Hotel.'
"Okay; you have to join duty tomorrow. By the bye, I will show you the alterations I made in your portion. Come with me." The house owner unlocked the door and led them inside the room. When he opened the door, to their surprise, the room was entirely changed. Yes, the whole room was white washed neatly and a new fan was hanging at the centre of the beam. The ceiling of tiles was completely covered by cardboard, neatly painted. Bath room was altered and neatly painted with new door. New taps were fixed and the floors were cemented properly. The kitchen room was also altered into a new one having shelves, cupboards and black slab for cooking in a standing posture. A ventilator was provided at the top of the wall and the floor was cemented neatly and properly. Two bed rooms were painted neatly and the floor was also cemented neatly and properly.
Kesavan and Jayasri flattered him:" How nice it looks. It looks like a mini paradise. You have changed the entire portion into a new look. Thank you so much."
Their flattery worked out well. The house owner was immensely satisfied with their flattery and with a broad smile on his face, he said:" It's my entire new plan. It incurs nearly fifty thousand rupees for complete alteration. Hereafter it's your responsibility to keep your portion spic and span. Moreover, Lalitha rang up to me in the

morning and conveyed all information about you and the immense help you did for her marriage. But it's unfortunate that she is not satisfied with the Lawyer whom you chose for her as a life partner because he stipulated that she should resign the job and rake care of his daughter born to the first wife. So she said to him that she would consult with her parents and tell him the result very soon. She asked you to ring up to her and contact her as soon as you come here. So, ring up to her."

When they heard that the alliance with the Lawyer was chucked, their eyes met together and then they called back the vatic words of the theurgist: ***The lawyer you chose is not a suitable match to your bosom friend who is physically handicapped. God has chosen another man for her life who is residing at the place you are going to work under him.***

It amazed them that vatic words came true.

On seeing their amazement, the house owner and his wife thought that they concerned for the misfortune of Lalitha.

His wife in a sad tone told them:" Out of five daughters, he got four daughters married in a good place but unfortunately, Lalitha could not get married due to her physical handicapped. But she is a very good girl and having helping tendency. No one knows what is written on her head. We feel very sad for her misfortune. "

After a pause, his wife said:" You can occupy this new portion not now unless you do certain rites. As soon as your parents come here, they know how to perform the ***warming ceremony.*** So today night, you both occupy one of our bed rooms. Take rest and get ready to get up early to catch the train to Chittoor. Good night."

With their luggage, Kesavan and Jayasri entered the ***Hymeneals room, Thalamus (Shanti Mugurtham)***

"First of all, I should ***freshen up*** myself. "saying, Jayasri undressed her dupatta, slung it to the corner, then her tops through her slender shoulders and then finally her bottoms so as to remain in sexy dress-swimming dress, bikini dress while, he removed all dresses except his briefs. Both went into the bath room to freshen up themselves.

Jayasri didn't feel any inhibition to remain in that sexy dress, ***brassiere and Thong*** only to hide her sexual organs.

While she was laving her face, Kesavan stood behind her and kissed her back.

"After ringing up to Lalitha and talking to her only, remaining matter be ensued." Jayasri was strict all of a sudden.

"Okay, Princess, okay" Kesavan ***bopped*** at her ***callipygous/callipygian*** butts gently.

"Please don't stimulate me now by doing this. Then you 'll suffer."

"Suffer? Why?"

"You've to work hard to satisfy me, can you?" Jayasri laughed at him while wiping her face with a towel.

"Time has changed everything and everyone." He spoke irrelevantly.

"What change do you mean?

"During the last generation, we, males, we're longing for the girls but now it is entirely subversive."
"Sexual thirst is common to all human beings irrespective of any caste, religion or any country, isn't it?"
"Yes."
"Why don't we, ladies, expose our feelings overtly instead of hiding our latent feelings?
"Hi, you have started speaking wisely nowadays."
"It's a universal truth. Then why should I hesitate to be frank?"
"You're perfectly correct, Jayasri. I won't mistake you if you come forward to ask me for coition."
"I won't care even psychologist calls me as nymphomaniac lady for I am a sex- fetishist "
"Similarly I am least bothered about if any abuse me as a ***satyriasic (***Having or relating to *satyriasis.***"***
"Good boy," she played ribaldry by laughing. Then she added:" After having a talk with Lalitha, I will be your feast. Take my word: **"I AM AS FREE AS A BIRD."(***I am completely free to do as you like)*
Her candid expression astonished Kesavan who had never expected. He spoke his mind to her by lingering kiss on her cheek:" Generally, ladies conceal their lust into their heart and simulate as if they're not affected by libidinous feeling. Moreover, they expect the gents to initiate them for humping But you're exceptional which I like very much, darling."
"But you're partly responsible."

"How?"

"You stirred my latent libido by cunnilinguing which has become an engramma for ever and I've been enslaved by that sexual mores." She expressed overtly what she kept in her mind.

Libido (/lɪˈbiːdoʊ/; colloquial: **sex drive**) is a person's overall sexual drive or desire for sexual activity. Libido is influenced by biological, psychological, and social factors.

Though the orgasm is ephemeral and seems to be risqué to others for they are diehards or diehard conservative and inflexible, yet it is unique of all kinds of strata of feelings, human feelings dominating everyone.

"By **cunnilinguing,** I obtain orgasm from you and when you wriggle like a worm due to effusion of pleasure, it delights me. Moreover, since you attire brassiere I am prevented from seeing the bare boobs and I would like to suggest you that you need not wear brassiere because your boobs don't sag but erect as a twin flowers. May I suggest you to be devoid of wearing brassiere when you're at home and when you are out of the house, you can don brassiere as you please." Kesavan said courteously.

Jayasri replied:' Okay; I would like to wear ***balcony*** **bra**, or **balconette bra**, *(a typically a half or three-quarter coverage* ***bra*** *that covers the nipples and lifts the top half of the breasts. ... Also sometimes called "half cup* ***bra,"*** *a* ***balcony bra*** *is designed to enhance the look of the breasts, often with a bit of push-up or padding in the design.)* When we are out of the house I would like to don the balcony bra and I like your suggestion." Then after a pause, she asked him," Don't you like this brassiere?"

"Of course, you're ravishing in bra-cum Thong. But you are more charming when you are devoid of brassiere and thong. "He was ogling at her brassiere.

"Are you penchant for my boobs?" Jayasri asked laughingly and her eyes and face turned into ***cerise*** *(moderate to deep red.)*

Kesavan was a fetish for *mazophilia* and specifically Jayasri's for which he was longing for **floobing** her ***bathykolpian.*** Kesavan didn't reply orally but winked at her with a smile.

"What is your wish is also my wish. I don't have any kind of disagreement with you in this matter. They are with me to be played by your only." She spoke without nervousness or shame or any inhibition.

"Okay, darling; Ring up to Lalitha and inform her you wish to say quickly." Kesavan urged her to contact Lalitha.

Jayasri rang up to Lalitha. "Hello, Madam, How do you do? Here we safely reached at four in the evening. After taking snacks in the hotel, we reached home. By dint of the house owner, we come to know the result of the alliance. But we actually have never expected that he would be a selfish man. What you did is correct. Madam, a miraculous incident took place during our train journey." She began to narrate the profound details to Lalitha.

Lalitha, on hearing her narration of events, was stuck in wonder and expressed her wonder:" Is it? I wonder at this miracle. Jagan Moghan Reddy is my class mate He sought my love but since he belonged to Reddy caste, I shunned his offer. Yes, he carried the torch. After leaving the college, we were parted. Through Face Book, he contacted me after one year. We became Face Book friends but so far he hasn't expressed his desire to marry me. But, the theurgist you met predicted that Jagan Moghan Reddy is going to be my life partner. If it is the will of God, none can alter it. All is well that ends well. By the bye, take care of your health. Work sincerely and earn a good name from him. He is a very good man. What else do you want to talk?"

"Nothing particular, Madam."

"Well. Keep in touch with me now and then. As you said, it is better to shift your residence to New Colony. I will deal with my uncle and aunt. I will send the amount to the account of Jagan Moghan Reddy. He will give you the amount. Make use of the time and money to your favour'"

Okay, Madam."

"Good Night."

"Good Night."

It was eight.

Jayasri sighed and said to Kesavan:" I feel rather ***peckish*** (slightly hungry) even though I had had heavy tiffin items at the hotel. Shall we go to any other hotel nearby this area?"

"Is it so? Get ready. Wear churidar and tops quickly. Let's go now."

They met the house owner and enquired about the hotel nearby the area.
“Why don’t you take meals with us? Come and take meals with us.” He gave a grand hospitality to the couples.
The wife of the house owner also offered hospitality and compelled them to rake supper. So, they joined them to partake of supper.
By nine they retired to bed. The house owner and his wife said, “Good Night’ and locked the door.
The bed room was attached with a bath room and ***john*** *(toilet)*
“May I strip down your dress?” Kesavan asked Jayasri eagerly. Jayasri was about to undress her dress.
“With pleasure.” Jayasri came near him.
Kesavan fling off her tops through her shoulders to expose her brassiere, white colour brassiere that concealed her boobs but revealed the contour of the size of the boobs. Then she showed him through eye contact the bottoms to be removed completely for which Kesavan took the role of Duchasana, brother of Duriyodhana who was stripping down the mantle of Drupathi.
Now she posed him with bra and ***thong*** where her ***camel toe*** was exposed through her thong, white colour thong as if she‘d worn the thong in her quest for the callipygian ideal. Thong is minimal clothing worn usually by strip teasers and it is a narrow strip of fabric that covers the pubic region and passes between the groin and it is supported by a waistband.
A set of thongs was given by Lalitha last week.

The contour of her labia through her ***thong*** invited his attention as there was a stain marked at the curvature and convergent point of her thong which adpressed to her vaginal **introitus**: The vaginal opening is called the **introitus** of the vagina. The Latin **word** "**introitus**" comes from "intro", into, within + "ire", to go = to go into. In anatomy, an **introitus** is thus an entrance, one that goes into a canal or hollow organ such as the vagina.. He ***peered over*** *(to look closely or carefully at it especially when he could not see it clearly)* that ***inguinal*** spot (The crease or depression of the human body at the junction of the trunk and the thigh, together with the surrounding region.)

"What is it?" Kesavan asked Jayasri pointing at the strain.

Jayasri understood what he mentioned but she felt shy to reply. So she chuckled and replied:" Nothing, particular."

Her vague answer interested him to know more about it. So he asked her again.

Again she replied the same answer.

Impatient Kesavan requested her to ***spread eagle*** on the bed.(spread hands and thighs extensively)

"Nothing, my boy." She avoided telling the truth but her coy smile revealed the truth.

"Don't I deserve to know what it is?" He appealed.

"Liquid" she blurted, pouted, looked at him ***coyly and demurely*** and then covered her face with her hands.

Kesavan could not suss out still.

Skene's glands are seen as two small ducts superior to (above) and on either side of the

vagina between the vagina and the urinary meatus (the opening where urine comes out). They produce lubrication and mucus for the vagina during intercourse and are thought to be the source of the 'squirting' when some women orgasm. Skene's glands are embryo logically related to the prostate gland in men. Bartholin's glands are similar in size and appearance but are inferior (below) the vagina and before the labial frenulum and perineum.

Jayasri whispered in a soft tone:" Whenever I crave for humping, I squirt. It is a usual activity."

"It facilitates me for smooth coition, isn't it" Kesavan asked her winking at her.

Jayasri nodded smiling coyly.

"Don't you wonder at the unusual act of our parents who sent us together as couple 'prior to our legal marriage? Kesavan cuddled her.

"During our previous generation, there was no custom of registering marriage in Sub-Registrar's office or temples. So, they follow the old tradition trusting upon us. My mother found out that I had pre-marital intercourse with you but she didn't ask anything about it. She may think I have no qualm for it." Jayasri replied acknowledging his ***cataglottism*** *(lascivious kiss)* when he osculated over her shell neck.

Afterwards there were no sweet-nothings.

Raining kisses over her neck and verge of her boobs, he encircled her waist and then unhooked her brassiere at her back. Her white brassiere fell down like a severe head on the floor. Then he buried his mouth into her bosom and clipped her dextral boob.

No sooner did he bury his mouth into her ***bosom*** than she reminded him of the 'wheat Halwa' and 'Gulab Jumun' bought from the hotel.

Jayasri with semi-naked dress helped him in searching for the sweet items they bought and finally, they got the sweets.

As soon as Kesavan held the 'Wheat Halwa' packet in his hand, Jayasri stripped her 'thong' and kicked it to the corner. Now Jayasri was in ***cuerpo querpo*** *(naked)* and opened the packet. The delicious sweet was soaked with pure ghee and before eating it, Jayasri cut into two, one for him and the other for her. Then she cut the half from each share and gave them to Kesavan with the intention of smearing it throughout her naked body.

Kesavan directed her to lay abed which she obeyed imminently and then started smearing the ghee halva from her neck to knees. While smearing the halva over her erect bare breasts, he found that she closed her eyes. He took much time in smearing the ghee halva upon her erect boobs which looked like anointed naked statue.

Closing her eyes as if she're in a trance, she was enjoying the pleasure being smeared by the ghee halva. Yes, it was a **"Gemutlich"***(comfortable and pleasant experience*)to both of them.

Holding the ghee halva in his dextral hand and smearing her boobs, was a nice experience to both of them. While smearing them, Kesavan found

that her boobs were ***orbicular like statuesque beauty.*** He began to laud at her ***beau siens***.
"***How bangable your bathykolpian are!*** Is this the reason that many great emperors won many kingdoms but not win their minds and desires. Is it due to your boobs and beau corps? Even the great sage, Viswamithra was enamoured by the wiles of celestial angel Menaka as he was entranced by her gracious curves of her body and boobs. God created 'Lust' and keep it common to humans and animals but man is fundamentally different from an animal only because of the faculty of reasoning. It's this ability that places him as the crown of all His creations. The more I see your boobs, the more is the stirring of concupiscence in me. Fire can be extinguished by pouring water but my concupiscence of fire cannot be extinguished by any liquid matter or any means. It is aflame in my energy, mind, subconscious mind and all the corpuscles of my blood. If the kismet makes me part you from me, I prefer death to life. **I can't be without you as well as doing it...."**
Can there by anyone who can be exceptional to ***majophiliac?*** From the time memorial, no human being is exempted from this paraphilia. As civilization grows, lust also grows simultaneously. **Now we see the extant of what is legal has become illegal and what is illegal has become legal.** The term, 'Chastity' has been strangled with definitions. None can follow the norms and conditions of chastity as prescribed by our ancestors. A government school teacher, teaching

Biology tempted his student, girl student and stimulated her base feelings and humped her to make her pregnant at the age of fourteen. At the age of sixteen she got married to another man. Still there are many people humping using preventing the pregnancy by using abort ideal drugs. By using '***Duloxetine" and 'Fluvoxamine" , Mifepristone*** *(drug used to terminate early pregnancy in its earliest stage)*nowadays, they prolong humping.
What Kesavan ***over emoted*** while he was lapping her bare boobs which were smeared with ghee, all were heard by Jayasri who was also levitated during the process of foreplay by her spouse whose ***panegyric*** *words* ***pandered***(give satisfaction to) Jayasri who had been ***jouncing*** her whole body while he was smearing and lapping her bare boobs, ghee-smeared boobs. It could not be decided which factor was responsible for rendering her orgasmic pleasure either his encomium or foreplay.
Kesavan felt her hands racking through his head and appressed to her chest and with a sigh she emoted: "I can't endure the ***Lustprinzip*** that I procure from your foreplay
And I feel elated to be proud of being born as a female to be enjoyed by you."
Kesavan, while lapping her tits, expressed his upsurge of emotion through the honeyed words:". Even in my dream, I have never dreamt that I will get you as my spouse. Possessing such a great charming beau siens, I must be a lucky fellow to have you with the most beautiful, bathykolpian breasts Aha! What a stunning boobs you have to

stir my concupiscence! Your breasts look like a mango to satiate the man who is hungry of concupiscence"

Moghana gave her repartee by appressing his nape to her breasts: While I am unable to endure the heaven of hell, I don't imagine how I am going to wriggle like worm when you perceive the door-sill of my Heaven. I don't know how I am going to jounce when your tongue perceive and play with the guard of my Heaven below my navel.

While burying into her broad chest, Kesavan prolonged his sweet nothings:". I have already sussed out why you desired to buy the cylindrical shaped Gulab Jamun. It is not only your desire but also mine to worship the Phallus by penetrating into the Gate of Heaven."

On hearing his words of lust, Jayasri laughed and said:" Let your effort be commenced now itself."

She pushed his head downwards towards her ***hypogastric*** region.

Jayasri eagle-spread to facilitate him. The **eagle**, or **spread eagle**, is a sex position which involves her lying on her back, **spreading** her legs really wide, to allow him to hang over her. The eagle sex position is when one partner lies on their back with their legs spread apart, or spread-eagle. It's said to be similar to missionary but with the person lying down having their legs wide and in the air, rather than straight and flat on the bed. There are variations to the position, such as lying face down with legs spread, similar to doggy style. Another variation is for the receiving partner's legs to be closed, and the penetrating partner's to be wide apart. As soon as she eagle spread, Kesavan penetrated the piece of 'ghee Halwa' into her foramen of vagina and then opened the plastic cup in which six Gulab Jamun pieces were ready to be used up. He dabbed the fingers into the sugar syrup of jamun and then began to smear it at her ***bazongas or bazooms*** to titillate her and then her navel, an ***erogenous*** region..

"It's difficult to judge whether your ***busters*** taste sweet or Gulab jamun tastes sweet when I lap yours." Kesavan bantered.

Jayasri laughed gently but in a low voice as she became aware of the situation that the house owner and his wife might hear their secret sweet-nothings.

"Shall we take a selfie in this position, dear?" Kesavan asked her burying his mouth into her bare chest.

"With pleasure." Jayasri showed him green signal and then added," Prior to that, could you finish eating the ghee halwa that has been placed into my paradise?"

Fortunately, Kesavan didn't prod the piece of ghee halwa into the foramen of her genitals and the half of the piece was lying inside while the rest was outside the Labia. The orifice of Jayasri genitals was of the same dimension of her buccal form in a vertical form. The piece of Ghee halwa was little bit broad and hence it was very tight when it was penetrated into the orifice of her vagina.

Jayasri taught him how to operate her smart phone especially camera and after following her instructions, he clicked and caught the pose into the camera and it was serialized in the photo gallery.

"Could you take snap shot when I clip the piece of ghee halwa by my mouth?" Kesavan asked her eagerly.

Jayasri nodded coyly.

Next moment, Kesavan dilated her thighs gently so as to have a glimpse of the ghee halwa inserted into her foramen and when he stooped to bite it, she snapped her smart phone camera which recorded that scene. Then by holding the piece in his mouth, he moved his mouth near her mouth so that she could bite the remaining piece.

"I would like to see the profound organs of your genitals; could you extend your cooperation, Jayasri, dear?"

""First of all, switch off the light and with the help of smart phone torch light, you can view them. " Jayasri replied.

Kesavan switched off the light and with the help of her smart phone torch light, he began to do research on her genitals.

Focusing torch light upon her patulous vulva, he saw her Mons Pubis, Labium Majus, Labium Minora, Bartholin glands and Coleus Feminus.

His sight fell on her Mons Pubis, a rounded mound of fatty tissue that covers her pubic bone. At the time menarche, the whole area is covered with hair and it contained sebaceous glands that release substances that are involved in sexual attraction. Next, his attention was invited to her pink Labia Majora what're fleshy folds of tissue that enclose and protect the other external genital organs. He could see sweat and sebaceous glands which produce lubricating secretions where hair grows and it was epilated by her recently. Then he dilated her Labia Minora to expose her "Labia Minora, very small and it's width was below two inches only and surrounds the openings to her vagina and urethra. It was in pink colour because of the rich supply of blood vessels. But he did not know that during sexual stimulation, these blood vessels engorge with blood, causing the Labia Minora to swell and become more sensitive to stimulation. Then he could view her perineum. He saw the opening to the Vagina called the Introitus, a gate way to allow the "Membrum Virile" during coition and the exit for menorrhea. Finally, his eye fell on her "Coleus Feminus' located between her Labia Minora at the upper end and a small profusion which is very sensitive to sexual stimulation and can become erect.

"How great it is!" Kesavan could not be without wondering at the structure of her pudendum which was neatly epilated and ***couleur de rose. "So*** small it is, but how sensitive it is!" He thought himself and expressed his mind to Jayasri who was lying by dilating her thighs on the bed.

"What about 'Gulab Jamun, darling? It should not get wasted." Jayasri reminded him of the jamun he bought in the hotel.

"I won't get it wasted, dear." Kesavan replied, taking the plastic cup in which six pieces of cylindrical shaped jamuns were kept soaked in sugar syrup.

He poured the entire syrup over her breasts by which the sugar syrup began to flow slowly towards her navel and then eventually to the depression, her pudendum. Then he began to smear the entire region from her chest to her pudendum with the sugar syrup. Now he got ready to lap her boobs which shone in the torch light.

But Jayasri insisted him to switch off the light for which he switched off the torch light of her smart phone, Now darkness embraced the bed room.

Nothing could be seen as it was pitch dark but by her moaning and sighs, one can understand what Kesavan was doing with her.

The next day morning, by six, both got up from the bed.

Kesavan, who helped her in laving her naked body, was also in the bath room. Now she looked like a fresh rose.

After wearing a new dress, both came out of the bed room to wish the house owner and his wife.

The house owner was kind enough to supply them with coffee and urged them to catch the train at Katpadi junction.

Kesavan and Jayasri went to the Vellore Fort where Agilandeswari temple was located. Both prayed sincerely and then Jalagandeswar.... Then went to the Amanda Bhavan Hotel to have their breakfast. After breakfasting, they caught bus to Katpadi junction.

A passenger train from Katpadi to Tirupathi was waiting for their arrival.

After fifteen minutes, it started its journey towards Chittoor.

By eight thirty, they reached Chitoor railway station and by share auto, they reached Maharishi Vidhya Mandir.

Mr. Jagan Moghan Reddy welcomed them and gave them the Appointment Order. "I would like to introduce you to my Staff after prayer. Then you can go to class as per the time table. Moreover, after a weak, you will be given an initial amount for your monthly expenses."

The strength of the school was about one thousand both English medium and Telugu medium. But the number of students in Telugu medium was lesser than English medium.

Everyday there held assembly and in the assembly brilliant students sang Prayer song followed by speech given by the students, trained by English Department and Telugu Department.

After initial speech, Mr. Jagan Moghan Reddy introduced Kesavan and Jayasri to the assembly and asked them to speak a few words.

Kesavan and Jayasri had no experience to extemporize in the public that too, in presence of scholars of that institution. They were quite embarrassed when they were coerced to speak a few words about them.

Kesavan and Jayasri could not speak very well but stammered to discommode the entire atmosphere. Jagan Moghan Reddy was also embarrassed but he understood their foible.

After dispersion of assembly, Jagan Moghan Reddy called them and advised them to take it easy since it is their first experience to address in the public meeting.

He gave them time table; as per the time table, Kesavan was given thirty two periods per week to handle, VIII, IX X, XI & XII standards English while Jayasri was given

Kesavan was given the Intermediate Final year class to handle English while Jayasri was given Intermediate first year class to handle Maths and science.

The class room was spacious and on seeing Kesavan, a new teacher, the students were very happy and expressed their happiness by greeting him.

Kesavan started teaching English Grammar in a very simple method which the brilliant students understood pronto while the dunces could not follow his teaching and remained indifferent.

All girl students easily followed his teaching but the majority of boy- students could not follow him because they didn't have fundamental knowledge in Grammar. On seeing them, Kesavan recalled Jambu, his tuition students, the dullest student of the universe, and said to himself:" Jambu, you are omnipresent and you are in their minds and forms. How can I forget you?"

One day before leaving Tiruchy, he met Arumugam, father of Jambu and told him about the employment in Chittoor, his father was very sad while Jambu was very very happy. When Kesavan reminded him of the tuition fees, Arumugam carelessly replied:" Oh, I've forgotten. I will send the money through the bank. At present, I have no single paisa with me. What to do? There's an unexpected loss in my business.

Don't worry. I will send the amount through the bank "

Dissatisfied Kesavan, cursed him by himself and left the house quickly.

Jayasri was very good in teaching Mathematics and earned the reputation from the students. As usual, girls' students quickly followed her teaching and felt happy to have that teacher.

Both had three periods out of four periods in the morning session and the same in the afternoon session; so totally six periods out of eight periods per day.

Since meals were free for all the teachers in the afternoon, Kesavan and Jayasri lunched along with the students and Principal.

In the morning session, fourth period was free for Kesavan and he took rest in the Staff room where some teachers welcomed him while one or two teachers turned wry face at him. Similarly, Jayasri faced the same kind of experience in the ladies' Staff Room where some of the lady teachers turned wry face at her and didn't speak with her but pretended to be very sincere in their correction work.

JEALOUSY IS EVERY WHERE IN ALL WALKS OF LIFE.

In a month, second Saturday and fourth Saturday are holidays.

Next day, being Second Saturday, all teachers were very happy for they could enjoy two days consecutively. Kesavan and Jayasri were not exceptional to this.

At four in the evening, they left the school by the school van to Chittoor railway station. They had five o' clock train towards Katpadi and they were waiting for the train. They reached Vellore by seven after taking snacks at Amanda Bhavan.
They exchanged their experiences between them.
Next day, Saturday, to their surprise, Lalitha with the parents of both families appeared before Kesavan and Jayasri who were exhausted throughout the night as Jayasri ***double decked*** Kesavan (pulled down his pants and upper dress to make him naked) and obtained orgasmic pleasure from his foreplay mores. "
Wow!" Jayasri exclaimed on seeing Lalitha and hugged her, while Kesavan welcomed them with an affable smile on his face.
Lalitha said:" Saturday and Sunday are holidays for us and moreover, I would like to help you in arranging things for a new house. "
Kesavan and Jayasri led them to their new portion of the house which couldn't accommodate for all of them. The house owner and his wife offered them the best form of hospitality. The house owner, being her paternal uncle, was very free to speak with his niece, Lalitha and made enquiries about her and her father and family matter.
When the house owner came to know that the couple's parents were going to stay with them, he felt sorry for he could not accommodate for six persons in that small portion. So he advised Lalitha to seek a better and spacious apartment in New Colony for them.

All ladies occupied the house owner's portion while Kesavan, Jayasri's father and Kesavan's father occupied the rented portion.

At about nine, all went to the New Colony in search of a decent apartment and very easily they got the spacious apartment which could accommodate even ten persons. They were very much satisfied with the facilities available in the apartment.

The house owner was in North India and he agreed with them to give accommodation to them and Lalitha fixed the house rent which the house owner agreed and in an hour, Agreement paper was made and Lalitha signed on behalf of Kesavan and Jayasri. She paid the Advance amount to the house owner.

The new apartment consisted of treble bathrooms with toilet, treble bed rooms with all facilities, spacious kitchen room with a separate dining hall, one main hall, balcony, and an open space at the side of the Entrance door.

After taking lunch in a Star hotel, Lalitha and Jayasri went to Chittoor to meet Mr. Jagan Moghan Reddy while others returned home to take rest.

What the theurgist vertically pronounced came true in their life.

Kesavan and his family were immensely happy to get a decent apartment in the New Colony which they never expected.

In the meanwhile, Lalitha and Jayasri went to Chittoor to meet Jagan Moghan Reddy who never expected their arrival and was blissed out on seeing Lalitha after many years. He gave them a warm welcome to them and offered the best form of hospitality.

Jayasri whispered something in the ears of her friend and left the place to see the students staying in the hostel.

Rajendran and Lalitha reminisced their college life, halcyon days in everyone's life and both were shedding happy tears from their eyes. Then he explained how he strove to start that school with the help of Maharishi and made it as an illustrious institution in Chittoor city.

Then Lalitha narrated him how she had striven in her life and the crossed the rubs and worries of life. Rajendran sympathized with her and sighed.

"I thought that you'd have married by this time." Lalitha said.

"Marriage!" he sighed and said:" I have been living with your memory, sweet memory, Lalitha. I have never changed my mind."

Lalitha became emotional and blurted out her latent mind to him through her mother tongue: "Who will come to marry me at this stage since I am a lame lady? I am running forty years and reached the stage of menopause. I am counting my days. When my own sisters neglected me and made fun of my situation for my ridiculous position, what is there in my life and why should I live on this earth? I wish to die when my father dies. I am very much vexed with my life. …." She blubbed as she could not control her feelings.

Rupendra comforted her: Don't say such words, Lalitha. I am also running of the same age. I repeat the same word that I uttered in the past. If you give me your tacit consent to marry me, I have no objection. I won't coerce you against your will. If we are united together in the life, we can work hard to meliorate the standard of this institution. Take your own time and reply me at your earliest convenience. I am looking forward to your positive answer." He said assertively.

"Is it true, Rajendran what you have said?"

"Don't you still believe my words?"

"Decision is yours not mine." Lalitha flexed her head.

"This Reddy won't cheat anyone. I will always keep my promise. My decision has already been revealed to you, Lalitha."

"I won't even believe my own father in this matter but in your words. "

"You can believe my weeds, Lalitha."

Next minute, Lalitha buried her face into his chest and sobbed blissfully.

"DON'T ASK ME WHETHER ANY ONE CAN SOB BLISSFULLY. LALITHA SOBBED BLISSFULLY. THAT'S ALL.

The return journey from Chitoor to Vellore was the happiest journey to Lalitha and Jayasri.

Jayasri informed her husband, Kesavan about the good tidings and asked him to convey the same to all except the house owner and his wife. But her paternal uncle guessed what would have happened since he knew about the amatory affairs between Lalitha and Jagan Moghan Reddy during their college days.

When Jayasri gave the house owner and his wife sweets and informed them the good news, they were very happy and congratulated Lalitha. The news about her marriage with Jagan Moghan Reddy was delivered to Lalitha's father who had been clinging to conservative type of life and he was dead against the ***'inter caste marriage.*** But her paternal uncle persuaded him and proved that her selection is the best one which the God has blessed. At last he agreed with his words.

Next day was Sunday.

The enthusiastic family made arrangements for the simplest marriage for Kesavan and Jayasri in the temple in the Vellore Fort. At the sanctum of the Goddess Akilandeswari Kesavan garlanded Jayasri and she, garlanded Kesavan. So it was the simplest type of marriage held with the consent of their parents.

Then ***'House Warming Ceremony*** 'was performed at the new rented apartment in the New Colony. In the meanwhile, previous day, Lalitha ordered for the entire household articles, vessels, furniture including LPG cylinder.

Suganthi took charge of cooking the delicious food while Neelavathy was assisting her. Kesavan's father and S's father helped them in cutting vegetables bought from the market.

On an auspicious day, Lalitha wedded Jagan Moghan Reddy and settled her life in Chittoor. Kesavan and his wife were regularly travelling by train from Vellore to Chittoor and were working in the institution under the guidance of the newly wedded couples.

Have you ever seen such a true friendship between Jayasri and Lalitha?

End

PART -TWO MARRIAGES ARE MADE IN HEAVEN

Childhood is the best period of one's life which decides one's future. Parents have much responsibility to inculcate in the minds of their children not only the sense of discipline but also pave the proper way to them to earn much knowledge, failing which, it will be a case of a twig drifted along with the course of the river. The childhood shows the man, as morning shows the day.
WILLIAM SHAKESPEARE

The 'Silver Jubilee of Sri Saradha Autonomous College "was being ***jubiliated*** (celebrate jubilee) conspicuously in an opulent auditorium which was deluged with college students, ***the dignitaries, panjandrum*** (important and influential persons), from ***Vicenarians to sexagenarians,*** Education Minister, I.A.S. Officers, local politicians, above all, popular actor and actress (their fans***) and*** common people by which the clamant was at is apex.

When the '***Mistress of ceremonies'***, a vicenarian sylph, announced the names,

"***Shyamala and Nirmala ,*** in front of the podium, on the dais, the uproarious merriment ripped the air , to imply that it's a premier and conspicuous programme and she continued" "We are proud to present before you the epulation in the form of "Bharatanatyam, a unique ***orchesis****(art of dance)* by the' ***twins' Shyamala and Nirmala, B.A. English Literature final year.***

The whistlers, both boys and girls, expressed their joy and pleasure by whistling and clapping and twist dancing by remaining in their seats to invite the attention of the audience.

In a trice, the curtain got dilated to expose a set of marble statues, in the form of Bharatanatyam traditional gesture to baffle the audience whether they were one or two, as the two marble statues were of splitting images, twins, Shyamala and Nirmala who were identical to one another, ravishing blondes, to trance the hearts of youngsters and cause even the sexagenarians drool over them

வருகிறாள் உன்னை தேடி"a mellifluous, mellisonant and a dance competition song, based on ***Atana raga***" sung by the Late M.L.Vasantha Kumari and Soolamangalam Rajalakshmi sisters,, an ace, adept, champion, genius, hotshot, maven, megastar, sensation, star, virtuoso, whiz, and Carnatic wizard, was played for which the twins began to dance according to the song, in such a manner that the audience was enthralled and thought whether the celestial dancers, Rumba and Urvasi, in the court of Devandra ,returned to the mortal world and dance on the dais.

It continued for ten minutes and those ***Brummagem*** (*cheap and showy)* spectators whose interest pivoted to ***scrawny*** (*inferior in quality*) music such as 'dappangkuthu as well as folk dance, indulged in poking fun of Carnatic music and dance while some of ***Melophile*** (lover of music) whose horizon widened around Carnatic music and classical dance, a component of orchesis, were ***engrossed tout a fait*** (*completely and were* ***exhilarated*** *(filled with sublime emotion)* and reminisced to compare the dance with the dancers in that old Tamil film. The Education Minister was ignorant of Carnatic music and Bharatanatyam and engaged himself with his P.A, an IAS. Officer in discussion about the opposition party, some of the conservative girls students engrossed their attention and enjoyed the pleasantness of the music and dance, the majority of the audience was eyeing up the dancers, the gestures of Bharatanatyam and the gorgeous appearance of Shyamala and Nirmala.

One of the dignitaries whispered to his wife:" The twins must be Brahmin girls, aren't they?" and his wife gave her repartee:" No

doubt in it. Our daughter is fit for 'dappangkuthu dance and music only"
On hearing their comments about the twins, another dignitary conveyed his opinion:" Generally Brahmins bring up their children according to their traditional way. These Brahmin girls are really ***gumption*** *(shrewd or spirited initiative and resourcefulness)*
A leading lawyer appreciated the dance:" Good. Very classical dance and music. The twins dance nicely."
Finally the music and dance ended with thunderous claps and whistling sounds.
After the consecutive folk dance and dappangkuthu dance programmes, the 'Mistress of the ceremonies" in her gorgeous dress appeared on the dais and announced:" There is an axiom that Old is gold. We feel delight in inviting the Prince of our College, Mr. Baskar, M.A. English Final year, who is going to feast us with his mellifluous voice.
When it was mentioned, 'The Prince of our College" , the dignitaries and the Education Minister and the I.A.S officers were eager to see who Baskar is and in the meantime, the girls students were whistling enthusiastically while some boys students clapped their hands to express their pleasure.
In three minutes, Baskar appeared on the dais in his gorgeous dress, dressed up for the occasion. The entire audience except the college students, was fascinated by the ruddy complexion of Baskar who tranced their hearts and one of the dignitaries suggested to

his wife:" He seems to be the 'Kaliyuga Arjuna' and if God willing, he'll be the suitable match to our daughter. What do you say?"
His wife sighed and replied:" Oh! He is.....Madhu used to say about him. But I haven't seen him so far. He is the son of Sivasankar, the only son of his parents. As you said, if God willing, he can be our son-in-law. He is the perfect match to our daughter. "
"What's his father?"
"Computer Engineer in an I.T.Company. His mother is a teacher in a private school.
"How do you know all these?"
"By means of Madhu."
"Is she....?
"You mean boyfriend?"
" No, she ***carries the torch***."*(Have one sided love)*
"After this ***mellow*** conversation, followed the applause that ripped the air and after dying the applause, Baskar ***descanted on*** (a decorative musical accompaniment added above a basic melody) Moghana raga' "மோகமதே எழிலா...கண்ணனின் ....in his mellifluous tone as if A, M.RAIAH in the ghost form entered into his soul and began to sing a **man's** falsetto **voice**, the **voice** produces a sound that is sometimes described as "otherworldly". Baritone. A baritone is the most common type of **male voice** whose range lies midway between the high tenor **voice** and the low bass **voice**.

Of course, it's a matter of one twenty five seconds only, he crooned and made the entire audience spell bound, fascinated, transfixed, bewitched mesmerized and bound them in the musical fort. Usually, there're some ***feckless*** (of a person) having a weak character; not behaving in a responsible way) students who used to ***tease*** **(***to laugh at sb and make jokes about them, either in a friendly way or in order to annoy or embarrass them)* those who performed against their taste and interest but since the majority of the audience was in favour of Baskar; so they kept quiet.

Then followed a number of programmes and at the end, there was an announcement of the best programme for which the judges appeared on the dais and after a brief speech about the performance of the students, one of the judges declared: "All programmes were very excellent but we have been directed to choose three programmes only which deserves the first, second and third position. The 'Folk dance ' stands the first position, entitled to receive Five thousand rupees cash award, and "Tamil Drama" stands the second position to be entitled for the cash award of 2000 rupees and finally " "Karagottam" has been selected to be in the third position and entitled to receive thousand rupees. ....

As soon as the result was declared there prevailed **commotion** (sudden noisy confusion or excitement) among the audience and some overtly **commented (**to express an opinion or give facts about sth)**.**" The son of the local politician takes part in the above three programmes and so the judges selected the undeserved programmes as they were corrupted.

Baskar and the twins were ***stung*** (to make somebody feel angry or upset) by the corrupted and blemished judgment.

The twins with bleary eyes burst out:" Hereafter we won't participate in any of the college programmes and Baskar cried and reported to his parents:" As long as politicians are, we can't change the world into a right path. Had I known already that this college is under the control of the local politician, I wouldn't have participated in the vocal song competition. The judges are debased, debauched, demoralized, bribed and greased the politician's palms. I will never participate in any of the college programmes hereafter."

The twins and Baskar were unaware that this malpractice judgement is a blessing in disguise since it paved a way to unite them together in the ***Bond of Love.***

After this hapless incident, on the next working day, the Principal of the College convened an assembly and all the students assembled in the open ground and then he began to address:" ***I take delight in congratulating the students who participated in the Anniversary Day programmes and Tamil Alagan was declared to be entitled to receive the***

first, second and third prizes and I congratulated him for his best performance. At the same time, I cannot be without congratulating the twins, Shyamala Devi and Nirmala for their superb performance in "Bharatanatyam 'and I feel they are eligible to receive the cash award of Five Thousand rupees. I request them to come to the dais and receive the cash award."

This was like a ***bolt out of the blue*** by which the twins were overwhelmed, thrilled and drenched in the torrential rain of joy and they were phasing towards the dais followed by applause by the students who were in favour of the judgement.

After awarding them, the Principal continued:" ***I am not an ace or maven in Carnatic music but penchant for A.M. Raja who is a maestro in Carnatic music and composer and playback singer and our Prince of the College, Baskar, a dux, Final year student of M.A. English is hereby declared to receive the cash award Five Thousand rupees and on behalf of Committee members of this college and you, I congratulate him for his wonderful performance in crooning the Carnatic song by A.M. Raja. I request Baskar to come to the dais and receive the cash award.***

It's ***a peripeteia*** *(a sudden change of fortune in one's life)* in the life of Baskar for which he was ***flabbergasted, boggled and dumb stricken*** for some minutes and then he ***minced*** *(walked daintily)* towards the dais. All the girl students and boy students who're in favour of Baskar ***applauded*** till he received the cash award and shook his hands with the Principal.

The countenance of twins and Baskar exposed that they ***kvelled*** *(felt happy and proud)* for being awarded by the Principal with the laudatory remarks. The assembly witnessed that the twins and Baskar were blissfully delighted and the reason for they blissed out and the ***oblectation was*** not for the money they got but the victory they got in the competition in which the bribed judgers are said to have become ***bedrock of corruption and bribery*** for they gave their partial verdict.

The trio was so handsome, smart and adorable that they're such a ***beaut.*** ***(****Person of great beauty not only on the outside but also inside)* and their floridity added to their pulchritude.

The ***Amor*** *(God of Love, counterpart of Greek Eros)* darted an arrow at the twins by whom they'd a ***lucid dream*** in which they met Baskar at ***Shangri-La,*** a fictional place as well as a mystical harmonious valley gently guided from a lamasery, enclosed in the western end of Kunlun Mountains.

Next day, when Shyamala met Baskar in the College, she greeted him, "Good Morning, Baskar." for which he reciprocated by greeting her and extoled and applauded her," Your dance performance was superb like that of Kumari Kamala. It's an engramma."
Arrided by his complimentary words, Shyamala replied:" Thank you for your compliments. Similarly, your crooning was so mellifluous that I was fascinated like **kine** (cows**)** on hearing the flute music played by Lord Krishna.
At the same time, Nirmala appeared there who was in search of her sister and on seeing Shyamala with Baskar, she guessed something and greeted Baskar for which Baskar reciprocated her by wishing and said:" It's very difficult to identify who Shyamalais and Nirmala is. What a splitting image! "
Nirmala blushed and said:" Even my dad cannot identify us exactly. "
"Oh, is it? Well, really it is very difficult to differentiate between you both. Bye the by, your dance performance was very superb and it's inerasable in my mind."
"Thank you for your compliments, Baskar. Your crooning is also very excellent and I was very much fascinated by the honeyed voice. But the corrupted judges gave their verdict wrongly. Is a folk dance equal to Bharatanatyam? Can a folk dancer dance Bharatanatyam? For lamenting song and senseless words are called duet song. The cadre of the judges has been exposed through

their taste. We couldn't digest it and were upset very much. The committee members realized their mistake and through our Principal, they made arrangements to honour us. ***We feel happy now for the truth triumphed at last."***

Baskar spoke his mind to them:" What's the use of exposing our skill and ability to the undeserved? We should habit to the deserved but not to the uncultured. We made a mistake without knowing the fact that it is not a suitable place to show our ***feat***.(an action or piece of work that needs skill, strength or courage).Had you shown your feat in the ***dance ceremony*** or Dance performance, you would have been honoured by the mavens of Noble Art; similarly, had I shown my feat in the concert, I would have been honoured but haplessly, we performed to the people who are blind and deaf. Anyhow, we've learnt a good lesson. Hereafter, I won't participate in our college function."(தகுதி இல்லாதவர்களின் முன் தம் தகுதியை காண்பிப்பது பெரும் முட்டாள்தனம்.

The twins realized the depth of truth in the Home truth Baskar expressed out of his own experience.

There held many meetings to the trio for discussion on several topics like Greek Literature, European Classics, William Shakespeare and John Milton, Francis Bacon, then politics, religion and philosophy.

Love burgeoned between them. Yes, Baskar was enamoured of Shyamala Devi and Nirmala and vice versa. Baskar was so ***besotted*** (so attracted by the twins that he was always thinking about them).that he couldn't hide his feeling from his crony who found out the change in him and asked him for the reason for which he revealed his secret love with the twins.

His crony said: "You say the twins are interested in a relationship with you, that you love both of them, and you don't want to hurt either one. That's not a bad problem to have, if you can resolve it well. I have some thoughts to share with you, if you are interested." His crony paused. Then he continued: You didn't give many details, but I am guessing that you aren't in a serious relationship with either of them, yet. It is good that you are trying to think about how to approach this, instead of just muddling through. My biggest suggestions are honesty and a lack of assumptions. Don't think you know anything about how either of them feels. Don't try to make decisions for either of them.

You need to think about this in terms of doing the best thing, not in terms of avoiding a bad thing. If you make a decision based on not hurting someone, you aren't making anyone happy, except by lucky accident. If you pick either one, you will make someone unhappy, so it is best to pick based on what makes the most happiness, not the least unhappiness. Human beings tend to make decisions based on avoiding negatives rather than gaining positives, and that often leads to a bad outcome. If you pick one based on not wanting to hurt her, what happens is you end up with the one who is needier, and least capable of dealing with adversity. That's not a great outcome. It ignores all the important stuff in a relationship, and puts you in the role of caretaker, or guardian. That's a terrible foundation for a relationship, and not a nice thing to do to someone you love. You need to assume that the twins are strong, resilient, and capable. Rejection hurts, but she can deal with it. Think carefully about your feelings for each of them. Don't agree to anything just to avoid hurting someone. Long term will lead to more pain, for you and for her. If there's one of them you don't want to be in a relationship with, you really do need to let her know that it's miserable having that discussion, but it works out better in the long run. I have made the mistake of getting more involved with someone than I wanted to because she was interested in me, and I didn't have any big objections to her. Easy choice at first, super difficult later. You say you are in love with both of them, so you may not have the easy out of picking one based on your own feelings, and in the long run, that is often easier. They both want to have a relationship with you. Do they know that you‘ve relationship with both of them? If they really do have feelings for you, and know you, and want the best for you (that is part of love), you should be able to talk to each of them about the situation. You should be able to tell each one, "I am struggling with a difficult situation here. I do love you, and I do want to be with you. I also love {other girl} and want to be with her, and you both have expressed interest in me. I don't want to hurt either of you, and I don't want to turn this into some sort of contest" etc. etc. Being honest and not making assumptions opens it up so they can be honest with you.

I would also suggest you read up on the subject ***of polyamory***.

Polyamory is the practice of, or desire for, intimate relationships with more than one partner, with the informed consent of all partners involved. It has been described as "consensual, ethical, and responsible non-monogamy". People who identify as polyamorous believe in an open relationship with a conscious management of jealousy; they reject the view that sexual and relational exclusivity are necessary for deep, committed, long-term loving relationships Polyamory has come to be an umbrella term for various forms of non-monogamous, multi-partner relationships, or non-exclusive sexual or romantic relationships. Its usage reflects the choices and philosophies of the individuals involved, but with recurring themes or values, such as love, intimacy, honesty, integrity, equality, comm unication, and commitment.

There are possible versions of your story where you don't have to hurt either one of them. It's a long shot, but it could happen. Assuming that you aren't going behind either one's back already, you are in a good position to start seeing both. Life is not a sit-com or a rom-com, where these situations always come down to a decision with one girl being wonderful and the other having some tragic flaw. You can pick both. In some ways it is the harder approach, but it has advantages too. Good luck and I wish I had not learned this stuff the hard way. If you ever go back in time, find me and beat this information into me until I get it.

Whether it's an ***advice, or counselling or guidance or admonition***, Baskar obtained clarity of his further action to execute.

In the meanwhile, Shyamala underwent the process of '***the Hell of Heaven'*** since the days that Baskar tranced her heart to make her remember the popular home truth:

First best is falling in love.
Second best is being in love.
Least best is falling out of love.
But any of it, it is better than never having been in love.

It's not known to Shyamala that her sister, Nirmala, like her, was enamoured of Baskar, and Nirmala, vice versa. Similarly, the twins were unaware of the fact that Baskar was **smitten** with them

On Sunday night, Shyamala rang up to Baskar to woo him.
"Hello, I'm Baskar speaking."
"Hi, Baskar, I'm Shyamala Devi."
"Hi, Shyamala Devi, how do you do?"
"How do you do, Baskar?"
""What's the matter, Shyamala Devi?"
"....I feel a little bit hesitation to express what I feel."
"Yes, I understand what you're going to convey."
"How?
Because I have the same hesitation."
"I would like to speak my mind to you overtly. Can you choose our tryst?"
"Why not? Golden Fort tomorrow evening after college."
"Okay, done."
"Have you been waiting for this occasion since all these days?"
"Yes, waiting for your call."
"Any other news?"
"Nothing particular. Rest in person at our tryst."
At this time, Nirmala was in search of Shyamala and stood at her doorsill and she ***eaves dropped*** her last dialogue.
Her abrupt arrival to her room displeased Shyamala but concealed her displeasure through her countenance
"Who is your boyfriend, Shyamala Devi?" Nirmala asked her with her smiling eyes and took a seat in front of her and gazed at her.
"What! Boyfriend? Who told you such thing?"

"There's no use of concealing your secret love from me because I overheard your last dialogue with whom you were speaking."

Shyamala tried to hide the truth but Nirmala was very adamant in knowing her secret love. So finally she nodded blushingly.

"Tell me clearly who your boyfriend is. Don't try to avoid answering my question."

Shyamala revealed the truth.

Shyamala expected that after hearing the name of her boyfriend, Baskar, Nirmala would make fun of her but Nirmala was shocked to hear the news from Shyamalaand in her shocking tone, "What? ....What did you say? You said the name of Baskar, isn't it?"

Blinking, Shyamala asked her," What has come of you"?

"All went wrong, Shyamala Devi."

"What are you telling, Nirmala?"

"We love the same Baskar. He wooed me in the morning when I rang up and expressed my love to him and he reciprocated my love and asked me to meet him at the Golden Fort tomorrow evening."

"Oh my god! He wooed me also."

Nirmala rang up to Baskar and she was hot under the collar and a froth:"Baskar, tell me the truth. Did you woo my sister, Shyamala Devi?"

In no minute did Baskar understand the situation and sussed our why she was ***stomachful.***

Baskar replied calmly:" I love you both and am going to marry you both. Rest in person tomorrow during our meeting." He rang off.
Both were wrathy and Nirmala particularly slated him and disparaged him in her flak" He is absolutely a ***sandbagge***r (One who deceives another about his true nature or intent in order to take advantage of another) as well as ***a con-man (***male who cheats or tricks the female by gaining their trust and persuading them to believe his words which are not true.) Tears swelled in her eyes. "He jilted me and has broken my heart. I am not going to leave him and I will retaliate very soon." She gnashed.
It's obvious that Shyamala and Nirmala trusted him, his words and never expected that he would cheat them as he mentioned that he loved both. The sense of possessiveness swayed their minds. And both thought that Baskar belonged to herself.
"Thoughts of possessiveness come when there is a fear of losing the loved one! It's not because they don't believe you, it's because they don't have on others who might take advantage of your sweetness.
"Jealousy in romance is like salt in food. A little can enhance the savour, but too much can spoil the pleasure and, under certain circumstances, can be life-threatening.
"A jealous girlfriend is faithful girlfriend if she gets jealous it's because someone has your attention, if she doesn't get jealous, it's because someone else has hers.

"Jealousy is the dragon in paradise, the Hell of Heaven, and the most bitter of the emotions because it is associated with the sweetest.

Their mother transpired their amatory affairs by dint of their resentment and freakish attitude towards her.

Their mother knew very well that the seed of love would grow in her daughters' nubile age and it's natural to everyone. First she garnered full details and then she pondered over the matter. She admonished her daughters:" There's nothing wrong that a boy falls in love with a girl but it is unnatural and leery if he falls in love with two girls or more. You both have been enamoured for he was the most handsome gumption. What do you know about his parents, his social status, and his character? You both blindly doated him and built castle in the air for which he is not responsible for your grief and disappointment. We dream many bad dreams and we don't feel sorry for it. Similarly, take it as a bad dream and abandon it. Say, 'Good bye' to his love and mind your business."

When the twins encountered with Baskar, he tried to persuade them but they loured by which Baskar sent sms to them: "If you are of the false opinion that I've jilted you, I am not responsible for your misconception; It's true, upon my god's promise that I love you to the bits. I would like to marry you both for which I wish to discuss with you today evening after the college. Hope I may be responded sincerely.....”

As anticipated, the twins met Baskar at the Golden Fort after the college.

With his fortitude and determination, Baskar asked them,” Now tell me, what your problem is.”

“You’re the problem; you created the problem but you are asking me what problem is.” Nirmala burst out.

“Okay; if you think that I am the problem to you and have created a problem, then let me know in details. Baskar asked them.

Nirmala replied:” You reciprocated to my wooing. But at the same time, you cheated me by wooing my sister, Shyamala Devi. Am I right?”

“You’re right that I reciprocated your love but it is true that I love Shyamala also. I mean I love you both. What’s wrong if I love you both, as twins? Is there any rule that I should not love both the sisters? Tell me is it wrong to love you both?”

Shyamala and Nirmala did not know how to reply.

Baskar reiterated:” Tell me what is wrong if I would like to marry you both? When you both are united together and marry me, what is wrong?”

“How can it be possible?” Both raised the question.

When the gods are polygamists why we, ordinary humans should not marry at least

two, that two, both sisters? I treat you as my both eyes. How can I lose one of my eyes? "
"I see, if we marry another boy along with you, will you agree with this marriage?"
"Certainly not; if the by whom you choose to marry co-operates with me, I don't have any objection."
"You can say theoretically but practically it won't be possible."
"I defy it. I have no objection if you wish to be a polygamist but what I wish is that I want to marry you both. It's a good fortune that you are sisters. You know each other and extend co-operation with each other in all matters. If any one of you happen to marry another boy, you have to be alone and there's no chance to be with us. But if you marry me, you can be happy with me. Am I right or wrong?"
"Can the polygamy legal?"
"There is a way for it. Sign the document asserting that you accept this marriage with whole heart. Even there are many concubines in the world. You are not going to be given the status of concubinage but legal wife. At the end of the street, there is a Brahmin namely Mr. Natesa Iyer, working in All India Radio. He has three wives. The first wife is nulliparous. So he married another and she gave birth to two children. Then he married another wife but she is residing separately. She gave birth to three children, is he not living happily?"
The twins were *baffled, befuddled, bewildered, dumbfound, flummoxed,*

gravelled, mystified, perplexed, puzzled and stupefied. After the perplexity came the clarity at the end.

At the end both realized what Baskar suggested was right and rued for their imbalance of mind as well as labile fettle. Both cuddled Baskar and apologized for their impudence.

"What shall we do now?" the twins asked Baskar.

It's our foremost duty to persuade our old parents who are steeped in the ideology of conservatism and bring them to the modern trend."

"If they don't agree...?"

"Let's get married and stand before our parents."

"Are you joking?"

"What to do? It's my congenital habit."

"Be serious, Baskar. If our parents disagree, what shall we do?"

"Think positively. We'll get positive result."

"No, Baskar. Thinking positively or negatively is not a main factor but it is nothing but our over confidence. What is to happen will happen and none can alter the fate."

"Let's wait till our parents give us permission."

"Do you mean at the age of seventy""

Baskar said something to them how to solve this problem.

Till the twins completed their B.A. course, they were levitating with Baskar by roaming all-round the places with the knowledge of their parents as well without the knowledge of their parents. It means, a few places with the knowledge of their parents and many places without the knowledge of their parents. So, their parents came to know their love affair.

Baskar and the twins were persisting their parents for their consent and at last Sivasankar, father of Baskar, being conservative, asked his son to get the horoscope of the girls for synastry. (Synastry, also known as relationship astrology, involves the comparison of two astrological charts to determine areas of strength and weakness in a relationship. It is a valuable resource for people who want to examine their relationship with another person based on aspects between each person's birth charts.)

Astrology is true but unfortunately there is none to predict the future exactly. This is the opinion of Baskar.

Unable to bear the persistence of Baskar, his parents contacted the parents of twins through cell phone for matching of horoscopes of their daughters and the twins parents partially agreed to this and invited the parents to their house with the boy's horoscope on an auspicious day.

On an auspicious day, Sivasankar with his wife came to the twins' house and after receiving the hospitality, gave the horoscope of Baskar to Sivasankar, father of twins. Then he invited the parents of twins to his house and they paid a visit to Baskar's house on an auspicious day and gave them the horoscopes of their daughters.

Both were discussing about the legal points for marriage as it's a ***bigamy. An*** astrologer was invited there for ***synastry*** who began to scrutinize both horoscopes.

The astrologer declared:" The horoscope of the boy is flawless and the Venus is powerful and occupies in a favourable place to the Moon. *Venus is the planet which if powerful and present in right house then, no doubt that the person has good power to attract females.* That's why the boy is the most handsome to attract the girls. There is no chance for arranged marriage but 'Love Marriage only. Well, let me see the girls' horoscopes." The astrologer took the horoscope of Shyamala Devi and Nirmala and began to scrutinize them. Then after clearing his throat began to give his verdict:" Venus and Mars are in one place, house and this causes friction in their family life. Sextiles and tines produce attraction that is not as insistent or competitive as the hard aspects. Rather, the attraction is smooth and pleasant. However, the square, opposition and quincunx can cause friction at the same time. There is considerable attraction but over this time, tis sexual energy can become disruptive when left unchecked. The square tends to be the most troublesome inter-aspect between Venus and Mars-sexual attraction exists and is powerful. But sex is often delayed as the couple tends to engage in arguments that take time to work out before they do what they really want to do. The square gives tremendous physical attraction and tension that is very often disguised and mis-channeled. The Venus person is easily hurt or offended by Mars. On the whole, this horoscope doesn't match with the boy's horoscope.

Sivasankar and Sivasankar were very happy to know that the horoscopes didn't match with each other. But Shyamala and Nirmala were in tears and sobbed in the Pooja room.

Sivasankar gave ample amount to the astrologer and sent him away.

Baskar suspected that his father would have made some tricks to make astrologer declare that the horoscopes won't match.

Sivasankar could not digest the fact that there's a serious flaw in his daughters' horoscope but however, he was immensely satisfied that the horoscopes couldn't match.

As soon as Baskar reached his house, he took his 'Astra' against synastry of horoscopes.

"Dad, I've no faith in horoscope. Do Muslims or Christians or Jains believe in horoscope matching? Do they have any horoscope? Do Americans believe in horoscope matching? Don't these people marry and live happily? How can you believe that an enemy planet can kill a couple? When a man is born the date of death is also written. In such a situation, how can the dead enemy planet kill the opposite person? It's sheer fake. Another example I would like to cite. Dad, your marriage was conducted after verification of horoscopes, isn't it? Does it match with my mam? Can you show me any couple without quarrelling with each other? Agreement and disagreement is always common in all families irrespective of any religion, caste or creed. It depends upon the co-operation that extended by the couples. Adjustment, patience, adaptability and mutual understanding are only enough for the peaceful living but not the horoscopes that decide one's family life. I have no faith in horoscope and synastry." Baskar paused.

"Are you a maven in Astrology? Sivasankar asked resentfully.

Baskar shook his head.

"Are you a theist or atheist?

"Theist."

"Well. On an auspicious day, let's all go to the Golden Rock temple dedicated to the deity ***Lalitha Devi***. Let's perform 'Cleromancy'. If Goddess permits, I've no objection in this marriage but if the Goddess gives negative reply, you are bound to it. Do you agree?"

"Can you explain how you are going to test the Will of Goddess?"

"Let two separate packets containing holy ash in one packet and vermilion in another packet. Let these two packets be kept on the feet of the Goddess till Archana' finished. After circumbulating the lit camphor, a small child is to select one of the packets. If vermilion is taken it means that the Goddess is willing for your marriage with the twins but on the other hand, if holy ash is taken, then it means that the Goddess is unwilling for this marriage. What do you say?"

"Can I have the freedom to test the Will of Goddess in my own way?"

"What you're going to test the Will of the Goddess?"

"Yes, I wish to know how the Goddess gives ***Her verdict."***

"How?"

"It's suspense. Please arrange for the occasion for '***Cleromancy'***

This kind of arrangement was delivered to the parents of twins who at first disagreed but after insistence by the twins, they agreed to participate in the 'Cleromancy' programme at the temple.

On an auspicious day, the two parties marched towards the 'Golden Rock Temple' dedicated to Lalitha Devi. Baskar, his parents, Shyamala Devi and Nirmala and their parents made up the party. The priest had come and lit the tall oil lamp before the idol of Devi Lalitha and a giggling baby of five years old was also present, a medium between the Goddess and the party.

They stood in the dim inner sanctuary and the priests enchanted "Sri Lalitha Astothram' and submitted some rose petals at the feet of the idol of the Goddess. As soon as the 'Archana' was performed, oblation, coconuts, plantain fruits were offered to the Goddess. Then a camphor was lit in a copper plate and the priest raised it very near to the idol by which the Goddess shone in the camphor flame and the priest circled it before the idol. One could see everyone in the party including the baby, the judge, was found with folded hands. At that time, the camphor flame flickered on the flower-decked image, by which the twins took it a mascot and fervently prayed to the Goddess to give the decision in their favour and to make the Mars, enemy planet, powerless. A few sparks flew from the wick of the lamp which they took it as a splendid omen.

Now came the time for the Goddess to give Her verdict.

One pocket containing holy ash and another packet containing vermilion were kept on the pedestal of the image as per the taboos of Cleromancy.".

The priest called the child and asked," Would you like to have a plantain fruit?"

The judge nodded with seraphic smile on her face.

"Very well, then," said the priest, "You see those two packets. Take any one and give it to me."

The modern judge asked the Priest," Why only one, why not two?"

"The Goddess wants you to pick up only one. "said the priest.

"Is it? But the Goddess didn't say to me to do so."

"The Goddess told me secretly that you should pick up only one. "

"Oh, secret message! Okay, I will pick up one of the two."

The child (Modern Judge) stood there just for a second, contemplating the two packets, little realizing the immensity of the part that she was asked to play , a medium between the Goddess and the man, a mouthpiece for Goddess to say whether Baskar could marry the twins or not. The vermilion was for 'Yes' and the 'Holy ash for 'No'.

Everybody held his breath and waited, the child stooped to pick up any one of the two, and Baskar as well as the twins, unable to bear the strain, closed their eyes.

When they opened their eyes, they saw the 'Holy ash' picked up by the child.

"She knows what is best for us." said Sivasankar and Sivasankar.

Shyamala and Nirmala with bleary eyes, closed their eyes but when they opened their eyes, they saw Baskar insisting his father to make another choice.

"Only one time in the court of Heaven." Sivasankar declared.

"You've agreed to my condition. I've my own way to test the Will of the God."

"What are you going to do?"

"Another chance to be given."

Sivasankar nodded resentfully.

Baskar asked the priest to try another time for which the Priest sighed and after seeing Baskar who signed to give him money, he smiled and got ready for the trial.

This time, the medium of God, the mouthpiece of Goddess, picked up the vermilion in favour of Baskar.

Baskar and his lovers were enraptured but Sivasankar demanded for another trial by which the priest got angry and said:" It is not a court to play in this way. The second one is valid.
Sivasankar denied saying:" No, I want it another trial."
The priest was baited with his adamancy and he said:" Do one thing. You play this game out of the temple not here."
At this time, Baskar slid a hundred rupee note into the hand of the priest and requested him to take two garlands from the image of Lalitha Devi but the priest demanded more. So Baskar gave him one five hundred rupee note as bribery. Immediately Baskar received two garlands from the priest.
"Pardon me, dad and mum. I've no other alternative way except doing this," He prostrated at their feet and in the wink of the moment; he garlanded the twins' neck and asked them to garland him which they did pronto.
"THIS IS THE VERDICT OF TRUE LOVE, BLESSED BY THE WILL OF GODDESS.' Baskar shouted out of joy.

CHAPTER No: THREE

The hour hand of the clock embraces the number ten while the second hand embraced the number twelve of the wall clock to declare that it was ten o' clock (night)and all the arrangements for the Hymeneals had already been made by parents of both parties.

SHYAMALA and Nirmala looked like the celestial fairies Menaka and Rumba, whose beauty and charm are splendidly described by the poets.

The Hymeneals Chamber was decorated with fragrant flowers and it was lit with oil lamp, as per the traditional way. Manifold sweet items and fruits items adorned the table along with a jar of milk and a cup of honey was placed on a small stool.

Like Lord Krisna leading his consorts, Rukmani and Sathya Bama, Baskar was leading his consorts, Nirmala and SHYAMALA towards the Hymeneals Chamber and then locked the door inside as per the directions of the twin sisters. Both were ravishing in their ritzy dress, sari, and blue sari matching blue bodice.

Baskar sat them on the bed and opened the conversation with them: "Anyhow, our marriage has been performed and henceforth we need not have stealthy ways of meeting and coition. What do you say, SHYAMALA and Nirmala?"

The twins heaved a sigh of relief and Nirmala said:" Yes, you're right; henceforth, we need not inhibit for anything."

"My mother has already ***accepted*** (to be satisfied with sth that has been done, decided or suggested) our request but my dad hasn't changed his mind but nodded resentfully." SHYAMALA said sadly.

Baskar excerpted the axiom:

We cannot please all people, nor can we set them right;
We cannot do the work of years in just a single minute.
But we can make one corner beautiful by humble patient labour.
We can be honest with our work and can help the next door neighbour.
I always remember this verse and it gives solace to my wounded heart. I think you can understand what I mean."
"Is your dad obdurate by nature?" Baskar asked the twins.
"It's his congenital disease grown in him. "Nirmala replied.
"Your father and my dad joined together against us." Baskar said sadly.
"How did you solve the problem?"
Your father ***sopped*** the priest and as per his instructions, the priest kept the holy ash in two pockets instead of vermilion in one packet and holy ash in another packet and so the child whatever packet takes, it will be holy ash. I guessed that it must be the base act of your father and I wish to boomerang for which I sopped the priest and instructed to keep vermilion in two packets. So I did tit for tat.
The twins felt that the shrine was desecrated by corruption and bribery and when they told Baskar that it's a great sin to perform such kind of fraudulent methods in the sanctuary."
"Are you not aware of the fact that God created Satan in 1924 in Tiruvarur district

and the Satan spoiled the entire world by spoiling the minds of the people to indulge in corruption and bribery and rowdies began to sway the country? That's why the priest became greedy and agreed with your father for doing such kind of plot against our marriage. "Baskar said.

Nirmala spoke her mind:" I feel this sari is too weighty to be borne by me."

SHYAMALA blushed and her cheeks turned aflame by coyness to add pulchritude to her and said softly," Yes, I too feel it."

Baskar laughed and said:" If it is so, better to strip off it." He understood that the twins made overtures by implying their desire. He chuckled himself for ***He made honest women of them.***

"We are not accustomed to strut ourselves in this ritzy sari but skirt or petticoat. It's simple and comfortable."

Their sari fringe slid from their shoulder and exposed their ***corsage*** which was transparent to expose the contour of their ***bandeau.*** At the sight of the exposed corsage as the sari fringe was slid from its place, Baskar felt prurient pleasure as they looked like the rotund rising sun and rotund setting sun. Baskar sussed our why the sage Viswamithra was allured by Menaka as he ogled her corset and her willowy waist and movements.

Though Baskar had seen their ***bangable and fapworthy*** boobs at many angles and stages, yet it's the newest one to see their boobs in corsage dress caged by bandeau which they used on this auspicious night but in other circumstances it was their wont not to wear brassiere or bandeau during their trysts so that it facilitated him to floob them. Shyamala, Having seen him ***perving on*** their exposed corsage, Nirmala and writhed in smiles and asked Baskar," Why are you ***ogling*** at them as if they're quiet new to you?"

Baskar replied by fingering at the verge of their boobs:" Has any one cloyed with the beauty of plenilune on full moon day? Similarly, your ***beau seins*** have made me an eye minded."

No sooner did his fingers touch the verge of their boobs than the twins thought:" How many times these fingers played on the verge of the boobs! Like two fragrant flowers canoodle in the waft of breeze, his fingers covered the surface of the verge of our boobs and canoodled the verge of our ruddy and erect boobs. How he made us long for stripping off our bodice!....Now he has commenced his foreplay."

Keeping Nirmala on dextral side while SHYAMALA on sinistral side, Baskar slipped his hands into the verge of their plump and chubby and bathykolpian boobs of excellence and then glided downwards to hide the eminent mammillae like covering the bright sun by black clouds. And their boobs spoke to his palms how much they 're craving for the titillation by which they expelled heat so as to make him know how far they were struggling to come out of the cage of bandeau. Hadn't his palms cupped their breasts and covered the profound region, they would have heaved; their breasts made a request to relieve them from the prison of brassiere or bandeau. Moreover, his palm felt their ***thelerithism for their thelium / papillae*** were imprisoned by his hot palms.

As soon as his palms imprisoned their boobs and especially papillae, the twins felt as if they're ***in seventh heaven*** and closed their eyes pleasantly.

In the meanwhile, their boobs implored his palms to set them free as they'd felt ***muggy*** for which his palms replied: "Let the bandeau be removed from the spot" and their bandeaus appealed to his palms to set them free from imprisonment. But his palms took pity upon them and unknotted the lace of the bandeaus at a time by which their bandeaus were set free from imprisonment and like a set of "Love Birds" they disclosed their appearance to his leering eyes.

As soon as their breasts came into view, Baskar ogled at them and was tempted to praise them: "Aha! What a ruddy complexion these breasts are! The design made by the bandeaus is impressed on this chubby flesh to make it look like a set of new and polished diamonds. Like a liberated slaves from the prison, how ***élan*** *(enthusiastic and assured vigour and liveliness)* they are! Like a treasure buried into the earth, these treasured diamonds were buried inside the cave of bandeau, zealous for freedom. Fruits are found hanging from the branches of trees but they won't protrude; but these fruits are not hanging or sagging but stand like a gorgeous fort and erected statue. Like the waves of the sea, these boobs are heaving. "

Like a normal human being, Baskar was ***mmazophilous*** *(excessive interest in breasts)* and like an ***opsomaniac person*** (person having extreme enthusiasm for a particular food), he'd an ***orexis*** *(physical desire or appetite)* for ***diddling*** *(manipulate manually)* his consorts, Nirmala and SHYAMALA whose breasts were exposed but hid the view of their breasts, partly since his dextral hand covered Nirmala's dextral breast while his sinistral hand, SHYAMALA DEVI's sinistral breast and the remaining could not be hidden by his palms for he had two hands only and had he four hands, he could have manipulated the four breasts simultaneously.

Prior to his foreplay, the sexual hormones in the twins such as ***testosterone, oestrogen, progesterone, oxytocin and vasopressin*** play an important role in stimulating their ***orexis and libido*** and as soon as his manipulation over their erect breasts commenced, these hormones intensified to augment their libido conducing to ***brazenness*** (*shamelessness)* by which inhibitory impulse in them got immersed and hence Nirmala asked Baskar," Your hot palm

is burning my breast due to over-temperature; so alleviate them by any means" and it was followed by SHYAMALA who was levitating said intoxicatingly :" Our body is burning with the lust of fire and it is in your hands to extinguish the fire by any means
Baskar smiled at them and said:" Yes, I understand." And continued," During one of our trysts, you came to my house during the absence of my parents and I alleviated your grief of libido, isn't it?"
Nirmala and SHYAMALA nodded at a time. Then SHYAMALA said:" We took photographs of our naked pose and they are preserved in our cell phone. We can't forget that day."
Nirmala continued:" Seeing our naked pose, you be rhymed about us. It's a wonderful day. Who can forget that day?"
Baskar reminded them what they did on that conspicuous day.
Yes, it was a ***memorable*** day.
As usual, the twins were waiting for Baskar at the rendezvous and as usual, our hero came late to that tryst and SHYAMALA was baited by his *punctuality* and made a tiff with him and warned him:" If you come late hereafter, we won't wait for you. This is the last warning to you."
"Extremely sorry, SHYAMALA and Nirmala. " He regretted and added," My friends compelled me to watch porno and so it's late."
"Are you also used to watch porno?"

”After ogling at the raunchy magazine only I watch porno.”
“Oh, you ogle at raunchy magazine?”
“”After stripping Anu only, I used to read smut stories.”
“What! Stripping AnuRadha”
“What to do, darling? It’s inevitable for me when she implored me to satisfy her biological needs. So, I helped her and satisfied her biological desire.”
Instead of quasi anger, the twins burst into laughter and commented:” You’re the master of white lies. Don’t we know that you quibble over the drooling girls?”
After persiflage, SHYAMALA asked Baskar,” Can you berhyme us?”
“Why not?”
“Take it a challenge and you are going to berhyme on us.”
”Can you come to my residence tomorrow?
“Your residence?”
”Yes, my parents won’t be available between nine and five. So we can make use of this opportunity. What do you say?”
After hesitation, the twins agreed to meet Baskar at his residence.
Next day morning, at about ten, the twins were present at the residence of Baskar who welcomed them and led them inside the house.
Both were in raunchy dress, tight banian, white colour and red lehenga and were ravishing in that dress.

Baskar led them to all the places in his house and offered them cool drinks. Then he led them to his ***man cave*** and asked them to refresh themselves in the bathroom. He whispered softly:" Lave it and stand before me nakedly so that I can berhyme on your beauty."

Though he twins restrained initially, after his persuasion, both gave their consent to do so as per his wish since they began to be aflame with lust.

His way of persuading them was strange; he French kissed them and dry humped them one after another till they were burning with sexual desire.

Baskar was waiting eagerly for them from the bath room. After thirty minutes, first, Nirmala opened the door and came out nakedly followed by SHYAMALA who also was buck naked.

It's their maiden experience to expose their nudity before their lover, Baskar; so, aflame with coyness, instinctual tendency with all ladies, the twins, writhed in smiles and adorning blushing to add pulchritude to their charming. Like all gents, his eyes fell upon their bare breasts and then their escutcheons where he could see cuneus or wedge shaped region below their navel which were constricted by their thighs and they laid their arms across their chest so that he could not see the full view of their boobs. Though Baskar could not see their bare boobs and vulva yet he could see the contour of their boobs and ***bouffant*** pubic regions. After bathing or laving, the twins looked like a fresh flower having ruddy complexion and especially their erect boobs and navels and genitals were so stunning and tempting to eff. Baskar requested the twins to relax themselves and pose in naturalisbus so as to take photos and video their naked pose for which the twins, initially were hesitant, but later on, they nodded and freed themselves from inhibition and stood nakedly so as to allow him to video their naked pose.as they ***wallowed*** *(be delighted in sensual pleasure)* and poured winsome smile during videoing. Now the twins emitted winsome smile and with sparkling eyes with pleasure as they feel an indescribable pleasure to expose their nudity in presence of their fiancé. *Their gestures and postures became more wanton and provocative.*

During outing or field day of the tryst, Baskar could frottage and cunnilingue when they're ***habilimented*** as they were scared whether they could be found out for which they did ***Anasyrma and flashing*** but now they felt full freedom in the secured place, his residence without any disturbance, and ergo they were encouraged to expose their nude body to their fiancé.

The twins tittered and asked Baskar," Could you tell us how we are in this naked posture?"

Baskar described:" Not only are your parents lucky but also me for you are rendering me the epulation of lubricity by exposing your

beau corps which is an engramma and a mascot. While warping your image, the Lord Brahma took special care in beautifying you on the basis of the following aspects. It's unknown to me whether your slim and tall body is due to the exercise done for Bharatanatyam or congenital structure created by Lord Brahma. In His creation, everybody has some flaw but in your case, there is no flaw in your golden body. Like your moon-lit face, your sexual organs, I mean your erect breasts, spathic breasts and perky breasts as well as your puffy crotch are sizzling and have the power to stir the latent lubricity of the onlookers, especially youngsters. I like your growth of hair where it is necessary and where it is not necessary. Like the gloaming with golden rays, your naked body shines to brighten the surroundings. Generally, gents prefer rotund face but I prefer oval space with which you are bestowed. I like your ***pompadour*** which you coiffed for this occasion. Your forehead is broad which signified that you are genius and I've already written my name on your forehead with my lips and osculation which you pronto responded to me. Like a ruby diamond your tilak on your glabella has got adorned to add your pulchritude. I have been amorous of you both for you are bestowed with aesthetic eyes that have the power to enslave even a great warrior. I feel delectation by looking at your eyes which are pleasing to your personality. The sparks of love and

lubricity that your eyes emit incite my latent sexual desire. It baffles me many times whether the expression through your eyes is beautiful or your mouth which springs honey for my slaking the thirst of sex is beautiful. After canoodling, the French Kiss I imprint on your lips sweetens not only my lips but also my thought. Your cheeks are chubby for the reason I always basciate and engrave my love on them. Your chin is so smart that whenever I caress you, it serves my purpose. Then below your face, emerges your long neck in which I bury my mouth and convey my secret message through amorous language "
Now I would like to berhyme the remaining organs of your body.

I want to claim your breasts as mine
For their stiff nipples I do pine
To suckle them is my desire
My hungry mouth will never tire.
You bare them for my waiting eyes
To see them bare is no surprise
My fingers grasp those nipples taut
I have just found what I have sought.
One lovely nipple I now suck
The other one my fingers pluck
I'll try to suck some milk from thee

I'll suckle hard and we shall see.
I guess for milk you must give birth
And lose your rounded b3lly girth
I guess it's been too long ago
That from these breasts your milk did flow.
You've told me that these breasts are tough
That I should treat them very rough
You know I will fulfil that need
That from your breasts my mouth will feed.
Your nipples are now tiff and plump
Rotund just like your lovely rump
I tug them now, extend their length
I'm going to pull hard with all my strength.
Twisting now with thumb and finger
These hands will long time linger
Squeeze and diddle and then suckle more
You know that your breasts I adore.
I want your breasts to make you cum

And make your all of your body hum
Boobgasm is your special art
Which often cause your legs to part.
Orgasms of your breast're so fair
Do make you want your cunt to share
When tingling in your breasts do cease
Then cunt and cock will share a piece.
Your breasts're for me a place to start
To cause your lovely legs to part
To find your dear vulva wet
For it is soon a cock to get.
First I'll lick your clitty cherry
My lips and tongues may long tarry
You may orgasm ere we fuck
Yet still I will your totties pluck.
Now when your cunt is dripping wet
It's time for it my cock to get
Those lips wide open to my thrust
My many strokes now are a must.
Your cunt now knows my cock so well
Your whole bare body casts a spell

As prick and cervix meet and greet
Each loving thrust will be more fleet.
Each time we fuck there is an end
For semen my cock will spend
You feel cock pulsing inside
Your pussy takes my gift in stride.

Like twins, Baskar used to watch porno movies in which the Indian petite babies were found with dark complexion, their pair of breasts had the same skin colour and their pubic region was either black or dark colour while on the other hand the British and Russian girls had fair complexion, ruddy complexion and their well-developed breasts had ruddy complexion as well as their pubic regions which were epilated neatly.

Baskar ***found*** (to have a particular feeling or opinion about sth) the ruddy complexioned ***rotund boobez*** (round and fat boobs) as well as escutcheon region of the twins to ***adulate*** their conspicuousness and fame. He told them:" Unlike Indian girls, your perkiest boobs and escutcheon region are blessed with the ***couleur de rose*** complexion to augment the richness of its colour and gracefulness. "This laudatory remark perked them up and they felt proud of themselves.

Nirmala and SHYAMALA were arrided by his adulation for which prurient smile adorned their moon-lit face and added charm to their face. And they conveyed him the gush of thanks through their eye-contact.

“Though the vestibule of Heaven is small yet it is really great.” Baskar pointed out their cunts and went near them to walk them towards the bed and they eagerly walked along with him to achieve the heavenly pleasure.

Baskar cuddled them uttering passionately,” I love you to the bits” and while reciprocating him, Nirmala and SHYAMALA basciated Baskar and expressed their deep love saying,” Me too.”

Then, Nirmala bantered:” Are you now satisfied with the video?”

“Can it be without satisfaction, darling,” said Baskar and added, “I videoed on your cell phone and afterwards send the video to my cell phone by WhatsApp.”

Nirmala was eager to see the video.” I wish to see the video.”

Baskar gave her, her cell phone to watch the video in which Baskar videoed their naked pose in the ***john***.

Both watched the video to know how they looked in their naked body. Nirmala continued:” Why don’t you perform Pooja every day in the morning?”

“Not video but you.” Baskar gave them his repartee.

“: Live?”

Baskar nodded with his usual smile on his face.

"How?"
"You both stand erect and I will perform how to perform Pooja."
Both, Nirmala and SHYAMALA stood erect as per his instructions and Baskar took a cup of honey and ghee and told them:" In this way, I am going to anoint your sacred organs."
"***In this way, I am going to anoint your sacred organs."*** His lecherous words diluted with honey poured elixir into their ears and hence Nirmala asked him," How are you going to anoint them?"
As it's a novel experience which they hadn't heard of, they were eager to know how he was going to deal with their "***Fanny***" with honey. Baskar devised how they should do to get anointed. "You both lay abed and I will anoint you."
As per his novel idea, both Nirmala and SHYAMALA lay abed ***in cuerpo*** whose appearance looked like a ***coquette*** with flourished ***Mastos*** that became ***tumid***, stacked, voluptuous and shapely and their ***bedroom eyes (***sexually attractive look) incited his concupiscence.
Baskar ogled at his bed partners who were lying abed ***supinely*** (*lying on the back or with the face upward)* and took a cup of honey and poured upon the mounds of their chest as if a temple priest pouring or anointing honey over the Lingam by which the twins felt a tickling sensation and writhed in smiles. The poured honey percolated through their glassy and rotund

breasts towards the valley of their navel like stream of water flows down the valley from the hills. As he poured more and more the sweet honey made its way through their navel and like sea waves springing fast towards its shore, the honey flowed quickly to reach the slope of their escutcheon regions. The pilose pubic region got epilated recently by which they were shining brightly in the honeyed reflection.

As soon as the pouring honey over their ***fanny regions*** was over, Baskar began to diddle upon their erect breasts by standing between them cosily. As soon as his fingers started massaging and stroking their bare, rotund and erect breasts with that ***viscous*** honey, it rendered them ***boobgasm and*** they were eyeing up Baskar whose palms were oily and sticky. During the process of stroking and massaging their erect and bare breasts which were soaked with the viscous honey, the pair of breasts got adpressed to make many kinds of shapes. Similarly, whenever, his fingers passed through their thelium, a sensitive organ, both tossed their heads and sibilated by closing their eyes. His thenar and fingers played a prominent role in rendering them boobgasm by which Nirmala and SHYAMALA were enjoying the pleasure of his foreplay by closing their eyes like philharmonic players who're tranced by the mellisonant song, which was spreading the mellifluous voice to overflow the entire valley. Baskar was arrided with the lambent glow of their honeyed body and his simultaneous application of his hands on the twins brought them about the state of euphoria. Then his eyes descended from the mounds to reach their navel region which looked like a vortex or whirlpool and his thenar smeared from the verge of their breast descending towards their navel and halted there. His fingers began to stroke and massage their navels to make them mad after his method of foreplay and this was obvious from their wiggling of hips. Nirmala and SHYAMALA anticipated that his fingers were going to descend from their navel region, hypogastrium and in a few minutes, his fingers were navigating towards their escutcheon .and while passing through their escutcheon, his fingers perceived the little mound at the vestibule of their cunt, a fluffy and flossy mound and the curvature like a convex shape or bell-shaped like gibbose moon.

Like a flawless gold statue, their ***vulvae*** were Gynelophilous (hardwood floors) and blooming due to the application of viscous honey profoundly and like a double door their labia constricted the Heaven by lying ***interfemoral and exposing*** their sexual organs.

Both felt that his fingers began to smear their pubic region with honey and they expected that any time they would descend towards the vestibule of their vulvae.

Nirmala and SHYAMALA heard him say:" How small it looks but how great it is!"
The twins' eyes met each other and conveyed something with smile.
"Is it your wont to epilate periodically?" Baskar whispered softly.
Both nodded silently smilingly.
"What a couleur de rose complexion!" Baskar exclaimed
Baskar slathered their pudendum with viscous honey and clipped the dextral labia of pudendum with index finger and thumb and then made them splay so as to view their internal organs which were pink colour. Then his index finger and thumb clipped their sinistral side of their labia of pudendum and stroked them softly. They were tactile and he felt immense pleasure and expressed his mind as:" How tactile they are!"
Nirmala and SHYAMALA felt that his fingers were trying to dilate their labia and finally succeeded in his attempt. Then his index fingers of dextral hand and sinistral hand penetrated into the foramen of their pudendum simultaneously which were smooth and wet.
As soon as his fingers penetrated into their vaginae, both wiggled their hips and sibilated Then Baskar penetrated his index finger and middle finger into the vaginal tract of Nirmala while his mouth buried into SHYAMALA's interfemoral region.

In a few seconds, SHYAMALA began to wriggle and wagged her hips and sighed ecstatically.

The more Baskar cunnilingued her Coleus Feminus, the more she wriggled and got ready for the Cowgirl position.

Next moment, SHYAMALA formed cowgirl position and Nirmala took rest till her sister completed her coital act.

It's an adage that the speediest one in the world is nothing but our mind. Baskar reminisced the entire episode in a fraction of minutes and recovered from his Dreamland. The twins, Nirmala and SHYAMALA who were concupiscent, goatish, hot, hypersexual, itchy, lascivious, lecherous, lewd, libidinous, licentious, lubricious, lubricous, lustful, oversexed, passionate, randy, salacious, and wanton were ready for the coition

Baskar reminded them how he coitioned them in his residence and laughed.

Nirmala and SHYAMALA said:" Yes, it's a memorable day. On that day, you berhymed excellently. Now we are going to berhyme on our part. Could you listen to us?"

Baskar nodded with surprise.

Nirmala began berhyming:

"I prefer the young man for coition, and him only;
He is of courage full—he is my sole ambition,
His member is strong to deflower my virgin.

And richly proportioned in all its dimensions;
It has a head alike to a brazier.
Enormous, and none like it in creation;
Strong it is and hard, and with the head rounded off,
It is always ready for action and does not die down;
It never sleeps, owing to the violence of its love.
It sighs to enter my Heaven, and sheds tears on my belly;
It asks not for help, not being in want of any;
It needs no ally, and stands alone the greatest fatigues,
And nobody can be sure of what will result from its efforts.
Full of vigour and life, it bores into my foramen,
And it works about there in action constant and splendid.
First from the front to the back, and then from right to left;
Now it is crammed hard in by vigorous pressure,
Now it rubs its head on the orifice of my organ.
And he strokes my back, my stomach, my sides.
Kisses my cheeks, and anon begins to suck at my lips.
He embraces me close, and makes me roll on the bed,
And between his arms I am like a corpse

without life.
Every part of my body receives in turn his love-bites.
And he covers me with kisses of fire;
When he sees me in heat he quickly comes to me.
Then he opens my thighs and kisses my belly.
And he puts his tool in my hand to make it knock at my door.
Soon he is in the cave, and I feel the pleasure approaching.
He shakes me and thrills me, and hotly we both are working,
And he says, 'Receive my seed!' and I answer, 'Oh give it, beloved one!
It shall be welcome to me, you light of my eyes!
Oh, you man of all men, who fillest me with pleasure.
Oh, you soul of my soul, go on with fresh vigour.
For you must not yet withdraw it from me; leave it there,
And this day will then be finished free of all sorrow.'
He has sworn to God to have me for seventy nights.
And what he wished for he did in the way of kisses
And embraces during all those nights"

Baskar lauded them since their verse pivoted to real situation.

Nirmala said:" Darling, prior to our marriage, it's a thrilling experience but were inhibited whether we would be found out. But now we don't feel such inhibition as we felt on that day. We feel ***in seventh heaven and now you have made an honest woman of us.***

Then Nirmala told Baskar:" We would like you to let us know how you deal with the temple priest. It baffles our minds."

Baskar related how he dealt with the temple priest and astrologer. Your father, being a business man, wanted me as ***beenah*** to which my parents protested and my father turned against your parents. He sopped the astrologer to make him say that my horoscope has flaws and thus it won't match with the horoscopes of yours. But your mother was in favour of me and wished to give you in marriage with me irrespective of my consent for beenah or not. I met your mother secretly without anyone's knowledge and came to know the plot whetted by your father in cheating me .As expected the astrologer that your father fixed, played drama but he declared that my horoscope had no flaws but your horoscopes. My father felt happy with the verdict of the astrologer, a cheat. My mother was in favour of this marriage alliance and suggested for ***Cleromancy*** and convinced my father. My father and your father joined together against us and contacted the temple priest and sopped him with money to make this alliance null and void by any means and the priest suggested that he would keep holy ash in two packets separately. I met the priest and sopped him with more money than he expected and hew played drama as per my instruction. During the first Cleromancy, the baby took the pocket containing holy ash to mean that the Goddess is not willing for this alliance but I insisted for the second chance for which our parents excluding mother, opposed. But I insisted more and finally they agreed. This time, the priest kept vermilion in two packets instead of holy ash. So when he baby selected one of the pockets, it was the pocket containing vermilion and as per the signal given to me, I got a pair of garlands from the priest and garlanded you immediately. "He paused.

"How did you convince my father?" Nirmala asked Baskar.

"You mean for beenah?"

"Yes."

My mother and your mother joined together and persuaded my father to sell my house and planned to construct another two storeys with your residence so that all can live together peacefully. So there is no question of being beenah hereafter in our family. Your father changed his mind and befriended my father. It's a divine blessing to our family. "

"I couldn't believe how my father changed his mind." SHYAMALA surprised.

"It's all due to the good time." Baskar replied and hugged them.

(Continued)

CHAPTER NO: FIVE

Baskar and his consorts, Nirmala and SHYAMALA were in a state of Euphoria for they accomplished in their love affair and married successfully after eradicating the obstacles by the Grace of God and above all, the "***Sororal Polygamy*** "rendered them no problems as the twins gave up their possessiveness over their husband. Moreover sweet tidings awaited them.

There was a call from Sivasankar and Sunder for Baskar and his consorts and when they appeared before them, Sivasankar asked them to be seated before them and after they seated in front of them, Sivasankar opened the topic:" By the Grace of God, everything went on well. It's our family custom to send the newly married couples for honey moon. So we would like to ask you to which place you prefer to spend your Honey Moon."

That sweet tidings poured honey into their ears and the delectation they felt was ineffable and they jumped out of joy and conveyed their thanks to them.

Baskar replied:" What my consorts decide is my wish, dad."

"Oh, it's good. It'll be very nice when the ladies decide as they are expert in this matter." Sivasankar said smilingly.

Sundar nodded at them.

Nirmala and SHYAMALA suggested Los Angeles in Texas in USA but Sivasankar told them:" Of course, it is a nice place to visit but it is very difficult to get Visa to go to USA so it is better to choose within India. I would like to suggest you, Shimla." What do you say?"

Their faces beamed with delight on hearing the name," Shimla."

Sivasankar added: Recently I have been to Shimla with my friends in view of party arranged by one of my friends. I enjoyed like anything. So I suggest you this golden place. for spending Honey Moon. Further, it is the place where you are going to get rich experience with the insurmountable place, The Himalayas in all its enigmatic glory. Oh! What an excellent place to enjoy! It is an epulation to our eyes. The evergreen forests, rolling valleys, breath-taking lakes, gorgeous climate and colonial ambiance all come together to lend this hill station a charm of its own. With a varied range of attractions – natural splendours as well as man-made wonders – the place truly lives up to its reputation. First place to visit is The Ridge which is the heart of Shimla in terms of location and tourist attractions. This Shimla tourist spot is actually a wide-open street that runs along the Mall Road from east to west and connects it to the famous Scandal Point. What makes it such a popular destination is that it offers gorgeous views of the snow-capped mountain ranges that rise against the blue sky to border this paradise of a destination. The place is dotted with long-standing. The next place to visit is: "Jakhoo Hill and Temple Covered in a blanket of alpine trees, Jakhoo Hill is the highest point of Shimla and offers scenic views of the snow-covered ***Shivalik*** Ranges as well as the sister town of Sanjauli. Situated at a height of 8000 ft. above the sea level, Jakhoo Hill is the location of an ancient Hanuman temple that boasts of having the world's tallest statue (108 ft.) of this Hindu deity. Shrouded in legends and mysteries, it attracts devotees and the tourists alike. If the local legends are to be believed, the temple stands at the very spot where Lord Hanuman had rested for a while during his journey to bring the ***Sanjeevani Booti*** for Lakshman's revival during the battle with Ravana in Lanka.. Then the next third place to visit is: When it comes to places to visit in Shimla for couples, you can't give a miss to the Mall Road. Otherwise, also, the place is a hip and happening location in this hill station and attracts visitors of all ages. With a plethora of cafes, restaurants, showrooms, departmental stores, and shops selling trinkets and exclusive handicraft works, this is one place where you can soak in the spirit of Shimla in all its touristy delights. From jewellery and books to intricately crafted wooden articles, you can shop for a variety of items here. At the same time, you can explore a number of other attractions in the vicinity, like the Kali Bari Temple, Town Hall, Gaiety Theatre, and Scandal Point. What's more, since the road is closed to vehicles, taking a stroll here during the evening hours while overlooking the scenic beauty of the hills is a pleasure in itself."

Baskar and his consorts were gaping at Sivasankar who was recounting his experience.

"The Kalka-Shimla train ride is a highpoint of Shimla tourism and for a good reason. Built in 1898, this narrow-gauge railway has recently been added to the mountain railways of India World Heritage Site by UNESCO. Winding through the extremely scenic and mountainous route from the Shivalik Range foothills at Kalka (Haryana) to Shimla, the train ride offers spectacular views of the surrounding hills and villages. On the way, it stops at a number of tourist destinations, like Solan, Dharampur, Summer Hill, Salogra, Taradevi, and Barog, among others. The ride will take you through no less than 864 bridges, 919 curves, and 102 tunnels. The train ride in itself may not count as a 'place' to visit in the region, but missing the ride means missing out on some of the splendid sights that Shimla has to offer."

A ride of about 40 minutes from the city centre will bring you to Kufri, another must-visit place in the region. Located at an elevation of 8607 ft., this small hill station promises you panoramic views of the surrounding snow-capped mountains. But Kufri is not just about Shimla sightseeing. It is also an adventure hub that offers training and facilities for exciting winter sports like ice skating and skiing. That is why it is also known as the winter sports capital of India. Since Kufri experiences regular snowfall in winter, it ranks top among the places to visit in Shimla in December. The next place is a breath-taking natural dale near Shimla and Kufri, Green Valley stands true to its name. Set against the backdrop of snow-covered mountains and lush green forests of pine and deodar, the valley is carpeted in greenery. Away from the touristy crowd, the serene Green Valley is where you can witness nature in all its grandeur, which makes it one of the best places to visit in Shimla for honeymoon. Given its pristine beauty, the place also counts among the favourite Bollywood locations in India and has been featured in a number of Hindi movies. Although you can visit Green Valley all year through, the best time to visit it is during the summer months. Some temples are known for their religious or historic significance while others draw in visitors due to their architectural beauty. But there are some temples that score high on both counts.

The Kali Bari Temple in Shimla is one such place! Believed to have been built in 1845, the temple boasts of architectural beauty as well as religious significance in equal measures. As the name indicates, the temple is dedicated to Goddess Kali and houses a captivating idol of the deity. Located very close to the Mall Road, it is an ideal spot to spend some serene moments connecting with your inner self. An interesting thing to note is that Goddess Kali is known here as Goddess Shyamala Devi and it said that Shimla derived its name from Goddess Shyamala Devi. You may or may not be a religious soul, but while in Shimla, you must not miss out on visiting the Tara Devi Temple. Located atop the hill called Tara Parvat, this shrine is believed to be about 250 years old. Goddess Tara, a goddess of the Tibetan Buddhists and one of Goddess Durga's nine sisters, is the presiding deity here. According to the local belief, the wooden idol installed in the temple was brought from West Bengal. While the temple exudes a serene vibe, what draws tourists to this destination is its fine architecture. Nestled within the Glen Forests, Chadwick Waterfall is one of the most delightful sights that nature has bestowed upon Shimla. The waterfall makes a dive from a height of 86 meters and cascades down a huge gorge. Surrounded by a blanket of greenery formed by the deodar and pine trees, it presents an enticing sight. The best time to visit it is during monsoons (from June to September) when the water level increases and Chadwick seems to take on a life of its own. If you are not daunted by the idea of taking a dip in the cold waters, you can go ahead and splash around. "

Baskar asked him how to reach Shimla.

Sivasankar replied:" The best way to reach Shimla is to travel to Chandigarh by flight or train and from thereon, continue the 4-hour-long journey to Shimla by road. You can also reach Shimla via Kalka Railway Station on a toy train."

Sivasankar fixed a date for their journey to Shimla in view of their "Honey Moon" Till Sivasankar completed his description about Shimla and his superb ***design*** *(to think of and plan a system or way of doing sth)* to jaunt to Shimla in view of "Honey Moon" for the new couples, Baskar and his two wives, Nirmala and SHYAMALA DEVI, all were ***gawping at*** *(look with amazement)* Sivasankar who had visited Shimla several times prior to his marriage with his wife, Gowrie. After marriage, he went to world Tour with tourist party to spend 'Honey Moon" with his wife, Gowrie. Having rich experience in tourisms, he designed how to spend the Honey Moon holiday pleasantly without risks.

While Sivasankar was recounting the picnic spots in Shimla, Baskar and the twins were swimming in the ocean of Dream and they felt as if they 're in Shimla and jaunted to all the picnic spots as the description was so scintillating but not ***yammering*** which was not his wont.

At the same time, Sundar was watching his son, Baskar and his ***consorts,*** Nirmala and SHYAMALA

Devi (wife or husband, especially of a ruler) who were in sedentary pose on the couch; Baskar was between Nirmala and SHYAMALA to look like Lord Subramanian with his consorts, Valli and Devayani.

Baskar, an admirer (man who is attracted to a woman and admires her) and his wives looked like couple made for each other or *[of two people] very well suited romantic ally*. Or made for one another (perfectly suited) and rued for the disapproval of their marriage and conspired against them associating with Sivasankar and realized that what God has willed will come true, Marriages are made in heaven. Neither he nor his ancestors had the practice of Bigamy or beenah but during his generation, it transpired by which he had been in a qualm whether it would yield well if he would make marital relations with Sivasankar family. Further it was an ***arriere pensee*** that Siva gave up his egoism and sought to befriend him. Moreover, Sivasankar had known that his in-law was working as a teacher in a private school which was running at a loss like a sinking ship in the ocean and he wished to buy it to run the institution of his own for which he contacted the President of that educational institution and bought the school and registered in the name of Gowrie and formed partnership with Sundarasan, as the Correspondent, while Gowrie as Secretary and himself as President.

One day Sivasankar invited Sundarasan and his wife, Gowrie to have a discussion with them at the Star Hotel in view of future plans for which Baskar's parents met Sivasankar and his wife, SHYAMALA at the Star Hotel and during the ***alfresco*** dinner, he opened the topic

"Well, Mr. Sundar, I would like to discuss with you both regarding my future plan. Past is past and there is no use for ruing for it. My daughters are my eyes and they are patrophilic than matrophilic and gave up the idea of Beenah. Why can't we live together in our residence?" He paused.

Sundar:" Our residence?"

"Yes, my dear in-law; Hereafter my residence is your residence and vice versa. I am going to construct a double storey for your family. What do you say?"

"Do you want us to reside at your double storyed residence? " Sundar hesitated.

"I understand what you feel and why hesitate. I would like to suggest you another idea if you don't mistake me. Either can you sell your present residence or rent for it. If you opt for selling your present residence, I will buy it and deposit the entire amount in your name or to whomever you wish me to deposit the entire amount. What do you say?"

Sundarasan understood his stage. He replied:" It's an excellent idea to live together. I agree with your idea but I don't want to sell my ancestral house which is memorable to our family but I will rent the house. The rent amount will be deposited into your bank account till the cost of construction of the double storey is paid. Afterwards, the rent amount will be deposited in my bank account. If our friendship should continue, then monetary matters should be handled very carefully. This is my idea. "

Sivasankar had no other way except to acquiesce with his decision. He nodded.

Prior to amorant affairs of Baskar with the twins, an interesting incident transpired.

As usual, Sivasankar was on the way to his agricultural land by his car. It was about ten and the scorching heat of the sun was severe. At that time, he saw a pair of lovers chased by some goons who were with sickles and knives. He stopped the car till the lovers, elopers came near his car. As soon as they came near, he opened the back door of the car and urged them to get inside the backseat. As soon as they got into the back seat of his car, he scorched the car towards his land and the chasers followed he car. As soon as Sivasankar reached his land, he shouted at his workers to come quickly and attack the chasers.

The agricultural workers ran pronto with their spades to attack the chasers.

At the sight of the agricultural workers with their spades, the chasers fled from the spot and soon disappeared.

Thus he rescued the life of the elopers and asked them about their life history.

They belong to a village in Kerala and since they belong to different caste, their parents opposed their love. But the lovers, teens, planned to elope by train and reached the city but unfortunately the parents of the families with their men chased them. Hadn't Sivasankar succoured the elopers, they would have been caught by them and subject to ***crucifixion.***

Both fell at the feet of Sivasankar and the boy, aged nineteen, was overwhelmed and blubbered out. His name was Prakash Raj, son of a peasant and fell in love with the daughter of the owner of the land, Menaka a petite blonde, had completed her education up to tenth standard in Kerala. When their amorant affairs came to be known to the parents of both parties, severe punishment was imposed upon them. Thus it conduced to strengthen their love and paved the way for the execution for elopement. But unfortunately, one of the spies came to know the secret plan and began to chase them with his men. Even if they would have surrendered at the police station for protection, it won't last long and at any time, they might be caught for tribulation. So they abandoned the

idea and boarded into the Express train and reached the neighbouring State But the villains continued to chase the elopers.
"What are you going to do hereafter?" Sivasankar asked them after giving then tender coconut water and kernel.
Menaka with bleary eyes joined her two hands and implored:" You are our succour and we, refugee. We will do what you say. Our future is in your hands, oh God man."
"Even if I give you the work in my land, the goons will find out and wreck the vengeance at any time. So your life is always risky. I will take you both to my residence and my wife will decide what should be done. Would you like to remain with me in my residence?"
Both ***horripilated*** and in a melting voice they prayed:" You are our God. Till our death we won't forget your help. We pray you to allow us to remain with you and we will be loyal to you till our death. "
"Well, go and take rest there in that cottage till my return. None will enter without my knowledge, you will be safe there. Go and take rest there and if you like to take bath, go and lave in the tank of water." Then he directed one of his women to take them to the cottage in the middle of the fields.
It seemed that ***Amorasa*** (female lover), Menaka and her boyfriend, Prakash raj, both were teen aged and wearing rustic appearance; Menaka seemed to be an ***ingénue*** while Prakash raj, very innocent boy but the girl had ruddy complexion for she

belonged to Kerala. Generally the Keralite girls have long black hair and Menaka was not exceptional.

Both were dead tired and exhausted as they were chased by their villains and both had miraculous and narrow escape from their foes. The tender coconut water and kernel slaked their thirst and tiredness to some extent and their dress were grubby/grungy/smudgy and dirty and what they needed was laving first.

The woman servant who led them asked them whether they had another dress to wear after taking bath but they lost their luggage during chase and now appeared in a single dress. She wanted to help them for they had single dress; so she sent her sister to fetch dhoti and shirt for Prakash raj and petticoat and blouse for Menaka.

Both had alfresco bath and washed their old dress and after laving, they wore the dress supplied by the woman servant and they conveyed their gratitude.

In the afternoon, Sivasankar informed the police for his protection and told the entire details to the sub inspector who was known to him very well.

The police came there in mufti by motor bike followed by police van secretly.

As anticipated, the villains were waiting for the return of the lovers and the car on the way and when the car appeared to their eyes, they gathered together to attack Sivasankar and the lovers but the police in mufti surrounded them and arrested them. They threw them into the police van.

Sivasankar informed his wife about the incident and reached his residence with the lovers. There held direct interview headed by SHYAMALA and after satisfaction, she gave them the *honourable and unique position as 'Cook'* in that house. Initially, both had to work as an apprentice for some days and after satisfactory result, further benefits would be made.

What are the benefits for them to be bestowed by the Ladies in that house?

Menaka would join the school to continue her education in tenth standard for she had no certificate with her though she'd passed tenth standard examination in Kerala. In the case of Prakash Raj, he had to continue his education by dint of Open University. They had to live in the outhouse at the back of the house. They would be paid free meals, dress and five thousand rupees per head for their expenses. Sivasankar and his wife, treated them very kindly and even the twins treated them as their own sister and brother. Both commenced their culinary art in the early morning and finished the work for their breakfast and lunch before nine. Nine to four rest,; then tiffin and dinner before seven. By eight, their duty would be over and return to their outhouse.

When Sivasankar narrated this incident to his in-laws, Sundar and his wife, Gowrie, they appreciated them for his kind nature and his gumption by helping the elopers and made them cook in his residence.

Till the construction of double storey was over, the parents of Baskar were in their own residence but Baskar was in his father-in-law's house.
At eight, Sivasankar, his wife, Baskar and his wives took their seats at the Dining Hall and Prakash Raj and Menaka began to serve breakfast to all of them.
The breakfast was ***sumptuous/delectable/delicious/ scrummy and tasty*** and Baskar smacked the dishes and Sivasankar, when noticed it, laughed and said:" See, how nicely our cooks prepared! Even if they wish to leave our home, I won't leave them. How excellently they prepare dishes!"
Baskar replied:" You are really lucky to have them as your cooks. I have never tasted such taste in my life."
Sivasankar said:" God has bestowed us these cooks as blessings. Really it is an accidental meeting. I think your father didn't tell you about them." He told him how he helped Prakash Raj and Menaka and rescued them from the grave danger.
"Aren't they at stake?"
"No, the police crucified them in the station and let them free after warning them not to return towards South. So, there is no chance for them to come here and disturb them."

"Menaka is under age, isn't it? How is her marriage with Prakash Raj legally accepted?"
"Of course it is an illegal marriage but I am responsible for it. Nothing can be done."
After a pause, Sivasankar and his wife asked Baskar," Any grievance you have in our hospitality? If there is any, please do let us know."
Please don't use such words. You are like my parents and I am your son. I hate bloody formality. You can be free with me." Baskar replied politely.
SHYAMALA and Nirmala who heard their parents' concern, chipped in:" Why do you worry unnecessarily about us? We are very very happy and he is also taking care of us nicely. We must be lucky to have him as our spouse since he had the gumption as equal to his charm and striking beauty." Both extolled Baskar to the sky.
Their overt flummery embarrassed Baskar though it deserved and true also. It's ***idoneous*** to be lauded as the Prince of the College since he was Adonis and had the ruddy complexion and charm as Gemini Ganesan, Prince of Love'
Baskar had known that Sivasankar was doating his two daughters very much and they're his two eyes and being a cynosure, he might think that he would be a polygamist. So he wished to clarify his doubt for which Baskar asserted:" Uncle, you need not worry about us. As you doat them like your eyes, I

consider them as my eyes and take care of them well. "

Sivasankar replied:" I've no doubt, my dear son-in-law. I know that though my daughters make you irritated, you will be calm and quiet. They are still childish. Hope I may not be mistaken for using such words."

Gowrie smote her hands on her forehead as her husband was yammering and spinning him a yarn as he was overwhelmed and Gowrie understood that if it would last, it would end in forming an impression on her husband conducing to calumniation gradually. So she chipped in and said to her husband:" Like yapping on the cell phone, today you are yammering to discommode benedict and our daughters since they require privacy. Let them be free." Then she turned towards Baskar and said:" You please take rest in the upstairs. Nirmala and SHYAMALA DEVI, both of you go and help him take rest in the upstairs."

Her esoteric words brought the twins about aflame with coyness to adorn their faces with rubicund complexion and met Baskar's eyes meaningfully and he, tout de suite, sussed out why she chipped in their conversation, thus to make them relaxation from her husband.

Sivasankar, like a devotee, implicit obedient to an oracle, ceased his yapping and rose from his seat saying," Yes, yes,, go and take rest in the upstairs."

The twins led their husband, Baskar to their room and as soon as they entered into the room the door was locked inside.

"My mother wants you to take rest here in this room. What's your idea?" Nirmala asked her husband banteringly.

Baskar gave his repartee:" My idea in this matter is to consummate you regularly."

"Are you not tired?"

"I am not tired of you both." Then he changed the topic for conversation:" Are you used to be in lehenga and sleeved ***banyan*** (a loose fitting jacket) even at home?"

"Aren't we ravishing in this dress?"

"Certainly; not only ravishing in dress but also appealing."

"Generally all males are flatterers."

"It's the instinctual habit of ladies to be leery."

"All males are expert in keeping concubines."

"Yes, you're right. I want to keep one more concubine."

"If we come to know about it, there will be no trace of her in your life."

"Are you going to murder her?"

"Certainly; what's wrong in it?"

"Is it not illegal?"

"Is it legal in keeping concubine?"

"Don't you know that in the Goundan caste, they used to have concubine though they have wife legally and similarly, Goundachhis have (illegal) paramour. Don't you know?"

"But you belong to noble Brahmin family, isn't it?"

"So what?"

"Have you ever heard any Brahmin having paramour?" Nirmala asked Baskar.
"yes."
"Where?"
"There's a neighbour belongs to Canadian Brahmin. He is working in the Court, Judicial Department. His name is RamaRao and he has wife and five children. Yet, he has a concubine who is working as a clerk in his department. She is also a married woman belongs to that caste. His father, namely Venkata Rao, a retired teacher , when he came to know about his illegal affairs, he condemned his son but he turned deaf years to his father's advice and condemnation. Venkata Rao left his son and now he is living with his wife alone. Now both are away from their only son.
What about Rama Rao's wife?"
She is very innocent and now she is living with her children separately."
"Oh, God! It's a pity. Now what's she doing for her livelihood?
"My dad helped her eldest daughter by getting an appointment in his company. So the family is surviving with the help of the elder daughter's earning. What a world it is!"
Nirmala and SHYAMALA cursed Rama Rao.
"Such a person is like a black sheep in our caste so as to bring discredit to our caste. That's why other caste people make fun of us."
Baskar said:" There are a number of RamaRaos in all castes. It is not the caste that matters but the people. Our Upanishads

strongly condemn the practice of paramour. Moreover, our marriage is also against the martial Law against Bigamy. "

"Though our marriage is against the "Marital Law of Hindus, none is going to be affected. It's also true that you are uxorious and we are like your both eyes. What's wrong in it?"

"As long as we, three are united together, there's nothing wrong and there's no problem."

"Do you doubt in our unity? SHYAMALA asked Baskar directly.

"It's not the question of doubt or confidence or non-confidence or over confidence but my suggestion in this matter. That's all."

"In the name of 'suggestion,' don't fuss over the matter." Nirmala said by basciating Baskar and as her right over him as a husband, she sat on his lap. Then she called his sister, 'SHYAMALA DEVI' to be seated on his lap and SHYAMALA rose from the seat and sat on his lap.

When Nirmala and SHYAMALA sat on their husband's lap, Baskar garlanded his two hands over their necks and slipped his hands into their banian and cupped their breasts gently. His cool palms perceived their hot breasts to cool them.

At the touch of your hands, the bud gets bloomed," SHYAMALA bantered.

"Who said yours are buds? They are well developed bathykolpian..."

"What a splitting image of your both boobs are!" Baskar exclaimed and continued,"

They're so tactile that I am always stirred to play with them in my own style."

Like a boobficianado, Baskar was floobing their breasts with his two hands, dextral hand- SHYAMALA and sinistral hand- Nirmala whose boobs were spathic and flabby. The twins didn't endue with bandeau or brassiere to cage their boobs by which it facilitated to Baskar to floob cozily. His fingers felt their boobs erect, soft, smooth and rotund. While Baskar was caressing their thelium, both closed their eyes and propped their cheeks to his shoulder on both sides, enjoying his foreplay. During his caressing their boobs, his palms were squeezing the chubby flesh of their breasts gently and in a few minutes, he made them strip off their banian themselves to bare their breasts. It's his usual style to make the twins strip off their dress by themselves and he won't strip off their dress on any account.

As soon as their breasts were exposed to him, Baskar ogled at their shapes and wished to enjoy them as he liked for which he asked the twins to come close to him so that he could mouth at them as an epulation to his tongue.

SHYAMALA looked at her sister and said something through her eyes for which her sister, Nirmala nodded her head slightly and then SHYAMALA kept her boobs over his mouth as per his instruction. It was not her maiden experience to SHYAMALA to be ***lambered*** by ***him*** even prior to their marriage. Yes, the twins had experienced his

foreplay pre-martially. Like a tasted cat, the twins became the fetishists for boobs-licking. In their ***intoxicated*** attitude, both uttered simultaneously: "Don't we remain in this same position throughout our life?"
Baskar heard what they uttered in their intoxicated mood but he didn't say anything, He knew very well that Nirmala and SHYAMALA were enchant for boobs-lambering as well as cunnilingus, especially Nirmala was very much fond of cunnilingus.
It's the special method of Baskar to make the twins long for coition by dint of his foreplay and as anticipated the twins were the victims to the lust and prior to his foreplay they used to hug him and basciated him followed by French kiss.
No sooner did SHYAMALA adpress her sinistral breast to his patulous mouth than Baskar clipped the entire mass of her chubby breast by which he could hear her sibilation and sigh. In order to facilitate her, Baskar was below her while she was on the top of him thus forming cowgirl position but she did not splay her thighs for penetration. SHYAMALA hugged his head violently so that her breast could be adpressed to his mouth and in her boobgasm, she sibilated and closed her eyes while Baskar, like an infant, expectant of its mother for suckling, to slake its hunger, nibble the nip-nops, dilated his mouth widely like a python to swallow its prey and caught her chubby flesh of breast into his mouth. Though SHYAMALA could not see how her

sinistral breast got buried into his mouth to be grabbed instantly but felt her sinistral breast resorted to his mouth for play.

Like a voyeur, Nirmala was watching how Baskar and her sister was inclined into foreplay and she was tempted to watch keenly and was laughing at them. "How you're smacking like a mango fruit!" she bantered at them.

Having heard her bantering, SHYAMALA gave her repartee:" Podi, you're a knave and mind your business." She simulated to be in quasi-angry.

Baskar understood her cravings for coition and foreplay by which he asked Nirmala to get ready for the coition. He expressed his lubricity by his words:" Could you slake my thirst by rendering me the elixir of lust? Please come here to render me the epulation and keep the oblation of a pair of mangoes to me."

Sitting on the bed, Baskar stretched out his two legs for his wives as the seats to be seated which they sat on his pair of legs. Then he hugged them or necked them strongly, French kissed and nip-nop shit their breasts one after another.

"Your breasts are sweeter than mangoes." Baskar extolled them while lambering their erect breasts.

"Such kind of boobgasm have we never experienced so far. The more you play with our breasts, the more we feel boobgasm. We couldn't sleep at night for this feeling haunts our minds." Both reported to Baskar

Baskar expressed his mind:" One day both pooned in such a manner that while strutting, I watched how your breasts were bouncing jouncing. From that moment onwards, I became your boobfiend."

"We're not conservative but liberal and trendy like modern girls of our age. Do you know how many students were drooling over us?"

"After our tryst, rendezvous, you sent me several ***boobfies*** that were taken in a span of a week through WhatsApp and it spoiled my sleep at night." Baskar replied sucking their breasts.

Next, SHYAMALA asked another question:" Are you penchant for this only?"

Baskar understood what she meant and smiled at her by floobing her dextral breast while squeezing the sinistral breast of Nirmala gently.

Baskar whispered softly:" Cunnilingus. "He paused and then continued," Cunnilingus or coition?"

SHYAMALA replied blushingly: "Cunnilingus."

"Why not coition?"

"Coition lasts only for a short span of time, matter of five minutes or maximum en minutes but cunnilingus lasts even one hour." Nirmala whispered softly without seeing his face.

SHYAMALA nodded and said:" What she said is true. During our tryst, I mean rendezvous, you made a request for ***anasyrmos*** *(gesture of lifting the skirt of kilt)* and we inhibited at first but you made us for the anasyrmos by genuflecting before us. Do you remember?"
"Yes, yes..." said Baskar nodding and then added," It's my maiden experience to see your transparent briefs by which I could see your ***camel toe. It was wet also."***
Most forms of vaginal wetness come from one of two places. 1) Bartholin glands. 2) The cervix. Bartholin glands are two small, pea-sized glands located just inside the vagina. They help lubricate the vagina to prevent excessive dryness. They also produce moisture when a female feels arousal and during sexual activity thus decreasing the risk of painful friction and injuries. Higher oestrogen levels can increase vaginal wetness by causing the Bartholin glands to produce more fluid
"We had never expected that you'd strip off our brief gently."
Baskar laughed at them: "What a funny talk! When you both lifted your skirt and showed me your briefs, how can I be without stripping off your briefs to see your genitals?"
Nirmala gave her repartee:" Without laving them, how can it be fresh for cunnilinguing?"
Baskar reminisced, pondering over that incident.

Baskar during sweet nothings, dry umping and then cupping their breasts by sliding his hands inside their shirts in order to make them sexually aroused, expressed his freakish desire:" If I am not mistaken, may I see your pudendum now?"
His minced words of request stirred their lust but they inhibit for ***alfresco anasyrmos*** but lust won at last and they agreed to lift their skirt above their navel to expose their briefs to his ogle eyes. Without looking at him, both, Nirmala and SHYAMALA lifted their long skirts up to their navel and exposed him their transparent briefs which they endue with for special occasion. Since it was transparent briefs, Baskar could not understand what purpose they were endued with such transparent briefs or thong. He thought that it might be the fashion of the day. He could not see the colour of their pubic regions but pudendum through the briefs they wore. Like a greedy man, his eyes with crazy looks, spotted the curves of their pudenda since they were distinct as the Bartholin glands secreted liberally to moisten the vaginae. He could see the moisture at the ***crotch of their briefs*** which the glands secreted for lubrication. Next moment, his fingers stripped off their briefs from their pudenda simultaneously and exposed their pudenda which were neatly shaved, having couleur de rose complexion as it was not tanned and it looked like a bosomed flower, fresh flower with splayed petals. He could not

see the profound view of their pudenda because they constricted their thighs thus prevented him from seeing the full view of their pudenda except their ***coleus Feminus.*** As soon as their pudenda were exposed, they gave out fishy smell which Baskar smelt and had known the reason for such foul smell. He thought by smearing their coleus Feminus, the moisture could change the fishy smell; so he smeared their Clitorises with his fingers by which they felt thrilling sensation at his touch of their sensitive organs. No sooner did his fingers smear than their thighs got dilated like a flower splaying their petals. Yes, it looked like a lotus splaying its petals.

Baskar dilated their labia by clipping them with his thumb and index finger and his ogling eyes spotted the inner view of their vaginae.

Baskar had seen their naked-selfies which they sent though WhatsApp while they were taking bath in the bathroom but in the naked photo he could see the profound and distinct view of their breasts but not their pudenda as the focus was not at their pudenda. Bur now he could see the clear view of their pudenda in reality. He could discern the view of their naked body through the photo and the reality when they exposed their nudity.

Baskar made them levitate by dint of ***onanism and by maritating.***

(Continued)

CHAPTER NO: SIX

The night glided into day.

The "***Vishnu Saghasranamam***" by .M.S.Subbulakshmi was echoing in all parts of the house which indicated that the Keralite couples, Menaka and Prakash Raj, after ablution, had started their culinary

The Keralite couples were very busy in the kitchen preparing for breakfast and lunch. Menaka and her husband Prakash had already prepared wheat dough for 'poori' for the next day and the only side dish they had to prepare was 'masala' and it was very easy for them and Menaka engrossed her attention in preparing 'masala' while her husband, Prakash was preparing 'poori' and in half an hour, the breakfast was ready and then they engaged themselves in preparing for 'lunch' and as per the timetable they prepared with the help of the Queen of the house' they began to cook.

Onion Sambar was the opsonium and Baskar was opsomaniac to onion sambar and Prakash Raj was an ace in preparing this recipe and while tasting it, he began to laud Prakash Raj and told his father-in-law," You've appointed a suitable person for preparing this recipe. I've never tasted such kind of recipe in my life so far."

Arrided by his extolment, Sivasankar said to Prakash Raj:" Very soon, I am going to open a restaurant in your name and you're the owner of the restaurant. It's your full responsibility to bring it to the sublime position. I will invest the capital amount and I don't want any share in the profit. It's yours. You've to send us breakfast, lunch, tiffin and supper daily by parcel through a person. I will bear the entire cost and give it to you at the end of every month.

Menaka and Prakash raj were overwhelmed on hearing his plan for their prosperous future and realized the depth of his kindness upon them. Like refugees, they eloped and chased by their foes up to the neighbouring State, and narrowly escaped by the succour of Sivasankar. They started their carrier as cook in his house, a stepping stone and got promoted gradually to the highest stage in life.

Menaka, sixteen years old teen aged girl and her husband, Prakash Raj touched the feet of Sivasankar and with bleary eyes, they wept for joy and said:" Like deer chased by wild animals of foes, we fled from our State and hadn't you succoured us, our life would have been snipped away but you showered your grace and protected our life for which we will be faithful throughout our life. Even you drive us out of this house, we won't go.. Remember, we are your faithful dogs.....Their voice melted and weakened at the end.

Sivasankar replied:" If this succour is considered as virtue, let it go to the Heaven and please the Almighty. ". Then he turned towards Menaka and said:" This is the age for education not for cooking. So from today onwards, you start to school along with my wife. Study well and come up in life. Had Prakash Raj studied at least tenth standard, I would have not appointed him as a cook in my house but .....Anyhow, he can come up in life as the owner of Hotel and save you as a protector of your life. "

When Menaka was endued with long skirt and shirt, school uniform, she looked like a small girl and no one would believe that she's a married girl.

Prakash Raj wept bitterly in the kitchen and whimpered:" Had I followed the advice of my parents, I would have continued my education but due to bad association, I wasted my precious life and my life is a lesson to those who discontinue studies. "

Baskar comforted him saying," You haven't lost your life. You have the flair for cuisine and you can develop your skill and ability. As my uncle planned, you are going to be the owner of a big restaurant. You are going to settle your life. Why do you worry? When we are here, there's no need to worry, Prakash."

Prakash was so overwhelmed that he held Baskar's hands lovingly dabbed them on his eyes to express his gratitude.

Baskar patted him and encouraged him to have fortitude. Then turning towards Menaka, he said:" It's your first day of the new school. You pray to God in the pooja room and then accompany with us."

Menaka nodded and went to the pooja room to pray while, the twins whispered softly:" How small girl she is in this school uniform dress! Will anyone believe that she is a married girl?"

"She has a new lease of life. So far her life was around the kitchen and cuisine. Now she is going to see a new world." Gowrie told her daughters.

"Devoid of Mangalyam, how can she be?" Nirmala raised an issue.

Next moment, Gowrie went to her room and returned with a golden chain. She asked Prakash to come to the Pooja room and adorn her neck with that gold chain as a symbol of Mangalyam

Prakash adorned her neck with the golden chain of Mangalyam in presence of the family members.

Gowrie advised her:" Menaka, on any account don't reveal the fact that you are a married girl for you know why I advise you to do. .I need not advise you to take much care of this golden chain of Mangalyam."

Menaka nodded.

"How will she go to school daily? Does she go by walk?" Nirmala raised another issue.

Sivasankar replied:" Next week I will get her a new scooter. Let her go to school. Hereafter it is the duty of Prakash to drive scooter and leave her in her school and get her back in the evening by scooter. "

"If anyone asks about him?"

"Tell them he is her fiancé."

Then the entire family members marched towards the school while Baskar's parents had already been waiting for them.

Sivasankar explained to his in-laws about the recent arrangements he made in the family and got ready for the "Parents' meeting"

Very few parents only attended the meeting. The strength of the school from first standard to tenth standard was exactly one hundred ninety only and many students left since the standard of teaching and infra-structure were not satisfactory.

"Is it possible to run the school with this scanty number of students?" Sundar doubted.

Sivasankar smiled and said:" Now, see the effect of my business trick." Saying, he announced:" If you bring any new student for admission in any standard, he or she will be given the cash award rupees, five hundred on the spot. "

As soon as he announced this, all the parents, especially women, clapped their hands and welcomed his scheme.

At the end of the meeting, Sundar asked Siva," Is it not a financial loss to you by introducing this scheme?"

"How much we are going to collect school fee for each standard? For an example, we are going to collect one thousand rupees for first standard per term. Now add five hundred rupees and make it as one thousand five hundred. Our people don't know this trick played by the management. We are at a profit by this scheme."

Sundar gaped at the business tactics of Sivasankar.

Sivasankar introduced many attractive schemes to encourage the parents for joining their wards in the school and as anticipated, within a month, the number of students admitted augmented to fifty more.

Sundar came to know that Sivasankar had marriage halls, own cloth shops, partner in jewelry shops and cotton mills and above all he was running the wholesale business of the products produced from his land.

About five in the evening, Menaka returned from the school and before undressing her school uniform, she recounted her rich experience at the school to her husband, Prakash who, was, on hearing her narration, in the seventh heaven.

Afterwards, she asked her husband:" I am going to take bath. Could you help me bathing?"

Prakash understood what she meant indirectly.

Menaka batted her eyelashes gracefully and paced towards the bathroom followed by Prakash.

Menaka faced him so that he would unhook her shirt and whispered softly:" Why are your fingers lazy without unbuttoning my shirt? Don't you know my shirt reeks filthy smell due to sweating? Do strip off my shirt pronto."

Her overt directions to him surprised him a little bit; however, he was chuffed with her candid expression since she was craving for coition. Previously, Prakash used to initiate for copulation with her and then only she allowed him to get her dress stripped off but now, she changed herself and asked him for sexual copulation and especially she was penchant for boobgasm and he had known very well which her sensitive parts were to make her mad after him. Previously, she won't allow him to strip off her dress complexly to make her ***in puris Naturalisbus but without undressing, he used to perform foreplay and finally coition.***

"I find some change in you. May I know what it is?" Prakash asked her cupping the protruding part of her shirt.

"What change do you find in me?" Menaka asked Prakshraj with blushing smile.

"Do you want me to mention it?" Prakash squeezed the protruding part of her shirt gently.

Menaka blushed and with smile adorning her face, she whispered into his ears:" This morning, it happened to me to see the coital scene performed by Baskar with his wives."

Shocked by the news, Prakash in a warning tone said," Oh, God! What a risk you encountered! Do you know what would have happened had they seen you watching them?" He withdrew squeezing the protruding part of her shirt.

"It happened accidentally." saying, she held his hand and kept it upon her protruding part

of her shirt and adpressed his palm to her shirt.
“How?” Prakash asked her and cupped her protruding parts of her shirt in which caged a pair of breasts by a bandeau and his fingers could easily feel the mass of flesh in a cone form and even his palm perceived the presence of her thelium.
Leaning against his broad shoulder, Menaka asked him,” Do you like me to have pubic hair without epilation periodically?”
Prakash wondered that her replay was not idoneous to his question and could hardly suss our why she evaded answering directly for which he asked her again,” Have you forgotten what question I asked you?”
”Do you think I can answer to your question in this position?”
“Well, I will relax my hands from your mounds so that you can be free to remember the question posed.” He took away his hands from her protruding parts of her shirt.
No sooner did he relieve his hands from her mounds, than she forced his hands to keep back upon the mounds of her shirt and in her graceful sexy tone,” If you take away your hands from my mounds on my shirt, I won’t answer.” She stipulated.
It was a riddle to him for her freakish behavior. Yet, he kept patience and asked her again:” What is the relevance between the epilation of pubic hair and the incident happened accidentally?”
“Yes, there’s relevance.” asserted Menaka.

"How?"
"Do you like me to have pubic hair without epilation periodically?" she repeated the same question to him.
Prakash sighed as he lost patience but endured; then he shook his head since he didn't like to answer vocally or orally.
When he shook his head, she basciated him and continued: "Baskar also didn't like his wives with pubic hair without epilation periodically."
Still he couldn't understand her implied answer. "Well, continue."
"So, at the time when I made my appearance there, I saw him epilating the pubic hair of Nirmala and he's a virtuoso with the ***clit-flick***. I was ogling how he was squeezing her clit between two fingers; he was flicking the clit with his other hand repeatedly until broozing.
Prakash, being aversion to ***pubephilia,*** expected Menaka to depilate her pubic hair periodically and she was depilating her pubic region neatly so that it remained as '***hardwood floors***' which he liked to be.
Menaka told him how she happened to see away the coital scene. It's her wont to keep the washed clothes to dry in the hot sun by hanging to the *clothes line* at the top floor but accidentally Baskar was depilating the pubic hair of Nirmala who was exposing her pudendum by lifting her nightie. As he cleaved himself to his wives especially to be in the hardwood floors, he engrossed his

attention towards depilating the pubic hair of his wife, Nirmala who directed him to depilate her pudendal hair and he willingly did it. At that time, Menaka came there with the basket of washed clothes, with the help of washing machine, to dry them in the hot sun by hanging them to the clothes line and she never expected that Baskar was busy in depilating the pudendal hair of his wife, Nirmala who was exposing her pudendum to him. Had he been depilating her pudendal hair inside his private room, there won't have been any chance for Menaka to see away the sexy scene but since it was performed alfresco depilation, Menaka chanced to photo the scene to her heart as an engramma.

Menaka shot him with her stag eyes in which lust was swelling to drive Prakash mad and when she informed her craving for the depilation of her pudendal hair by him hereafter, he gladly agreed and nodded gently. Then she complained that she could not execute the work of depilating her pudendal hair perfectly and sometimes she slashed at her groin by which stubs' were left unshaved.

When Menaka remarked that there were stubs left unshaved, Prakash commented:" True. Rose has thistles and how it can be tasted when there are thistles." He began to unbutton her shirt one by one and finally stripped her shirt completely to expose her bandeau which caged her fair breasts.

Menaka, a teenager adolescent, was stunningly charming with her ***boobez,*** perky and squeezable breasts, and she was like a rose flower in the hands of her husband, Prakash, a handsome hunk, and when his fingers moved through her back, Menaka understood that his fingers were going to unhook her bandeau which so far had caged her breasts and incarcerated them.

As anticipated, his fingers unhooked her bandeau and freed the twin of birds from the cage. He slung away the cage to the corner of the bath room and cupped her breasts profoundly by French kissing her and whispering," ***Beautiful breasts in the beautiful body"*** He lauded her.

Like a mermaid, she was standing semi nakedly before her husband whose fingers were busy in squeezing her breasts, which were ruddy like her naked body.

In the passion of lust, both sunk and forgot their duties; it's a tiffin time to serve Siva and his family members.

Baited by the delay, Gowrie knocked at the door of the outhouse, shouting, "Prakash, Menaka"

Bewildered by the voice of Gowrie in which the fire of anger broke out, Prakash and Menaka opened the door after a minute and they saw Gowrie staring at them and then turned away from that place by which both rued for their dereliction of duty and scared whether it would spoil their future life. So both hurried towards the kitchen room of

Siva's house where they saw Gowrie preparing for the tiffin items.
Both fell at the feet of Gowrie and begged her to pardon them.
Gowrie did not expect that they would fall at her feet and implore; so her heart melted and asked them to get up and said:" Be aware of the time and do your duty accordingly."
Sivasankar was out of station and Baskar and his wives were at the residence of Sundar for they expected them to reside with them. So Gowrie was alone.
Gowrie recollected her amatory experience with Sivasankar and tittered. "I was also like them, forgotten the world."
After preparing the tiffin items, Gowrie asked Menaka to come to her woman-cave and said politely:" I am not against your marital life to part you both and extract work from you. What I would like to advise you is, you are now a student and vested with much responsibility. Till you complete your studies, be careful not to become pregnant for it spoils your entire **academic career. Use condom to avoid pregnancy. Come up in life and be happy."**
"***Use condom to avoid pregnancy***"
Menaka had never expected such words from Gowrie and she blushed and flexed her head, nodding and her plump face was wreathed in smiles
Nirmala and SHYAMALA were not happy for they're coerced to reside with the parents

of Baskar after the end of the parents' meeting held in the school.

Meenakshi understood why the twins were sad and she desired to eradicate their grievance for which she patted their shoulders and comforted: "This house has everything you can desire. Be free as you feel at your home with your parents. We're your second parents and we don't expect any formality to be adopted and expect a cordial relationship between a mother-in-law and daughter in law. Hope you understand what I mean."

The twins had never expected such words, soothing words from Meenakshi and hence they fell at her feet and were too overwhelmed.to speak any words but looked at her with bleary eyes. When heart knows another heart, then no words are necessary.

While cooking, Meenakshi was discussing about the improvements to be made for the school and the twins were helping her in the kitchen.

Baskar was very busy with the books in his study, a room for studying books as a small library in his room.

He was penchant for George Eliot especially her short novel, Silas Mariner" and he took the book and opened the pages.

George Eliot was the pen name of the novelist Mary Ann Evans. She grew up in Warwickshire at a time when industrialization was transforming the countryside. Her mother died when she was

17, and in 1841 she and her father moved to Coventry which she would use as inspiration for the fictional town of Middlemarch. There she joined a circle of free-thinking intellectuals, and lost her Christian faith. After her father died in 1849, she travelled abroad before settling in London working as an editor at the left-wing ***Westminster Review***. This led to her meeting the philosopher and critic George Henry Lewes, married but separated from his wife. Eliot lived with Lewes openly and started referring to herself as Marian Lewes, in defiance of Victorian notions of propriety.

Lewes encouraged her to write fiction, for which she adopted a male pseudonym, partly in order to avoid her work being judged in relation to her scandalous domestic situation. Her first Warwickshire-set tales, profoundly influenced by the interest in ordinary people typical of both Wordsworth's poetry and contemporary genre painting, appeared in ***Blackwood's Magazine*** from 1857; they were published as ***Scenes from Clerical Life*** in 1858. ***Adam Bede*** followed in 1859, and ***The Mill on the Floss*** **in 1860. She published three more novels in the following decade, including Silas Mariner (1861), as well as some poetry. Her most famous book, Middlemarch, was published in eight installments from 1871 to 1872.**

A year and a half after Lewes's death in November 1878, Eliot married the much younger John Cross, but she died from kidney disease within a year.

After the kitchen work over, the twins appeared at the doorsill of Baskar's study and their shadow distracted his attention and turned towards the entrance door where he saw his wives who were ravishing in their purple ***lehenga*** devoid of dupatta.

He tittered as he knew why they came there; he closed the book, stood up and paced towards them, held their hands and led them in to his study, saying," "This is my study arranged by my dad and I used to be immersed in the books, Literature which loves me very much as I love them...."

"Sorry to disturb your privacy." Nirmala said.

"Disturbance!", he exclaimed and added," It's a great pleasure to see you here and kvell of you as you are also Bibliophilist . The treasure of knowledge welcomes you here."

It's a spacious room stacked with beaucoup books, especially English Literature, and in the centre of the room, there hung the photos of William Shakespeare and John Milton on the wall in the middle of the study. Below the photos, there engraved the famous quotation from William Shakespeare as:" Love all, trust a few, do wrong to none.

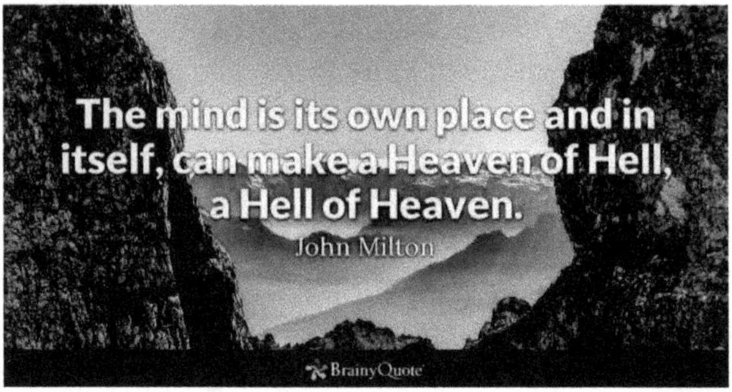

And below the photo of John Milton, there was engraved the above quotation. It's not known to the twins that Baskar was a *Bardolator (one who idolizes Shakespeare)* or ***Miltoniclatrist*** or both. *The* twins began to analyse about John Milton with Baskar. Certainly the time was spent usefully.

As the three were ***linguaphile especially in English Literature*** as well as ***philocalis***t they spent their time usefully by exchanging their ideas on the great works of celebrated English poets and writers.

After this, Baskar asked them," How do you feel this environment? Do you like this?"

Nirmala nodded and with wreathed in smiles, she replied:" If I am not exaggerating, I like this new milieu for our mother-in-law treats us more than her own daughter. We haven't been so far accustomed to adopt the Brahmin culture for we are pampered by our dad and we used to laugh at our mother who insists to adopt our culture but when our mother-in-law approaches positively how we have to perform our duties in our daily domestic affairs, the mystery behind our credos, and the scientific reasons. "

SHYAMALA continued: "Yes, after ablution, we are taught how to worship God and Goddess in the Pooja room, and we are learning by heart the Vishnu Saghasranamam and Lalitha Saghasranamam. What she told us is true, yes; we feel composure after '***parayanam***'. Do you perform Vishnu Saghasranamam every morning?"

Baskar was discommoded by her question for he hadn't performed parayanam every day which he must do it as per the creed. His silence proved that he failed to perform his duty as per the Brahmin culture and creed.

Nirmala asked another question:" Do you perform ***Gayathri Jabam*** daily?"

Baskar shook his head by flexing his head.

"That's alright, Baskar. Hereafter you can start doing Gayathri Jabam as well parayanam regularly." Both said together.

For Dravidians, Vedas are the spiritual capital and Gayathri Devi is the mother of all Vedas.

Gayathri mantra is made up of 24 letters. Even if one does not know how to chant the Gayathri mantra, merely the process of meditating on Her will help one reap the dividends of spiritual equity. Just as how a mother is very special to a newborn—even more than a father—similar is the efficacy of Gayathri.

Gayathri manifests as three entities—Gayathri, the repository of wisdom, Savitri, the life force (who brought back her husband Satyavan from the jaws of death) and Saraswati, the supreme dispenser of knowledge. Thus one can be assured of good thoughts, a good life and great wisdom if one were to meditate on Gayathri every day. In essence our *trikarnasuddhi*, or the three characteristics of *satva*, *rajo* and *tamas* can be turned to better use if we meditate upon Gayathri at the appropriate time. It is said that on an average, a human being is governed by *satva* traits from 4 am to 8 am and 4 pm to 8 pm. From 8 am to 4 pm, one is more likely to be under the influence of rajas; from 8 pm to 4 am one is likely to be experiencing tamasic qualities. And since Gayathri is the master of senses and wisdom, it is best to meditate upon her during the *Brahmamuhurtam* of 4 am to 8 am. This is the reason elders extol the virtue of studying early in the morning to children, and physical trainers often suggest starting the workout regimen during these hours. It is the best time of the day to think of spiritual aspects, meditate or focus the mind on a certain aspect and also be physically active. As Andal says in one of her pasurams, "Sing aloud with your mouth, mediate deeply and pray by showering flowers." Gayathri is present in all these forms.

Why is Surya important for Gayathri?

Surya is the *adhidevata* for Gayathri mantra. He is the energy provider for all life forms on earth, and protecting us along with the Sun God is Gayathri, who is depicted as five-faced and ten armed. Her five faces represent the five elements—air, water, earth, fire and ether, and together with Surya, she endows a devotee with all essential benefits.

The essence of Gayathri mantra is found in the Ramayana. It is said that Vyasa, the compiler of Vedas, summoned Valmiki and instructed him to deconstruct the Vedas so that everyone can follow the essence of those teachings. Valmiki even took the name of Ramayana from the important letters of the names of the four Vedas. He also narrated the entire epic in 24, 000 verses, each numbering a thousand, representing each of the 24 letters in the Gayathri Mantra. Therefore, those who do not know the mantra or lack the time to chant the mantra can read or hear discourses of the Ramayana. In Kerala and in many other states, the reading of the Ramayana in the month of Aadi is a common ritual. Children especially will greatly benefit from reciting *AdityaHridayam*, figuring the Ramayana.

Baskar's father, Sundar had no time to do 'parayanam or Gayathri Jabam as he was tied up with his work as he was working in a corporate company by which he was earning the income more than required. But his wife, Baskar's mother was punctual in performing 'Vishnu Saghasranamam as well as 'Sri Lalitha Sagasranamam'on alternative days. During weekend holidays, he was very busy with his friends and he hardly enters into the pooja room.

Baskar determined to do Gayathri Jabam as well as Vishnu Saghasranamam Parayanam punctually by which the twins were arrided.as well as ***kvelled.***

Meenakshi, Baskar and the twins went to the school and took classes and they impressed the students. Then they returned home by five.

Prakash Raj sent the tiffin items to Baskar family in the evening.

Yes, it was his duty to send the meals, tiffin items and supper from his restaurant by a van and so there is no kitchen work in both houses.

After returning from the school, Baskar bathed in a canal nearby his house and enchant "Gayathri Mantra' in his Pooja room while his wives, enchanted Sri Lalitha Saghasranamam.

Baskar and the twins went to the nearby temple and returned by seven.

At eight, they received food items for supper sent by Prakash Raj.

At ten in the night, Baskar entered into his room followed by his wives.

Nirmala locked the door inside while SHYAMALA flicked on the switch of the Air-conditioning machine as well as night lamp.

Baskar lay abed while Nirmala on his dextral side and SHYAMALA on sinistral side of him Baskar interlocked them with his both hands and conversed with them about the school and the students to whom he taught English.

The three were conversing and exchanged their experience about school and the ways to meliorate the standard of teaching.

Baskar said:" As you said, I feel a sense of euphoria and a phantom of ecstasy after doing Gayathri Jabam as well as "Parayanam'. By the Grace of God, I expect a Female child to be born to you both."

"What!, female baby!"

"Yes, what's there?"

"No, we are expectant of male baby."
"No, female baby." Baskar shook his head.
"Male or female baby, both are okay for me." Said Nirmala.
"Why do you prefer female baby to male baby?"
SHYAMALA replied:" Nowadays we are very affectionate to our parents as well love our father much. But on the other hand, boy is attached to his mother very much but not to his father. So generally males prefer girl baby to male baby."
"We expect a male child because he will be as charming as you are." Nirmala expressed her mind while his sister nodded and said," Yes, what she said is true."
Baskar laughed and asked them," Is there any symptom for pregnancy?"
"How is it possible?"
"Why?"
"You use 'condom', aren't you?"
"Yes, as per your wish only."
"We agree. We don't need any pregnancy now. Let's enjoy the life at least for two years. Then we 'll see for the necessary things."
Baskar said:" Next Sunday we are leaving for Shimla. Flight ticket is available."
"Ten days only."
"Enough ten days."

"What shall we do now?" Baskar asked them.
"Let's do for procreation." Nirmala whispered softly while her sister laughed.
"How to procreate?" Baskar asked her, slipping his hand inside her blouse and laughed
SHYAMALA held another hand and slipped it inside her blouse and said: "Dry humping and cunnilingus."
"Your ***clit-flicking'*** is marvelous." Both ***cleaved themselves*** to Baskar.
Baskar ogled at Nirmala who pulled her nightie upwards p to her navel and exposed her pudendum while her sister also stripped her nightie completely to expose her nudity.
Baskar formed prone position and began to cunnilingue the pudendum of Nirmala while his fingers started clit-flicking the pudendum of SHYAMALA DEVI, thus began his foreplay.
Nirmala and his sister, SHYAMALA felt as if they were levitating in the air and sunk in the ocean of delectation.
The twins were not cloyed with his foreplay as they felt like a thirsty man who craves for water more and more. Both indulged in his foreplay but not coition.
By eleven, the twins squirted and afterwards, Baskar performed coition with Nirmala who

dilated her thighs and signed for coition while her sister took rest.

It's Divine Grace that Sundar had a chance to familiarize with Siva and started living a luxury life. They had to wait till the construction of the new house, adjacent to Siva's bungalow and in three months the construction was over and a "House Warming ceremony day was fixed.
Prior to "Honey Moon to Shimla' the "House warming Ceremony was enjoined and the whole family was ebullient.
The admission of students gradually increased and Meenakshi administered efficiently for the improvement of the infra-structure and the melioration of the standard of teaching.
Prakash Raj was given full freedom in running his own restaurant and his income also got augmented gradually.
Menaka continued her education in that school and was a dux in the school.
It was Sunday.
Baskar and his wives with fewer luggage got ready for their 'Honey Moon' and Sivasankar drove the car in his car along with the whole family.
Baskar and the twins said 'adieu' to their parents.

LET'S WAG OUR HANDS AND GREET 'HAPPY JOURNEY TO THE COUPLES.

CPSIA information can be obtained
at www.ICGtesting.com
Printed in the USA
LVHW020949251122
733912LV00017B/807

9 789356 754195